THE MOURNERS' BENCH

ALSO BY SUSAN DODD

Mamaw

Hellbent Men and Their Cities

Old Wives' Tales

No Earthly Notion

THE MOURNERS' BENCH

A Novel

Susan Dodd

WILLIAM MORROW AND COMPANY, INC.
NEW YORK

It is the policy of William Morrow and Company, and its imprints
and affiliates, recognizing the importance of preserving what has been written,
to print the books we publish on acid-free paper,
and we exert our best efforts to that end.

Library of Congress Cataloging-in-Publication Data
Dodd, Susan M., 1946–
The mourners' bench / Susan Dodd.
p. cm.
ISBN 0-688-15799-8 (alk. paper)
I. Title.
PS3554.0318M68 1998
813'.54—dc21 97-52564
CIP

Printed in the United States of America

First Edition

4 5 6 7 8 9 10

BOOK DESIGN BY OKSANA KUSHNIR

www.williammorrow.com

For Rosanne

ACKNOWLEDGMENTS

For the gifts, countless and immeasurable, of faith, hope, and charity that allowed me to complete this book, my abiding thanks and devotion to Rosanne Desmone and Michael Dawkins, Richard Bausch, Joe Hurka; my colleagues and students in the Bennington Writing Seminars; Dr. Lori Polacek and Dr. Arnold Herman; Joe DeSalvo, Rosemary James, and the Pirate's Alley Faulkner Society; the heroes, lost and surviving, of the Literature Division of the National Endowment for the Arts; my brave and wise new editor, Claire Wachtel; my fierce and loving friend and agent, Esther Newberg . . .

And from the beginning, to the end, now and forever: Richard Ziff, Andre Dubus.

Who is the third who walks always beside you?
When I count, there are only you and I together
But when I look ahead up the white road
There is always another walking beside you
. . . who is that on the other side of you?

T. S. ELIOT
"The Waste Land"

THE MOURNERS' BENCH

PROLOGUE

ROUTE 17 CUTS DOWN from Virginia to penetrate North Carolina at what seems a particularly tender spot. The trees are slow to disrobe here. Suggestive foliage lingers, giving one ideas: how lush and secretive this passage must be in spring, in summer how sultry and redolent. But it is November now. Limbs not quite naked arch and entwine above, splayed before an ambering late-day sky.

Many missed seasons are implied. It has taken ten years to bring me this close to Leandra. Now, within a breath of her, again I circumnavigate, I idle. Is she preparing a meal? Lighting a lamp, perhaps. When I picture her house, I see a cramped space that cripples light. Little as I've possessed, I could have offered her more. . . .

My collection of North Carolina leaflets and maps fills two shoe boxes in a closet crowded with clothing I have left behind. What will my wife, in Massachusetts, make of the stash when she finds it? I regret but one pair of shoes, burnt-umber brogans I've owned for more than twenty years. They need resoling. It would have been impractical to bring them here. One should, in any case, have something left behind that's worthy of regret.

For more than a decade, I sent away for tourist brochures, collected schedules of seasonal events and dimly limned maps. My tongue has tripped and fallen over names I could not have dreamed, imagined making itself free with their syllables and elisions—Currituck and Albemarle, Perquimans and Pasquotank. Pitches sweetened for developers have made my mouth water.

This is no promised land. Its waters are sour, its soil exhausted. There is a leveling flatness to the terrain that bespeaks hopelessness. The Chamber of Commerce painted the Sound bright blue, the outlook rosy. The palette I encounter brings to mind parchment and rags, old brooms and older photographs.

She could have lived with me within sight of mountains. In autumn she'd have seen fire on the slopes . . . such scathing greens in spring . . .

No public monuments distinguish my trail, no markers. The roadsides are lined instead with bygone abundance: FRESH PEACHES . . . OUR OWN MELONS . . . VIDALIAS HERE! . . . SCUPPERNONGS NOW! Crude altars to such deities have been dismantled, boarded up for a winter one can scarcely envision in so temperate a zone.

What holds her here . . . what keeps her? Somehow, surely, I shall find my way to her door. But shall I knock? That is the question.

Another hour and a half south, and I might be in the fabled territory of the Lost Colony—Dare County, a locale whose name has always appealed to me. *Do I dare . . . and do I dare?* Indeed, there will be little time left to wonder. I am not, in any case, called to travel so far. I have already found my celestial county: Currituck. The name, I have read, means Land of the Wild Goose in the Algonquin tongue. I suspect being lost may be the very cornerstone of human experience. Can one traverse this life without getting mislaid in it? The local legends are too obvious, their current applications facile.

A land riddled with metaphors . . . avoid one and you merely careen off another: I am perhaps half an hour from my destination when a sign lures me into the irresistible reaches of the Great Dismal Swamp.

This ghostly landscape might have been invented to stymie the great. George Washington dropped his venture capital here, founding a lumbering cartel meant to corner the market in cedar shingles. Profits were stingier than projected. A century and a half later, Robert Frost, budding and sappy and bowed by first love, traveled here from New England. His intent was to do away with himself. He ran afoul instead of a boisterous gang of fishermen from Elizabeth City, rowdies who rehabilitated the lovesick youngster's spirit with generous doses of whiskey and fried chicken and boys'-night-out camaraderie. The profitability of the poet's venture was, like Washington's, dubious: Frost went on to marry the young woman who'd spurned him, and the outcome was less than blissful. A swamp is a dark and tangled thing, of course. Its beauty smacks of chaos.

Would you suppose me a man resistant to such temptation?

I pull into a crude picnic area overlooking a mossy ribbon of water. My car's engine ticks—merely cooling, yet it sounds as if it's marking time. A pair of wood ducks drifts past in the mutual oblivion of a long-married couple eating a desultory meal. *Might I, in time, have neglected to notice her, had she only been beside me all these years? Assured of her love, might I have discovered in myself other longings, my heart moving off in some new direction, leaving Leandra behind?* I can no more imagine it than I can imagine myself another man, this body vessel to a stranger's heart.

Leandra the given of my earthly existence: it should be the simplest of matters, going to her now . . . it ought to be elemental. When one is face-to-face with death, I am learning, life ceases to be a terribly complex thing. One's desires shrink in number and size, coming down to a single highly concentrated spot of insistent wanting. All the rest one has striven for fades, first from view, then from memory. I'd have thought that by the light of a death sentence, life would become my one true desire. But I find it is not so. I want now only what I have ever wanted. I want *her*. And if I can have Leandra for these last months, I will not dissipate what remains of desire by wishing for time, by yearning for anything *more* or *else*.

She is, Leandra, my last wish. She has always been.

PART I

i

THE AIR THESE NIGHTS, though it is already November, just shivers with mosquitoes. And the stinkbugs! Sometimes late at night it sounds like a Ping-Pong game, those tough little shells tock-tocking against the screens. What you reckon I got in here they could want or need?

That's anyhow why I didn't get up right off and run to the door when the tapping started. Figured the bugs was just hankering after something again. But when the screen door rattled, I knew somebody had a mind to open it.

"You stay right where you are," I said. "I mean it."

"Leandra?" My name blew in from the porch on a breath of a breeze that had cooled down to just right for sleeping.

My heart knew right away who it was, but the rest of me somehow refused the knowing. I set down the scrap of doll's dress, a bedragglement of loose lace hem, got up. I kept the needle in my hand. I didn't move one step closer to the door.

"What business you think you got here?" I said. I was staring hard for some reason at the dolls lined up on the mourners' bench, its stern length taking up the wall between me and the porch. The dolls come in earlier that week—the afflicted, the sick, and the sorry, waiting to be saved. A pitiful sight, the lot of them, mostly stark naked and some in pieces. One lady in a mildewed petticoat was holding her head in her lap. I'm grown right tired of trying to work miracles, I thought.

"Leandra?" The whisper again, door rattling. "It's me."

"Had better not be," was all I could say, and my hands were shaking.

Then I heard the laugh, knew it for Wim's, and with it, like always, came the end of any good sense I ever had. I went and unlatched the screen. But I didn't open it. I was not about to hold open the door for a man could only be here because he intended to ruin my life. And his.

—∞—

April it was when I first went to Massachusetts, but it felt like winter to me. I was twenty-one years old and had never once been out of North Carolina except up to Norfolk, and my mama gone but six months. It might have calmed me down some had Branch been there to carry me to the airport. But Branch was off at Fort Bragg that year and not available to be leaned on. When Miss Maude Ellen's nephew Vern put me on that plane in Norfolk, I very nearly cried right out there in public. I'd never gone even so far as to picture myself on an airplane.

"You make it back in one piece, I'll maybe try it myself one day," Vern said.

I asked him did he want my ticket then and there.

"I ain't in no hurry," he told me, his doughy cheeks bunching up in a grin.

All that was ten years ago now, but I don't guess I'll ever get over it.

Where I flew to was Boston, and it still about strangles my heart to recollect how close that airplane come to landing on sheer water. They ought to build airports in a place gives a little more seam allowance, is what I think. This man was sitting next to me—wearing a brown suit and a spotty necktie, I recall—and he patted my knee when the plane bumped down and sighed with more relief than I myself was prepared to feel.

"Terra firma," he said.

I nodded. "Pleased," I said.

A few minutes later, the man helped me get Mama's vanity case down from the curved bin above our seats, and I said, "Thank you kindly, Mr. Terrafirma," and I never got the gist of his giddy smile, not at all like a businessman, until way later when my brother-in-law, who is Wim, or was then, began hectoring me about words and languages and such.

Terra firma is solid ground: I know that now. But it feels like something I haven't stood on since I was a child.

—~—

The yellow porch light I thought I shut off hours before made his olive skin look brassy. It jaundiced his eyes and coated his teeth and tainted the streaks of white in his wiry hair. The only thing that yellow bulb didn't do was keep the bugs away like it was meant to. The chinch bugs bounced off the screen. The mosquitoes and moths congregated around his face. Wim stood there in all that mess and stared in at me like I could save him.

"Just what do you think you're doing here, I'd like to know," I said.

He nodded like he was agreeing I had every right to ask. He looked like something the cat dragged in . . . *rode hard and put away wet, through the mill, to hell and back,* were other ideas that occurred to me.

But Wim, who teaches English in some fancy-britches school in the country where all the boys are rich and no girls are allowed, who once even wrote a book of poems printed in New York City when he was scarcely more than a boy himself and can't seem to get over it . . . well, Wim is death on what he calls clichés and he's made it hard for me not to notice them and it seems like my mouth has never worked right since. If you're disallowed to call a spade a spade, what in the world are you supposed to call it?

So I just stood there gaping at him, my mouth like a drain that was all clogged up with these words didn't have a thing wrong with them except they'd been used a bit, like something you'd run across at a rummage sale on a lucky day.

Another long minute went by. Then Wim came to, I guess, because he slapped at a mosquito on his forehead and his hand came away bloody and a red blossom bloomed above his eyebrow, blackish in the yellow light. He smiled a smile that looked like it hurt his face. My God, he's grown to be a beautiful old man.

"I guess you'd best come in," I said, "seeing as you're here." And I did hold the door for him; it was only common courtesy.

—∾—

It seems like only yesterday . . . that is a cliché for certain. They suck the blood out of language, Wim says, which is why we need to kill them. But plain English is all I got to tell this, and words like that, ready made, are only shortcuts to get you quicker where you want to go, is what I think. And seeing as I don't care to dawdle overlong in dark places, I got to tell it in my own quick way. Don't I?

That April winter up north is something I caught a chill from and my bones still feel it, is all I can say. It was Good Friday when I got there. Everything was slicked in ice. My sister Pammy Jo—Wim called her Pamela and still does—was waiting on a baby, and things was going poorly. Wim, the husband she'd been married to for eight years but who I never met before (and Mama never did), had to fetch me from the airport due to how Pammy Jo had to keep in bed for the last weeks before the baby came. Which was, Wim said, forgetting himself, no picnic.

He knew me right away. I figured Pammy must have showed him my picture, maybe he'd studied it before he left to the airport, memorizing my gray eyes that I wish was a bit wider apart, my plain straight hair that's the color of the weathered slats of Kepners' tobacco barn, my mouth that Pammy said once would make a good advertisement for the kissing booth at the county fair (only now, with harassment and all, it's only the mayor and the tax collector in that booth—them that gets paid to get harassed, Branch says). My mouth anyhow, even I can see, is about the best thing I got to look at. After Mama passed on I'd started wearing a touch of lipstick. It made me look different, I thought. But my sister's husband who'd never laid eyes on me picked me right out of a crowd.

My eyes had passed him by, an older man in a dark-blue overcoat, with little drops of water spotting the lenses of his eyeglasses. But he come up to me straightaway. "You're Leandra," he said. His voice and his face were so full of certainty, all I could think was it would be awful to have to tell him he was wrong. But Wim isn't wrong much. Not about small things.

"So I am," I said.

When I try to think back how his face looked to me that first moment, seems like all I can recollect is shadows. They filled in the hollows in his cheeks and under his eyes. They set off his slightly beaky nose and chin and thinned his lips. His hair was clipped close so you could see the shape of his skull. That and his beautiful hands and the careful still way he seemed to hold himself almost put me in mind of a statue, the likeness of somebody lived long ago, done something now forgotten that seemed important at the time.

He took my vanity case, heavy with home-cooked food, from my hands and set it down. He started to shake my hand, then halfway changed his mind and give me something meant to be a hug but never quite turned out as such. Wim is tall and I am not. I wound up with my head sort of caught in his armpit.

"I'm William," he said. "Obviously."

"Pleased," I said, trying to sound as certain, as unsurprised, as he was. But him being so old was the last thing in this world I expected. Pammy Jo was ten years older than me, and Wim (which is what she called him, so after a while I did too) was thirteen years older than her. Unlucky. Plus it made them having a baby kind of an embarrassment, I thought.

"How'd you know me so quick?" I asked, like I was changing the subject.

He looked me up and down, but not in a rude kind of way. I was wearing last year's Easter dress, a pale-yellow cotton with a drop waist and little cap sleeves. My shoes and bag were white patent leather. Mama's good gray poplin raincoat that she outgrew was draped over my arm.

My brother-in-law looked like he was trying too hard not to smile, which got my goat. I figured my nerves was still frayed from landing a foot from the water.

"Is something the matter with me?" I said.

Wim laughed and didn't look the least bit sorry.

"Well?" I said.

"It's twenty-nine degrees," he said. "Something just told me you'd have to be from the Tarheel State."

"Twenty-nine?" I said. "Ain't nobody told you folks up here how to put on a proper springtime?"

Wim laughed again, right loud this time. "You may be the sunshine we've been waiting for," he said. He didn't look near as old as I first thought. I was still kind of disappointed, though, that he hadn't studied my picture. Mama'd sent Pammy a new one every year.

I didn't much care for the way Pammy's husband said "the Tarheel State," either. It was like you'd talk about a place you'd never been and already made up your mind it wasn't worth the trip . . . kind of how I felt about Massachusetts before my sister that I hadn't seen in a dozen years called up out of the blue to a neighbor's house and when I called her back all tongue-tied and my heart thumping said in a voice just barely familiar how she needed me to help her, she was having a baby and she needed me. . . .

Or like Mama was that time way back when I was in third grade and Pammy Jo said she was going up north to Boston and go to school and it wasn't going to cost a penny because of a scholarship. And Mama said, "Massachusetts? If you're of a mind to go there, girl, you'd best not get a hankering to come back. . . ."

Oh, she could be like that, Mama, *hard,* you know, for years after Daddy got killed. He was working for the state, which seemed like all the safety a man could need—steady work plus overtime and health assurance and a pension waiting down the road. That bonus for working away from home come as pure blessing, Mama said. "Be gone but six weeks, they promised, and there were such things as we wanted for you girls, wanted so bad. . . ."

But then they got to blasting out there in the western part of the state, cutting a new highway through the mountains. . . . Well, it seemed like those boulders just crushed Mama, too, and coated her with a bitter dust.

Mama was only a mite when her own mama, not yet thirty years old, passed on. The baby she died having, Mama's little sister, Lacey, didn't last a month. Then it was only Mama and her daddy, him traveling hither and yon for farmwork, never so much as a full season in the same place nor a house to call their own. "No life for a child," was mostly all Mama'd say about it. But you could see the past was a dark place she never quite quit living in, especially once Daddy wasn't there to coax her out into the here and now.

Mama came around to mellowing a good bit, though, seeming to soften as she grew stout. You ask me, it was a downright shame Pammy Jo never got to know that lady, never found her way to the tender heart cushioned in that big soft body. They really might have done one another some good over time.

Mama, plain as salt, must have been frightened to find herself with a child so amply given to make-believe. Pammy Jo's imagination, huge and bold and brassy, seemed made on a different scale than what most of us get born with. I was, as a child, only too happy to let my sister make up my life for me.

With our daddy taken from us—and Mama, too, gone in her

way, gone all dark and distant—Pammy made it her business to provide for us. Over time her longings endowed us with whole generations of kinfolk. We acquired rich uncles in Baltimore, Maine, and Saudi Arabia, frail cousins with fatal diseases, maiden aunts with museums for namesakes. The various grandfathers Pammy dreamed up were inclined to be judges with Old Testament names—Micah and Samuel and Obadiah. We mostly called them Pawpaw. Not a one of them failed to dote on us, of course.

Pammy's specialty was grandmothers, though. She saw to it that we had at least a dozen. All those righteous judges that were so fond of us must have worked themselves into early graves for Justice's sake. Because our grannies were always widows, stern old ladies who made up in feisty independence what they lacked in means. You'd think it might occur to a judge to make better provision for his family, but that didn't seem to concern Pammy. My sister was always rushing us into the shriveled arms of grim necessity. Our grandmothers, every one of them, had a flair for hardship and a wealth of hidden talents.

No matter how weighty the fibs my sister hung on her family tree's flimsy branches, I never took issue. Fact is, I loved her tales, found comfort in dreams of a world crawling with beloved strangers just waiting for us to track them down so they could claim us. If Pammy's habit troubled me at all, it was only from fear my own puny imagination might let her down, betray her. But such dazzling stories are apt to daze folks dumb. I was hardly ever asked to confirm them.

I was too young, of course, to recognize my sister's family sagas for the sad and desperate thing they amounted to. It's only lately, in fact, Mama and Pammy now so long gone their faces go a little transparent when I conjure them, that I see the dire need behind an imagination I admired, even coveted, for its boundlessness. My sister's imagination must have known bounds. How else could Mama have fallen so far beyond them, her thrifty but durable love something Pammy just couldn't see?

Which maybe explains why she couldn't stop looking, stop hoping somehow to find all she needed in what she'd simply made up.

—∞—

Pammy and Wim lived, thank goodness, in a small town a good distance north and west of Boston. From the glimpse I got of the city, all grime and hubbub, I wanted no part of it.

The way home wasn't much more than seventy miles, Wim said. Maybe a tenth of such distance as I'd already come? But what with all the ice on the road, it took us near three hours, twice as long as my plane ride, to get there. Wim didn't have much to say for himself along the way. The little conversation he made a stab at sounded like he wasn't half listening to himself. He gripped the steering wheel of his shabby gray sedan in a way that turned his tan knuckles white as the bone beneath. I told myself all my questions would be answered soon enough by Pammy Jo anyhow. Still, he might have softened the silence some by maybe playing the radio.

I could see anyhow that the driving called for every bit of his attention. All along the highway, cars were stopped crooked, any which way, some in ditches, even. We saw one car bellied up on the median like a big blue bug. I was sure that ride would never come to an end.

Finally, though, we skidded through the crossroads of a little town with a tall skinny white church and a general store and a row of shops painted barn red. Like the postcards Pammy sent me a couple times when she first got up there. *Scenic New England.* The ice was so thick on the shop windows I couldn't get much idea what might be inside. Then we were out in the country again, and the road, wandering through woods and scrappy pasturage hemmed in by low stone walls a cow could have stepped over, was slippery as bacon grease.

"We're nearly there." Wim sounded like he'd only then recollected I was along for the ride.

"Praise the Lord!" I sort of blurted out, because by then I had to go to the bathroom so bad.

Wim laughed again, which made me huffy.

"What is it about me tickles you so," I said, "you don't mind my asking?"

He seemed to dwell on it for a moment. "You're a good deal like your sister," he said. "When I first met her. You sound like she did then." His smile looked sad or . . . I don't know, maybe wistful's the word. I couldn't keep miffed anyhow, not with him looking that way. He had to been worried about Pammy and the baby.

"She sounds different now?"

Wim shrugged, keeping his eyes on the road.

"How did y'all meet?" I asked him.

"She didn't tell you?" He was trying not to sound surprised.

"Never did tell us much, Pammy."

"I was her teacher," Wim said.

"Teacher," I said. "At the college?"

He nodded, his eyes skating over the slick twist of road.

Well, no wonder Pammy didn't mention it. Her teacher? Mama wouldn't have cared much for that.

"I never met anyone like her." Wim sounded like an old man suddenly, all caught up in the past like it was a dream. "She was just so . . . fresh," he said.

I figured he meant she talked back, acted up some in school. *Fresh as paint.* It was not a thing I had trouble imagining.

"Perpetually asking questions," Wim said. "She seemed to have an uncanny facility for finding that one thing I couldn't quite explain. I'd try, though. Then she'd give me this look . . ." Wim's worn leather glove scrabbled at the frost formed inside of the windshield like his memories were freezing there and he needed to clear them away so as not to be blinded to the dangerous road ahead.

"Pammy always did have a mind of her own," I said.

I don't think he heard me. "There is something fearsome about that kind of intelligence," he said. I felt like I knew just what he meant.

But why had he married my sister, then, a man like him? It's a question I still, after all these years, got only guesses for, no answers. . . .

Why?

—~—

Leandra: My name lollygags on his tongue like something he can't get enough of. It's the sound he loves, Wim says. But if you ask me, it's more like the flavor he relishes, something he can hold in his mouth and make it last and last. He as good as admitted it once, though he tried to make it sound like a joke. "Leandra," Wim said, "you are an acquired taste."

This woman he's married to now is called Clio, which I always thought was a name for a dog because of this old TV program Mama used to like . . . before my time, she said. Only then it came on in reruns. Wim, I reckon, is before my time too.

Wim's wife weaves wool. . . . Could be one of them tongue twisters children love, saying the words over and over until the sense of them gets lost. *Wim's wife weaves . . .* I picture a big loom in the corner of their cold glass parlor, right where Pammy's piano used to set. The shawls and mufflers and throws Clio makes are dark and smell of sheep, a little dirty. Wim sends me something every year at Christmastime, a shawl, a table mat, a rough afghan once. I keep them in the cedar chest, where they'll be safe from the chewing moths. I wonder if Clio picks out these gifts, choosing such things as came out somehow on the disappointing side. Or maybe Wim filches them, leaving his wife to wonder where this or that prickly sprawl of wool has disappeared to.

That would be like Wim, I think. He told me once, no bones about it, that his hero when he was a boy was Robin Hood . . . Robin Hood, who if you ask me was no better than a common thief, never mind what he done with what he took.

Wim stands now in the center of the single room that is my

house and lets me see full how the thick middle of him sags, and he don't pretend his hands are at anything but a loss.

When he passed close to me, coming through the door, Wim smelled stale and sad. I wonder if he has come to steal from me, finding rightness in his greater need. Mama's silver iced tea spoons dangle in a swan-shaped wooden rack above the sink, right in plain view. But it won't be those. Wim ain't after anything so simple as sterling. I'd wager he hardly knows himself what it is he covets.

He lifts up his head and looks close at me for the first time since I let him in the house. I stare right back at him. The light in the room is not good. Dim rooms are restful of an evening, I think. I'll cozy up to one small lamp and let the rest of the room stay pitchy.

"I shouldn't have come," Wim says. "I know that." His voice shows no remorse, nor his eyes.

"Why did you, then?" I say. "After all this time."

He keeps his eyes trained steady on mine. "Nobody has ever looked at me the way you do," he says. "I need some looking into, Leandra."

I turn away quick. "You'd best quit talking nonsense."

Behind me, Wim laughs. He sounds like a sad old man, seasoned to his own foolishness until he scarcely minds it anymore.

"What do you mean to find here, Wim?"

"What might be left of me," he says.

I may not understand him, but he isn't lying. I know that much.

Pammy Jo and Wim lived, like I said, way out in the country. But their house was a kind nobody but city folks could abide. The high glass walls looked barely held up by the clumps of stone and slashes of raw wood that joined them. Indoors the rafters were left stark naked, like in a barn, and the round stone fireplace belonged in some patchy campground if you asked me. There wasn't even a fire.

"Pamela?" Wim's voice had thinned out, seemed like. "Sweetheart, we're here," he said.

The house was cold and silent. It smelled of fresh lumber and nothing else, like nobody had ever cooked or eaten there.

"She sleeps quite a bit." Wim was nearly whispering.

"Reckon that's the best thing." I whispered too.

A murky narrow passageway cut off to the right of the fireplace. Wim started that way, then turned around and beckoned me follow. "She'll want to see you," he said. I wished he had sounded surer.

At the end of the passage, the icy afternoon light spilled in from outdoors again. The room Wim went into, and me after, was mostly glass. There was even a large patch of it up in the ceiling, though thick ice blocked off the sky. The room was big and square. About the same size as the room that is my house. There was hardly any furniture, which made it seem even bigger.

The one wall that wasn't glass, white as meringue, was all doors and shelves and drawers. The floor, blond wood, looked brittle with varnish. In the center of the room sat the biggest bed I ever saw, and in the center of the bed, under a heap of mayonnaise-colored comforter, was my sister.

"Sweetheart?" Wim said.

Pammy opened eyes that were dark, nearly navy blue, with lashes so long folks tended to doubt they were real. Eyes that big and dark in a face so white, so thin, looked almost freakish. Her hair, once unconscionably long and fiery, was cut to her shoulders and had gone a little dim. My sister was still beautiful, though. Never could Pammy not be beautiful, nor could I ever not know her.

I whispered her name. I thought I did. I whispered my sister's name like a secret I'd been sworn to keep until I died and now I was . . . *Pammy*. I felt my own life pulling away from me. But it was no more than a breath I let loose of, I guess, because neither my sister nor her husband looked at me and the air in the room stayed stretched tight.

"Where have you been?" My sister, staring at her husband, sounded fretful. Her lips looked parched and pale.

"The roads are a disaster." Wim seemed to shrink a little.

I expected him to go on, telling about the cars in ditches and how we kept having to stop and chip ice off the windshield when the wipers got too crusted to move. But it was as if Wim knew how little use there'd be in explanation. He spoke like a man expecting not to be heard. "The trip was slow," he said. "Are you all right?"

I kept waiting for my sister to look at me. The foolish thought popped into my head that she looked like the princess whose sleep got spoiled by a pea slipped under her mattress.

"I haven't had a thing to eat all day."

"Pamela—" Wim reached one hand toward her, then let it drop.

I could see he was embarrassed. I stepped up to the bedside, smiling. "You feel like some Carolina corn bread, girl?" I said. "Brought some okra too. Fig preserve and a pecan pie."

My sister shut her eyes for a minute. When she opened them again, she had put on a pleasant look as false and spare as the greenery filling in the gaps on a plate in a restaurant trying to be fancy. "Leandra," she said. "All grown up."

"Close to it anyhow," I allowed. I leaned down to kiss her, nearly toppling onto the bed because she lay so far from its edge. When I caught my balance by touching her shoulder, she shuddered.

"Good Lord, your hands are like ice." Her voice didn't sound the least bit familiar. She sounds right like her husband, I thought. Then I wondered if it was on purpose, each letter being so distinct, and maybe she was making fun of him.

I straightened up and rubbed my hands along the sides of my dress, but the cotton seemed even colder than I was.

"I'm a little flummoxed," I said. "Seeing you and riding an airplane and becoming an aunt and all."

Pammy looked away. "You had a good trip?"

"Tolerable." I rolled my eyes, made a face, hoping my sister would laugh, or at least Wim would. But their eyes were fastened on each other.

"Let me fix you a plate," I said.

"I'm past being hungry," said Pammy.

"You should eat something, Pamela," Wim said.

"I know." She sighed. "Did you really drag all that up here, Leandra? Figs and . . . " She trailed off as if the very notion wore her out.

"I did," I said. "Even sweet potato biscuits. That's one thing I'd never forget, how you couldn't get enough of Mama's sweet potato biscuits."

"You must have been a sight at the airport. Shopping bags, I suppose?"

"Honey," Wim said.

"I used the vanity case from Mama's Samsonite," I said. "I got so many things I been saving up to tell you, Pammy Jo!"

But my sister was looking at her husband again, like I was already gone and she had only him to blame.

"I'd best go make acquaintance with the kitchen first," I said.

When I glanced back from the broody passageway, Pammy was rolling over, showing Wim her back. He just stood there, looking helpless, as the huge bed bucked and swayed under my sister like a monstrous animal trying to lumber to its feet.

Later that evening, when Pammy was asleep again and Wim and I were eating warmed-over stew beef in the chilly white kitchen, I asked him about that bed. He told me it was a special kind. The mattress was filled with warm water. It was supposed to be soothing, Wim said.

I kept picturing Pammy's dinner plate, coming back to the kitchen as full as when I carried it in to her. One of the biscuits, garish inside as orange sherbet, had been torn in two. Like my sister had thought to trick me into believing a bite had been taken from it.

—ʌʌʌ—

The ice melted away in a day or two, but all that April and on into May the weather stayed raw and rainy. It seemed like maybe I wouldn't have been so homesick if I could just have got warm. My thin clothes never stopped reminding me how little I belonged in that place. Reckon I might have borrowed some things from Pammy, but I couldn't hardly bring myself to ask, her being so peevish. She'd never cared for me touching her things when I was a youngster.

I found this old zippered sweatshirt of Wim's anyhow. It lingered on a hook by the back door like a limp gray shadow. In the mornings after he left for school I'd put that on. It smelled a little musty, like a cellar, but also like him somehow. I was always careful to take it off and hang it back up before he came home. One day Wim got back early, though, and saw me in it. He didn't say anything, and I didn't, either. The next evening he brought me a red fleece jacket with the name of his school, St. George's, and a big dragon on the back. "Now you'll have a souvenir," he said with a twisted little smile. The dragon was breathing fire.

I looked for things I could do to brighten that house, but Pammy Jo wouldn't stand for much. She didn't care for what I cooked. Would only eat powdered mushroom soup that came in an envelope, frozen creamed spinach that came in a box, this special bread Wim brought from a bakery in town. The bread—wheat germ, he said—was rough as silage. Pammy Jo liked it, but only sliced thin and with the crusts cut off. I crumbled the wasted crusts and scattered them out back along the path by the kitchen door, hoping the birds would come find them. It always surprised me how few birds they seemed to have around there. You'd hardly know it was spring.

When the wind was high, the frail-spined house would whine and moan until my hair about stood on end. The sound came, Wim said, from how the place was built. There had to be some give in the glass, was how he explained it. To me, though, that house was just begging for some heat and light like a body naturally would in such weather. I'd thought, that first night, to make a fire. But the handsome brass-edged woodbox on the hearth was empty. Pammy didn't want soot spoiling the furniture and such, Wim said.

Well, keeping the house spick-and-span, that was surely something I could manage. The third day I was there, Wim off at school and Pammy sleeping most of the afternoon, I gave the white-tiled kitchen a good scouring, putting plenty of ammonia in the water. I took every last thing out of the cupboards and scrubbed the shelves down too.

My eyes were still teared up from the ammonia when Wim got home at five. You could see he was surprised at how I'd pitched in, and he about fell all over himself thanking me.

"Ain't that what I'm here for," I said, "to try and help out? Once she's got that little one, don't reckon Pammy will have much time for cleaning."

Wim looked distressed.

"Is something wrong?"

"No, no," he said. "Leandra, can we sit down?"

He slumped out of his heavy coat and hooked it over the back of a chair. A faded red book bag sat on the table, a battered thermos bottle poking up out of it. "Sit down," he said again. He pulled out a chair for me, then sat on the other side of the table.

"It's not that we don't appreciate what you're doing, Leandra," he said. "But we have a woman on Fridays . . ."

"A woman?" I said.

"Who comes to clean? Josie's been with us for years," Wim said.

I wanted to rub my stinging eyes, but I was afraid he'd think I was crying.

Wim looked down at the table, empty and shining in front of him. "Pamela can be . . . very particular," he said. "About the house. And Josie . . . well, she has her own way of doing things." He sighed. "Sometimes we have to put up with . . . We'd be lost without her, I'm afraid."

I nodded once, then looked away. I was thinking about my mama, always cleaning up after folks who were no kin to her.

Why, your mama's just a regular part of our family, one of them rich ladies told me one time.

"Leandra?"

I would not—could not—look at my brother-in-law.

Wim reached across the table, took hold of my chin, and turned my face toward him like he owned it. I wrenched it away. He looked straight into my eyes then, and I could see him seeing how he'd hurt me, seeing it and feeling it and taking it into himself. It was easy, for a moment, to hate him.

"What is it exactly I *am* here for, William?" I said.

He hesitated. "I'm not sure," he said.

"I thought it was to help out."

"You're not here to be a servant, Leandra."

"No, indeed," I said. "I'm here to be a sister. Only I guess it needs some explaining, what a sister is allowed to take on herself. Reckon I'm out of practice."

He flinched like I'd slapped him. "Forgive me," he said. "I'm not handling this very well."

I tried to look away, keep aloof, but I can't seem to hold a grudge if you clamp it in a vise for me. "Me neither," I told him. "Not well at all."

Wim sagged back in his chair, then we smiled a pair of woefully dim smiles.

"I thought if Pamela just weren't alone so much . . . "

"*You* thought."

Wim lowered his eyes. "We . . ." He shrugged.

"My being here was your idea, then," I said.

He didn't answer me.

"Pammy doesn't care for it one bit," I said. "Does she?"

"I don't think Pamela knows what she wants," Wim said. "Except not to be pregnant anymore."

I nodded. "To have the baby safe and sound. Of course that's what she wants."

I don't think I'd realized until that moment, when I saw it drop away, that there'd always been a veil across my brother-in-law's eyes. What I read in his newly naked look was that, old as he seemed to me then, a professor and all, Wim didn't have no more idea than a boy would how to comfort a wife. How to ease a child's passage into this cold world.

And I got an inkling too, maybe, that we all, Wim and Pammy and me and even that little creature whose foothold on this life seemed such a slippery thing, that all of us were already twisted up in some sorry predicament we couldn't stop or grasp or even see.

"Leandra, I'd be so grateful if you could just—" Wim took off his glasses and rubbed his big square thumbs across the ridge of bone that held up his heavy eyebrows.

"Tell me," I said. "I won't know what I'm even doing here unless I can help."

Wim has a heavy beard, and dark, even now when his hair's gone half white. There was only a silver thread here and there in his thick, close-cropped hair then. His cheeks and chin were dug out deep, though, and above his lip looked smudged late in the day.

"If you could get her to come back," he said. "She is so far away."

"I reckon she must be scared. Don't you think?" My voice came out small and unsure. "Those babies our mama lost back when—" I saw Wim wince. "Now I'm making you scared too," I said.

Wim, staring at his hands, seemed like he couldn't hear me.

"Pammy must have told you . . . about Mama losing some babies?"

He slowly shook his head.

"Three, I think. Or it may have been four."

Again Wim sighed, and suddenly I wanted to tell him all I never told to anyone, how all those many years later the pain of those tiny failed lives lived on in the eyes of a woman with two grown daughters, holding joy at bay and stunting love. *It wasn't she didn't love us,* I imagined telling my sister's husband, just how her love came to us worn, a little skimpy, like something handed down once too often.

But my throat and lips and tongue could not surrender so much, of course, not to a man I scarcely yet knew. Still, my sorrow must have whispered something of itself to Wim, because he reached across the table then and touched for just a second the back of my hand.

"Mama was still talking about those lost babies two days before she died," I said. "Past the time when she even remembered me." Tubes of icy bluish light slashed the ceiling of the square white kitchen. "I felt so . . . puny." The sound I made then, trying to laugh, was an embarrassment.

Wim just nodded, though. "Like you weren't even there," he said.

And when I looked into his eyes it seemed to be me I saw there. I glanced away fast, not wanting him to spy himself in me. But when I turned back, a small smile kinked his face, saying, *Too late, too late to keep anything from me.*

When finally I spoke again I sounded groggy, like somebody just shaken awake. "It all happened before I was born, those little lost babies and how after . . . I reckon it's what Pammy Jo's recollecting anyhow, maybe still seeing it like a small child would, how the darkness just swooped down and like to swallowed up her mama."

"Is that what she says?" Wim's voice was thin.

"She don't say much," I admitted. "You got to remember it's only a nine-year-old keeps me from being a stranger."

He looked at me like I was making no sense.

"Me." I smiled. "I was nine when she left. Just a child. I got no idea how much memory Pammy's kept of that child, let alone the least fondness. And the person I'm grown into? My sister don't know her one bit better than you do."

A pot of potatoes I'd set to boil on the range dripped onto the burner and hissed. I went to turn down the heat, keeping my back to Wim. "Did she ever talk about me? Used to, I mean?"

He made no attempt to answer. I understood then how honest

Wim could be when it was hard, and maybe started right there to love him a little.

"Never mind," I said. "Reckon it's us being sisters now that matters." I turned around and looked at him. "You just keep mindful of the sturdy baby my mama finally got around to having, though, because that one grew into somebody can put her foot down when darkness tries to take over a house."

It took him a moment to get my meaning. Then he tipped back his head, smiling only with his eyes. I saw Wim's eyes catch and melt the cold pale light from above. The glazed black windows were starting to cloud with steam. I wondered how causing his laughter could even for a moment have brought me a thing but gladness.

"Wim . . . You mind me calling you that?"

"I'm told William doesn't suit me," he said.

I considered that. "Don't reckon it does."

His eyes, even then, were a hazy shade, almost like doubt would be if you picked a color for it. I looked deep into them for a second. "Don't fret," I said. "I expect the child will bring her back to us if we can't do it ourselves."

I only half believed, of course, what I was promising. My honesty lacked the clear sharp edges of Wim's. But I tried not to think about that. Sometimes the lie you got to believe yourself is all you got to offer a soul in need. Later you might have to decide were you being generous . . . or just too proud to show your empty hands.

We stand, awkward as children at their first dance, in the middle of the room. The wainscoting is darkened by soot and smoke. I had meant to whitewash the walls in spring, but dawdled about it. Then it was summer and too hot for such ambitious work.

It's the rarest thing, now I think about it, that anybody save me gets much look inside this little house. There's Branch, of course, but he don't hardly pay attention, and I wouldn't rightly call him a visitor after all these years.

Now, though, all of a sudden, I find myself looking with new eyes at this place where I live, just because Wim is in it. Ain't the shabby furniture that vexes, the streaky walls and webby rafters. No, what's worrisome is, what does Wim make of all these broke-down dolls I live amongst? My livelihood, my calling. Does he look at the rows of hairless heads, the stacks of headless bodies, and see something like a little nightmare? Does he wonder how I've lived with so much maiming under my nose all these years?

A porcelain baby doll, a triangular gash in her head, is laid flat on her back on the bench. Her cloth torso looks pee-stained. Most of her fingers and toes are gone. Around her all the other dolls seem to be looking away, like mannerly children are taught to do when they run into a body that's afflicted.

Wim is staring out the doorway to the blackness of the porch, staring at nothing at all so far as I can see. I scoop up the dolls in one armload, clearing off the bench. The carton they came in stands on the floor in the corner. I drop them in, sliding the baby in last, and close the carton's flaps.

"You want to sit down?"

Wim turns, startled, and studies the bench. The narrow pine slab that is its seat has lost most of its finish. The back slats slant slightly forward at an angle to insult and torment the human spine.

After a minute Wim chooses the end nearest the door, sits down sideways, holding on to the back. He looks very small. The bench has room for at least another five men his size.

"Cozy." He smiles.

I nod. "My daddy's granddaddy made that. We claimed it back when the little Baptist church out past Barco burnt down."

"It doesn't exactly urge an old sinner to get comfortable," Wim says.

"It ain't supposed to," I tell him.

He looks up at me with skittery eyes.

"In the church, I mean," I tell him. "That's where a person sat waiting to be called up and get saved. You were supposed to pass the time counting your sins, I reckon."

Wim smiles again, a crimped little smile.

"There's other places," I say. "To sit."

I cross the room. The rag rug is lumpy under my bare feet. I take Wim's hand, draw him up, lead him to the old armchair. Around it, the pool of light where I sat, at peace stitching, a quarter hour ago seems distant as Raleigh, Asheville, Boston—places I've passed through without them leaving a mark on me. Soon it will be midnight. I haven't even been out tonight to check up on the moon.

"I thought I would never get here." Wim sinks into my chair.

"You must be right road-weary," I say. I think to ask how many hours he traveled, but I stop myself. I am not ready yet to hear what it took to get him here. Nor can I conjure up what it might take to get him gone.

"Do you want to wash up?" I ask him.

Wim touches his grimy cheeks with both hands, as if to make sure his face is still there. Blood has dried on his brow in the shape of a kiss. He nods.

I fill the old soapstone sink by the stove with warm water. I fetch a clean towel and washrag from the cupboard above, a new bar of yellow soap. Our hands do not touch as he takes them from me.

"The commode is just there." I point to a low doorway with a faded curtain strung across. "And the shower when you want it."

While Wim is washing, I go out and sit on the porch, taking the rickety straight-back chair I use mostly to set my feet on, leaving the wide-hipped oak rocker for Wim. That rocker is the only chair Mama could comfortably settle into after she gained her size. It used to sit beside the fireplace in the farmhouse up the road where we lived until she died. This house I'm in now was a sharecropper's shack on the same parcel of land, though it's been gussied up a good bit since then, plumbing and all. Both the rocker and the cabin have stood up to a lot of wear and tear.

"Leandra?" Wim sounds like a child just beginning to suspect he might have got lost.

"Out here," I say. "On the porch."

The night has finally got around to its cooling the last hour or so. It is, after all, November. I imagine myself taking the scratchy brown-and-russet shawl woven by Wim's wife from the cedar chest, wrapping the wool around myself, and setting here to outwait dawn, when Wim would drive off again, sunrise making a spectacle of itself behind him.

He is still in the house. Perhaps ransacking my belongings. As if the random object on a shelf or in a chifforobe drawer might make plain to him what he's come for.

"Wim?" I call softly. "Come out. The night is so fine."

He says something. *Yes?*

"There's a moon," I say. "Come sit with me."

I want him out here on the porch. The thing about having a man come to visit in a single-room house is that the bed is always right there in plain sight, staring at you like a dog that's waiting to be let out.

I hear his heavy footsteps moving toward the door. He must, by now, be longing to sleep. Not even a proper door on the bathroom and . . .

"Oh, Wim," I say. "You got to see the moon."

Pammy seemed, when she slept, to move not at all, as if she was petrified. But beneath her, the bed, so slight in its sinking and rising, seemed to breathe for her, for the baby too. Water is always moving, I reckon, even when you think it's not.

I dragged in a tufted white ottoman from the parlor and set it by the east wall, where I would feel the morning sun on the back of my neck, my shoulders. But the sun did not show itself often that spring, as I recall. Sometimes I would busy myself with the needlework I'd brought from home, a cross-stitch sampler with a border of little blue flowers I thought nice for a baby's room. But for hours on end, it seemed, I could forget the stitchery was in my hands and I'd just keep studying my sister. Looked to me like she was floating away from me on that bed, every day a little farther, and taking her baby with her.

Oh, I wanted that baby in the worst kind of way. Just couldn't wait to get my hands on it. I don't remember thinking at all about the babies I'd never have myself. I'd known it since I was seventeen and the bleeding got so bad and the pain that Mama took me to the doctor in Elizabeth City and he said this wasn't normal, no, something was amiss.

I bounced back quick from the operation, like you do when you're young, took the pills I was told I'd need to, and the news that there would be no babies scarcely touched me, or never seemed to, not then when I could hardly picture myself with a man, let alone a child. Not normal, and the doctor said he was sorry, sorry as could be, and I said that's all right and Mama said how babies were a kind of ruin anyhow, even if you loved them—*especially* if you loved them—and the best thing a woman could do was learn to look after herself.

"Some girls, seems like they're born with the gift of getting what they want." Mama's lips pinched tight together. "Lord knows we got no call to worry over your sister in that department. But you, honey . . ." Mama sighed. "Well, maybe you're best off this way, just makin' do with what life dishes up, not asking do you want it."

She could be right wise, my mama, but it seemed to me that time like she'd got both her children dead wrong. Never had me the least bit of confusion about what I did and didn't want, while Pammy . . . willful as she might appear, she was in something of a pucker about what she needed in this life.

But such thoughts lay only on the edges of my mind in the cold white light of that room where I watched my sister float away in sleep, her child wrapped sound if not safe inside her. Seemed like I barely thought at all. I just made pictures in my mind of a child that would love us back, all of us, same as we loved it, and I didn't until way later see how a kind of covetousness was maybe in my body and, not being in my mind or heart, might not even be sin but just something that couldn't be helped.

Most days Pammy would wake around noontime, but only long enough to eat some soup, nibble some shavings of bread. I coaxed her to try other things—a chicken sandwich, a jelly omelet she used to love—but my ideas seemed to distress her, and the worst thing for her condition, Wim said, was getting upset. So after a while I let my sister have her way in everything. It was best that way, Wim said.

She would ask me to put on the radio while she ate. The radio was hid, like something shameful, behind a secret panel in the white wall. The speakers, not much bigger than boxes of baking soda, were attached to the sides of the bed and stayed covered by a gauzy skirt. The station Pammy favored played complicated piano pieces that had numbers for names, and the men who announced them talked in the sad dignified way of undertakers.

I asked, a time or two, wouldn't she rather listen to something cheerful, but Pammy would shake her head, looking more scornful, I thought, than the question called for. I remembered how she loved Boz Scaggs in high school . . . how the year I started first grade she taught me a dance Mama said had the devil behind it. Whenever I think now of Massachusetts, I remember a sharp cold light and sorrowful music that seemed to move only very slightly, like Pammy's bed did.

After she ate, Pammy would almost always fall right back to sleep, and I would be left there alone with the music, whose sadness I could stand only so long and then I'd have to shut it off.

Later in the afternoon, around four or so, Pammy would wake again. She would let me wash her, tidy up her hair, and change her nightgown. She had the loveliest nightclothes, a whole drawerful, all white and eggshell and cream. And sometimes then, while I helped her to freshen up, she would talk to me.

Nobody—not Pammy and not Wim, either—had ever explained to me what the trouble was, whether it was with Pammy or the baby or if you could even separate the two. "Trouble," she said, that's all, when she'd called for me to come out of the blue. "A difficult pregnancy," was what Wim would say, when forced to mention it. "I hurt all the time, Lannie, everywhere," my sister would tell me. And I could see with my own eyes that, whatever else might have been wrong with her, Pammy was frightened half to death and Wim was too. Not normal, I thought.

I was frightened myself, of course, all the more with each long silent day that slipped past. Sometimes I would linger in the front room, pacing that length of glass that walled me in and watching the road out front like a sentry. Had to be neighbors, I thought, and friends, folks who'd come by with a covered dish or a potted plant or just a quarter hour to visit?

But the days frittered away, so slow, and there was no one. The mail was dropped by a gloved hand from a little white van into a green mailbox at the foot of the drive. The newspaper was tossed from a speeding bicycle by a youngster in a blue knit cap. Sometimes it hit the door with a thump. A man came once to read the water meter. I started to show him down the cellar stairs. He could find his own way, he said. It got so I could hardly wait for Fridays, when Josie would come to clean.

Josie Andrade was a small, tart woman with a righteous bun of gunmetal hair you could tell had had the curl scolded right out of it. She wore the same thing every week—a black sweatsuit with a thin electric-blue stripe down the pant legs.

The second she'd come inside, her big beat-up Buick jolted to a stop just shy of the garage door, Josie would pull a section of newspaper out of her tote bag and spread it on the floor beside the back door. Then she'd take off her fat plush-lined boots and set them on the newspaper. Next thing she'd pull out a pair of yellow terry-cloth bedroom slippers, the kind left to flap loose at the heels, and squeeze them on over her bulky wool socks. She'd never even think about saying hello until her feet been seen to. Not that Miss Josie's how-dos were the kind took much thinking about.

I didn't take one bit kindly, I must say, to the notion of somebody else cleaning the house while I sat around on my hands. But Josie made it right plain the job belonged to her and she wouldn't countenance nobody getting in her hair trying to help.

That Friday I first met her, I made her lunch—an egg salad sandwich and tomato soup and a dish of Jell-O with fruit cocktail and little marshmallows in it. I was feeling right pleased, especially with that Jell-O. Just the evening before, I'd worked up the gumption to ask Wim to carry me to the big store by the turnpike. If it was going to be me doing the cooking, those stern white cabinets were going to get filled up with food that had a little color to it. I saw Wim pressing his lips across a laugh when I dropped the sack of marshmallows into the cart, those tiny pastel pillows that resemble butter mints. *Laugh all you care to,* I felt like telling him, *so long as you give me a lift to the market now and then, because your kitchen is getting ready to open under new management.* But Wim didn't laugh and I didn't say boo; we just kept on about our business. He wouldn't hear of me paying for anything, even the shower cap and new toothbrush that weren't for anybody but me. First thing when we got home, I put that Jell-O together so it could set up overnight.

Well, Miss Josie brought her *own* lunch, thank you very much. I shouldn't have taken the trouble, she said. I wondered what she could have in that pea-green tote bag anywhere near as nice as what I'd fixed. I never got to find out, though, because at noontime that lunch got ushered down to the cellar. I pretty much made myself scarce after that when Josie was around.

The Lord must have seen the sorry state I was in, though, so fierce in need of a body to talk to, because the third Friday, He arranged to soften up Miss Josie Andrade for me.

I come out of my room in late morning to see about fixing Pammy Jo's powdered soup, and there is Josie hunched over the kitchen sink, crying so hard it looked like her tough little shoulders meant to split her body right down the middle like a chicken's.

So shocked I surely didn't stop to think, I just grabbed on and held her like nothing but my hands could hope to keep her in one piece.

Josie tried to shove me away. Her small black eyes, flooded with tears, were blusterous.

"What is it?" I held on, ready to get hit between the eyes.

Josie felt stiff and splintery as plywood in my hands. Then all of a sudden she went limp. She held up her left hand. I looked, expecting blood, flesh singed or torn, but all I saw was a small rough brown hand, some chipped pink nail polish, knuckles a little chapped.

"Miss Josie, *what*?" I said.

Her face bunched up like a squalling baby's. "My ring." She twisted out of my grasp and covered her eyes. "Gone," she said.

I recollected then what I'd seen without noticing: a thin gold band on her left hand. "Your wedding ring?"

Without looking at me, she nodded.

Finding things was a little gift I always did have, even as a child, according to Mama. Old folks especially was always sending for me to come over and poke through their belongings and help them get their hands on what they'd forgot where they'd hid. They'd give me cookies and colas and lemonade and even a quarter sometimes. One lady even told me I was a saint, a little Saint Anthony, she said. I asked Mama later what that meant and she said she wasn't sure herself, only Mrs. Gagliano was a Catholic and maybe a mite peculiar.

I took a grip on Josie's shoulders again, swiveled her toward me. "Now don't take on so," I told her. "Got to be around someplace, don't you think?"

She shook her head.

"You reckon a ring's apt to get up and walk away? Wander off into the woods, hitch a ride into town, maybe?"

I meant, of course, for her to smile. She looked at me like I was simple.

"Set down." I nudged her toward the kitchen table. "Now you just tell me what you been up to all morning," I said. "Start with the very first thing."

It took some persuading to get her going, but once she started, Josie had a memory wouldn't quit. I closed my eyes while she talked, trying to picture everything she done, the way she'd do it.

When she'd finished, Josie got to crying again. "It went with the water," she said.

Well, I knew right what she meant. Hadn't my mind's eye just been watching those small brown hands scrub out the toilets, scour the sinks? Before I quite knew myself what I was thinking, I was smiling.

"With the water," I said. I jumped up from the table and ran out the back door without stopping for a jacket or anything.

The day was bright, the air edgy with wind. My skirt slamming hard against my legs, I ran around to the side of the garage. There, tucked under a twist of bramble in some soap-scummed mud, the thin gold circle of Josie's wedding ring shone dully in spilled sunlight.

I heard her come up behind me. I turned around, smiling to beat the band, and held out the ring to her. "With the water," I said. "I noticed last week how you'd . . ."

Miss Josie didn't have a thing to say. She took the ring and jammed it down on the fourth finger of her left hand like she was just plain put out with the pair of them, that ring and her bony finger.

"Well, then," I said, turning back to the house.

Miss Josie stepped up and blocked my way. Slight as I am, she was way smaller, a tiny ferocious woman with a face tough and weathered as bark. She did not look up at me, she didn't say a thing. She just grabbed hold of my hands and—first one, then the other—she kissed them on the knuckles.

Then, walking in step, we went back to the house and got on about our business.

"A leopard," Mama was fond of saying (oh, some of her sayings would have tickled Wim!), "ain't likely to change his spots . . . unless the body talkin' him into it's right convictional."

Well, Miss Josie's spots weren't about to fade, let alone vanish. She stayed ever prickly about me getting underfoot when she was busy, still toted her own lunch. But Josie didn't eat in the cellar anymore; she sat with me in the kitchen. And sometimes if I made dessert she wouldn't mind a taste when she'd done with her tomato and cheese and onion sandwich.

She told me, one slow little piece at a time, how long ago her husband, Manny, was a fisherman in Rhode Island. He had his own boat, *Galilee Gal,* and when the tuna were running good off Point Judith, Josie said, sometimes Manny wouldn't come home for days.

Manny Andrade and his two brothers and the *Galilee Gal* went down in a storm near Block Island in 1974, Josie told, and the bodies were never found, just some pieces of the boat, and Josie all in pieces too, and only part of her left, so she lost the baby she was carrying, who would have been their first, her and Manny's, would have been her only . . .

And soon after that was when Josie moved to western Massachusetts, where maybe spring was unconscionably late and stingy, but at least she wouldn't have to look at the sorry sight of the sea another day of her life.

I wanted to ask Josie did she ever maybe think about getting married again. Then I remembered how she'd looked when she figured she had lost that ring kept her married to Manny, and I bit down hard on the question and tasted the foolishness of it.

I couldn't really talk to Josie about Pammy or Wim. That wouldn't have been right, and I didn't want to cause Josie any more reminding than could be helped of the little one she'd lost herself. But sometimes I would tell her about home. Carolina sounded like Portugal, she said, but when I asked how so, Josie just shook her head and crimped her mouth and said talking about it would only make her sad. And sad in Josie always sounded about the same as mad, but it got so I believed I could tell the difference.

I don't suppose there was much for Josie and me to talk about, especially if sadness was kept out of it. Still, I treasured Fridays for the simple comfort of another voice, another warm body besides my own in the cold hollow that my sister's house felt like to me.

Besides me and Pammy and Wim and Josie, the only ones ever seen in that house were the doctor, who came on Wednesdays around suppertime, and a nurse who stopped by three afternoons a week to check Pammy's blood pressure and such as that.

It came as a regular shock to me, at first, the doctor being a woman and the nurse a man. Dr. Hathaway looked to be about sixty, but right fit, sturdy for her age. Her hair sat tight against her head like a bathing cap and her shoes were mannish, but she wore a bright-red coat and fancied ruffled blouses and big sparkly collar pins. The nurse, whose name was Lester, was slender and brown and shy-eyed as a fawn. He wore a little gold earring, and once, passing by the bedroom door, I heard him call my sister "Ducky."

I was never invited to stay in the room, of course, when Dr. Hathaway or Lester went in with Pammy, and neither was Wim. I'd try to keep busy in the kitchen when they'd come, and neither one said much more to me than hello, how do, bye now. Wim mostly wasn't there when Lester came. When Dr. Hathaway would get ready to leave, though, Wim would always see her out to her car, a big cloudy-blue station wagon, and that was when she'd tell him whatever she had to tell him, I reckon.

It couldn't have been much. Wim was never out there for long. When he'd come back inside he'd look kind of peaked but more relaxed, and he would linger in the kitchen and say something to try and help stop me worrying, like *So far so good* and *No news is good news*.

Wim used clichés as playthings like that sometimes. His teasing was meant to ease my mind, I know. But it was never much good for that. It just bottled up my questions.

It got so I'd try to come back with things that would tickle him: *All's well that ends well* or *A penny for your thoughts,* and once, not stopping to think, *Don't count your chickens before they're hatched,* words so poorly chosen we both pretended I never said them and I went on peeling potatoes and Wim poured himself a glass of wine.

I'd been there a couple or three weeks, let's say—so Pammy would have been nearing her ninth month—when I came right out and asked her flat, would she mind explaining the trouble to me.

Dr. Hathaway had been in the evening before, and the whole house seemed to breathe a sigh of relief for a day or so after her visits. Plus the sun was out that afternoon. I was giving Pammy a sponge bath. Her spirits were about as good as they ever got, meaning she didn't twitch or cuss or swat my hand away like I was getting used to her doing when I ran the washcloth over her stretched skin. I made sure the water was nice and warm. She said the lotion I smoothed on afterwards felt nice. I figured it was a good time maybe to talk.

Pammy didn't get mad, just kind of wilted, when I asked my question. Her face, not near as fine and lively as I'd remembered it all those years, but still lovely, still young, looked very small above the big shiny globe of her belly.

"I don't like to talk about it," she said.

"Reckon you don't," I said. "But I'm scared white, Pammy Jo. And seeing as I'm the one stays with you all day, just seems like it would be . . . you know, *safer,* me having some notion what trouble we got here."

Pammy shut her eyes, sighing deep. Then she turned on her side to face the wall of glass, which had turned a sudden bright blue. For a second, hearing water slosh inside the mattress, I imagined a tide rushing in and wondered what it might be about to pull back out with it.

"Pammy Jo," I said, real quiet, "I'm your sister. Who else you got now to talk to? That's a woman, I mean."

She opened her eyes and stared at me. Those big inky eyes looked caught by surprise, like maybe it was only just now she noticed, yes, I was a woman too. Then her face slighted me. "It's hard to explain how you feel ashamed," she said.

"Ashamed?" My voice was splintery. She meant to tell me something terrible now, like maybe Wim wasn't her baby's daddy, some secret corner of her life that wouldn't bear looking into. . . .

"When your body's . . . when it doesn't work right." Then Pammy started to cry. "Maybe if I wanted it more . . ."

I leaned over the bed, took hold of her face, and tried to slant it in my direction. But she had set herself against me, and I could not bend her my way.

"Pammy, whatever it is, it's—"

"Don't." Her throat was thick with tears. "Don't tell me it's not my goddamn fault."

I didn't know what to say.

"Everybody tells me that, the doctor and—" She took a deep breath, grew calmer. "Maybe it's true," Pammy said. "It's just no help."

I sat down on the edge of the bed. It rocked and nearly tipped me off. Then, finding my balance, I started to move with the current, like I was floating. "Maybe you'd best tell me," I said.

Pammy rolled onto her side. The mattress lurched. Without thinking, I reached over and grabbed hold of my sister's shoulder. It felt like papier-mâché, brittle and nearly weightless, the bones like twisted wire underneath.

I had pulled off Pammy's nightgown to bathe her, and now I could see her start to shiver. Her breasts, rounder than the ones she'd left home with, were veined with pale blue. Her nipples, rose-gold coins, pursed tight against the chill.

I took my hand from my sister's shoulder and covered her up to her chin with the comforter, which was the shiny material of an old-fashioned wedding gown. "There," I said.

Pammy sighed.

"Tell me," I said.

After a minute, she nodded. Then, her back kept half turned on me, my sister explained how her womb did not seem to care to hold in the baby it was making. Something like the elastic in old underwear, Dr. Hathaway had told her, too much of the snap gone out of it, an excess of give, and so it could not be trusted. There had been an operation, Pammy said, something like a tiny hammock placed at the womb's opening to catch the baby if it started to fall. And when the time came, if she held together that long, they would have to cut her open to get the baby safely out.

"Cut you?" I said.

"And a great big old scar slashed through the middle of me," Pammy whispered. "You got any idea how that . . . I won't even be *me* anymore, Lannie, and Wim—"

"You think a thing like that's apt to matter to your husband, once he knows your baby's all right and you . . . ?"

My sister didn't answer me.

"Your baby *is* going to be all right," I said softly. "It could help if you believed it."

"You're just like Wim," said Pammy. "Don't care about a thing but the baby. What about *me*?" She sounded like she'd clean forgot it was her child we were talking about.

"Pammy Jo," I said after a while, "I know you must be scared, but—"

"You *don't* know," she said, turning toward me. "You can't."

"Not unless you tell me," I said.

My sister squeezed her eyes shut. Her mouth was like a small tight knot. "Wim thinks this is his first baby," she said. "There were two other ones."

"You—" There wasn't enough breath left in me to make another word.

"Got rid of them." She nodded, her eyes still closed. "He never knew."

"Oh, Pammy." I reached for her hand, but she yanked it away.

"I won't have you judging me," she said.

"You know me better." The second I said it, I realized how wrong I was, of course. "I'm no way like that," I said.

"Then you ain't your mama's child." My sister laughed, a hard-edged sound that hushed every argument my heart wanted to make and my tongue wouldn't fit around.

"I am your sister," was all I could say, not entirely sure I knew what it meant, knowing only the love in it outweighed any lack of understanding.

Pammy kept quiet for so long then I thought she was falling back asleep. I looked at my sister in that big bed, and my bones knew in an aching way how alone she'd have been, how scared.

"I'm sorry," I whispered.

Her eyes snapped open, startled-looking. "You are, aren't you?" She sounded amazed.

I reached over, slow, like you would with a riskish animal, and smoothed my sister's hair back from her forehead. Her skin was chilly and dry.

"I want somebody to take care of *me*," my sister said. "Can't anybody understand that?"

"You got every right," I told her. "To be sure."

"A child means ruin. Mama was always saying that, right?" For a moment my sister, her words turned soft and southerly, sounded like someone I remembered. Then her lips and tongue turned careful again, accounting for each letter. "I find myself thinking of her more than I want to, lying here."

"Mama?"

Pammy nodded. Her face looked floury.

"You'd be bound to miss her," I said.

"Miss her?" My sister tried to smile, but her lips bunched into a tight crooked line and lost their color. I thought she was about to cry, but I should have known better. "You can't miss somebody you never knew, Leandra."

"You didn't see her for a right long time, and that's a shame, but you knew—"

"That's not what I mean, not even close."

I waited.

"How much idea do you suppose we've got who that woman really *was,* that woman we called 'Mama'? What was she *like,* Lannie? You tell me if you can. What was Mama like before she got Daddy and me and all those dead babies and you to weigh her down and stretch her out of shape? You take away the grief and the worry, the pain and the want . . . you see anybody back there behind all that?"

"You think Mama wished she never had us?" The question left my throat feeling scraped, like the asking had taken cries and shouts and hours.

"What I think," Pammy said, "is there wasn't enough left of that woman to even know how to have a wish anymore."

"Then you are right about one thing," I told my sister. "You didn't never know her."

"But I know myself," Pammy said in a low, fierce voice. "And I know that having a baby is going to spoil every single thing I've made myself into . . . make off with every part of this life I've got with Wim." Her eyes moved slowly around the spotless room, as if it were filled with treasures and she needed to make an inventory. "He's got no idea, he really doesn't. And later, when he finds everything changed and not to his liking, well, he'll be free to go. Won't he."

"Don't sound to me like Wim."

"Maybe not," my sister said. "But he'll be different by then."

"There'll be changes," I said. "There'd have to be. But—"

"Look at me." My sister was clasping the embroidered hem of the bedsheet tight across her breast. "You think my skin will ever fit me right again?" she whispered.

"I don't rightly know," I said. "I expect it ain't your skin Wim loves."

"Men are so . . . Wim doesn't know himself what he needs me to be. But I do."

"Pammy Jo, it's clear as day how much he needs this baby,

wants to have a family with you. So maybe you weren't ready before, those other times. . . ."

"I told Dr. Hathaway." Pammy closed her eyes. "Everything. I had to know. The trouble has nothing to do with all that. It's just bad luck, she says."

"All right," I said. "You see? And in a few more weeks now you are going to have your baby. You'll hold it in your arms and look into its eyes and you'll purely forget how hard the coming was." I smiled. "Won't hardly mind if your skin does fit a little loose for a while."

My sister stared at me with eyes that did not look young anymore. "Wim will have *his* baby," she said.

"You can't—"

She silenced me with a shake of her head. "And I'll remember everything," my sister said.

—~—

Wim leans back in Mama's old rocker, resting his head against the high ribbed back, and closes his eyes.

I lean forward in my stiff-necked chair, elbows on my knees.

It seems like neither of us has said a word for hours, though I don't suppose it's much past midnight. The fields out back of the house, picked clean of the late crop of cotton, hum with insects, the night journeys of small animals, and I can feel the hunger of them, out there in the dark.

"You want something to eat?" I say. "There's greens left from supper, and I got plenty of eggs."

"You'd be amazed," Wim says after a minute, "how close my imagination came to this place. I've been on this porch every night for years."

"Pammy must have told you things," I say, forgetting my sister never lived here at all. It's easy, forgetting that, when she has always been so much with me.

Wim shakes his head without opening his eyes. "Your sister and her past were permanently estranged," he says.

Pain pierces my heart and spreads out from there. What is left of my sister's past—isn't that me?

I could not speak if I wanted to. Wim does not expect words from me. We learned a long time ago, Wim and me, to keep silence together, a language both of us could understand. Words do not help anyway, not to pass the time. They only disguise it, and sometimes disfigure it, fooling nobody.

I do not need to do a thing but wait. In his own time Wim will tell me what it is he thinks he is doing here.

—w—

The baby, my nephew, Will, was born a month early. My sister's womb gave way on the twenty-first day of May. It was first thing in the morning and there was not a cloud in the sky, but the close-clipped grass along the driveway was spangled with frost when the ambulance pulled away.

Pammy's face, as she was carried out the door wrapped in a thin putty-color blanket she'd never have allowed in her linen closet, was gray and bitter. But she was not to be blamed for that. One of the ambulance attendants, a curly-headed man with a rusty mustache, had given her a shot, and she wasn't really awake.

Wim and I followed in the car, but we couldn't keep up with the ambulance. The last thing I recall seeing clearly that day was a swirl of red light moving farther and farther ahead of us, finally disappearing around a bend thick with new-greening trees.

"She's going to be fine," I told Wim.

"How do you know?" He sounded grave, hopeful, like he believed I could prove it to him.

"If she wasn't, they'd use the siren, don't you think?"

Wim stopped staring at me only when the car bumped onto the shoulder of the road and claimed his attention.

—w—

I didn't see my sister again until dawn the next day. She was first in the operating room, then in the recovery room all through that night. And only Wim was allowed to go in and see her, just for a few seconds, twice. Both times when he came out, he couldn't seem to do more than nod at me, so that and praying were all I had to go on, to draw comfort from, and I felt like I was sucking on a stone.

By six the next morning, though, Pammy was in a clean white railed bed in a room by herself and the sun was coming up over a big green hill in her window. By that time I knew my sister was going to be all right, knew too that her son never would.

Will was born with something wrong with him that Wim said he would explain to me later, when the words wouldn't come so hard. But they always did, of course. No words could come harder, and not time or anything else in this world could ease them, ever, and it would be years before I could even believe them, let alone say them myself:

My nephew was born with his heart outside his body. I guess it's something that just happens sometimes. Once in a million, or something like that. There's an operation they can try, but Will was far too frail for such as that. The blood that goes up to a body's head carries oxygen to the brain, you see, and when enough's not getting there, well, Will would never have been right in any case . . . not normal.

The little creature lived two days, of a size to hold in one palm, except I never got to. Will died at three o'clock in the afternoon, in a little glass box in a room without windows, his father standing nearby, his big hands hanging helpless at his sides.

It was Dr. Hathaway, finally, who explained things to me, because Wim asked her to. Wim had gone into Pammy's room—I saw just his back for a second, his old gray tweed jacket, then the door closed. Then Dr. Hathaway was telling me, her good old face with stiff creases in it and her eyes steady on me, about the oxygen and the brain, and under the circumstances it was a blessing, she said.

Dr. Hathaway didn't tell me of Wim's useless hands, of course. Nor did Wim tell me himself. The doctor just said, I reckon intending to comfort me, that the little boy's father was right there with him when . . . and the picture of Wim's hands came to be a part of it and has stayed with me ever since.

Just as I have pictured, always, and always will, those tiny white baby hands cupped around a bright-red heart, dainty as a Valentine candy, and seen every day of my life since that one how the beating slowed and slowed and finally, with one gentle thump, just quit.

And told myself sternly, yes, what else could it be but a blessing?

—∞—

We cannot see the moon anymore, not from here. I reckon she's still out there somewhere, though, because the fluted top edge of Pandora's Hill is iced with a silvery light. It's the only hill for miles. Wim wouldn't likely know as much, being a stranger to this land. He knows names for all the stars, though, can call them from wherever he happens to be. Right now, while we are just sitting here, Wim could be teaching me to call the stars by name.

But the night feels like a breakable thing, as if, just by words dropping into it, the darkness could be shattered into a million pieces, like boiling water would do poured into a cold thin glass. And the stars up there look like splinters of what smashed and flew apart years ago . . . which I guess is what they are.

Wim dozes on and off, his head sloping forward, his breath a soft, soft whistle. He is a dark slump of shadow there, across from me, the night meadow flush at his back, and even the birds are sleeping.

I wonder if I dare leave him here. Just slip inside and switch off the light and sleep in my bed the same as if Wim had never appeared. I expect that come morning I might find him here, just as he is right at this given moment, only washed in a pink-wine light.

And in my mind that light is already on him, just so, when he lifts his head and looks at me. His eyes are clear as day.

"Leandra?" he says.

"I'm right here," I tell him.

"What time is it?"

"Three-seventeen A.M.," I say, then we both laugh, because I do not wear a wristwatch, never did, and we both know it.

Somewhere out in the dark a dog barks, just once, quick and sharp, and I feel rebuked for what we have done to the silence. We are vandals and looters, Wim and me.

When he speaks again, it is in a whisper. Wim has learned shame. "Do you know how long it took me to get here?" he says.

It is something I could never guess or calculate. He'd know that, Wim, if he stopped and thought about it.

"Ten years," Wim whispers. "I'm lucky I am still alive."

—w—

It was me and Wim buried his son, just me and him and the Unitarian pastor from a church up the road that looked like a ski lodge in a travel magazine, a squatty triangle of a building wound around by a big parking lot fringed with pine trees. You see houses look like that going up in the mountains outside Asheville now, and all along the Sound. Makes me wonder what folks could be thinking of, spending so much money to build such ugly houses in such beautiful places.

We didn't make much ceremony of it, Wim and that pastor and me. Wim didn't have a bit of use for churchly things, and Reverend Magnuson, who said I should call him Jack, looked plain too young to be in charge of such serious business, with freckles all over his face and a long fringe of fine fair hair hanging down the back of his neck. He didn't even wear a necktie, though he was dressed like an ordinary person, not a minister.

As for me, I just felt it wasn't my place to take charge. I feel a little different about it now, though, because Lord knows somebody needed to.

We never went into the church, just pulled up in front, where Jack was waiting for us to call for him. Wim and Jack were friends, it turned out, from playing tennis together somewhere. Also, Jack had a boy in Wim's school, which was maybe why Wim felt he could ask him to do this thing Wim couldn't do himself and wasn't altogether sure he believed in.

We drove in Wim's car to a big flat raw-looking graveyard out in the country, where deer tracks veered between the stones. Two young men from the mortuary were already there, waiting. They were both wearing gray suits and black ties and standing like soldiers at attention beside a dug grave so tiny it didn't look like a grave at all.

At first I didn't see Will. I wondered if he might be coming along after us in one of those great big black cars, all alone. But then we started walking toward the burial hole, and the two young men stepped aside.

The box, mother-of-pearl with pewter fittings, was not much bigger than a silver chest, except where it domed at the top. It stood so close to the opening in the wet ocher-colored earth that I had to stop myself from running ahead to pull it back from the edge before it toppled in and disappeared.

Wim, like he was reading my thoughts, took a tight grip on my arm, just above the elbow. He was hurting me, which somehow helped.

"It will be all right," I said. Reverend Jack, who mostly kept on a pleasantly blank sort of face, looked horrified. But Wim smiled at me a little bit and gripped my arm tighter, which was all I had holding me up for that moment.

The day was cool and overcast, with clouds dingy as the soapsuds that come out of a washer after the first go-round. The two young men from the mortuary nodded at us in a distant kind of way, but kindly. Then they moved off and stood under a maple, one of the few trees in the cemetery, and waited for us to finish with whatever it was we meant to do.

There was a kind of grace in it, what little we could do, maybe because we didn't know and hadn't planned it out and so had nothing but our poor fool hearts to rely on.

Wim walked up first to the grave, alone, and hunkered down beside the box like you would to have a serious talk with a little child. My arm ached where he had just let go of it.

We left him there, alone with his son, for a few minutes. If he said a word, I didn't hear it, and I'm sure he didn't cry.

Then, just like there was a signal between us, the reverend and I stepped over and lowered ourselves too, one on either side of Wim, who seemed not to see us, only when I went down on one knee beside him he leaned against me a little bit and we both found our balance that way.

Wim raised his hands and placed them on the domed lid of the box. I placed my hands next to his. That slick white curved surface had a million colors in it, like an opal. I expected it to feel cold, but it was warm, as if the sun had been shining on it until just before we got there.

"Let us pray . . ." Reverend Jack's young baffled voice made it sound like a question.

Wim answered it with the barest nod.

I figured the pastor would summon the Lord then, but he didn't, and I was glad. For I could see no comfort, then, in calling on a God Wim hardly believed in and I myself was disinclined to speak to, given such harm as He'd allowed. Well, the Unitarians, Mama told me once, when Branch's cousin Marcy married one, have their own way of doing things, and you would be hard-pressed to even prove they are Christians. This was meant, of course, as the severest kind of judgment when Mama made it. But on the day my baby nephew was laid in the ground up in Massachusetts, I was thankful there were ways of doing things apart from the Christian ones that didn't fit around what we'd been given.

"William?" Reverend Jack was looking not at my brother-in-law, nor up at heaven, but down at the box. He paused for a second, like he was making sure he'd got the little boy's attention. "You were hardly here, son," he said. "But leaving, you take so much away . . . the world all of a sudden seems sliced in half."

I closed my eyes, thinking of my sister, just a few miles away in a narrow white bed with bars around it, on a mattress that would not breathe for her. Wim felt like a small breeze blew through him, but he didn't make a sound.

"You weren't even here long enough to learn how sorrow feels." Reverend Jack shook his head slightly, like someone astonished. "Well, a while from now, when we can maybe understand things better, we'll try to be thankful for that." He sighed. "Truly, we will try," he said.

Amen, I whispered, but only in my mind.

"Could you help us heal, William? Move us to mend? I realize that's asking a lot of a little soul. Feels like asking the impossible right now, if you want to know the truth." He stared down into the hole in the earth. "It's really us who are buried, you know. Grief gets in our mouths and our eyes until we can't ask for what we need and we're blinded to heavenly grace. . . ."

The minister's voice had lost its steadiness. He stopped for a moment, thinking, I knew, of his own child. He took a deep breath I could feel inside me.

"I hope to hell the Lord is listening, kid, when you ask Him to help us live without you," he said. "Because if He doesn't, I don't know what we're going to do."

"Amen," I whispered.

And after a wait, Wim murmured, beside me, "Amen." Then he pulled his hands away from the humped top of that shimmering warm white box. He held his hands open in front of him, palms up, and stared at them like a man who'd just got scalded and still wasn't sure how.

—∾—

It was another week before Pammy Jo got home from the hospital. She was a slow healer, had always been. I remembered how when I was just a little thing and she was in junior high she took a spill from her friend Darlene's bicycle on the blacktop out back of the gym. It seemed like a year passed before the red scrapes on her knees and elbows went away, and even then her skin stayed pale and poochy where she'd hit the ground. Pammy would never wear shorts or sleeveless blouses for a long time after that, no matter how hot it got. She'd stand in front of the mirror and study the little white shadows on her skin, her face a sorrow to behold. Seemed like the slightest hurt marked her forever, I heard my mama say one time.

Wim went alone to the hospital to fetch her. I stayed behind to fix a special lunch, though it didn't take a minute to mix the powdered soup and get it hot, to carve out the bread in tidy little shapes. Wim wanted to go alone, I thought. I'd only have got in the way.

Forsythia had busted out all along the side of the garage. I snipped off some sprigs and put them in a green glass creamer I found in the dining room. It looked real pretty on the bamboo bed tray, beside the spring-green napkin, the sterling soup spoon.

I stood in the cold spare living room, peeking out from behind the heavy drapes that looked like burlap bleached out by the sun. I could never feel at home in such a place. But in the week since the baby was buried, I had made a kind of peace with the heartless rooms. They were full of grief, and so was I. Wim had taken the week off from school. We were at the hospital with Pammy much of the time. But in the hours we were alone in the house together, me keeping mostly to the kitchen, him in the room he used for an office or doing things out in the yard, I had started to feel less uneasy there . . . less unwanted, not so much a stranger. Wim didn't talk to me a lot, but I felt like he didn't mind my being around. He tried mightily to eat the meals I fixed for him. And he always told me they were good, even when he couldn't get much down.

Wim's car finally came up the driveway, then kept on going right across the lawn. I drew back from the window just as the front bumper came to a stop a few inches from the stoop.

Wim jumped out of the car and, without shutting his own door, dashed around to the other side, where Pammy was. I watched him lean inside. I watched him struggle to straighten his back. I watched him lift my sister out from behind the leaf-shadowed glass and into the sunshine. It looked, from where I stood, as if they both shut their eyes against the bright spring light.

I had seen my sister twice each day for as long as she had been in the hospital. She'd barely spoken, apart from asking Wim or me to hold her water glass, call a nurse, switch TV channels. Pammy slept a good bit of the time. When she was awake the television was nearly always on, but never with sound. Still, she would stare for hours at the glaring screen like it had something to teach her, something she needed to learn backwards and forwards before she could leave the bed, leave the dust-colored room, and step back inside the life she'd had before. I never heard her mention the baby, not even to ask about the burial. She must have saved such things for Wim alone, for the times I stepped out of the room.

I watched Wim carry my sister as far as the steps. Then I went to open the door. They looked, the both of them, so frail. But Wim, who had to struggle for balance, to keep on his feet and bear Pammy's weight, was the worse to see.

I stepped out into the cool blue and gold and green of noontime, backing against the door to hold it open wide.

"You're home," I said.

Pammy did not open her eyes.

"We're home." Wim's face was the whitish gray of modeling clay in a school art room. The gouges around his mouth and eyes and down his cheeks were deepsome.

"She's pretty weak," he said.

Wim's whole body was trembling as he made his way down the passage to the bedroom. I kept close behind, as if, should he stumble, I could catch them both before they fell.

Pammy could not eat, she said . . . or managed to let me know, anyhow, with her tightly closed eyes, the strict line of her lips, a weary toss of her head. Her hair was lusterless and crimpy.

"Could you just try?"

I reckon she didn't hear me.

The next morning the bed tray still sat untouched on the kitchen counter. Yellow forsythia blossoms lay in a limp circle around the base of the creamer, flat as embroidery.

—ᴡ—

You set down words and they stay that way and it changes the way you remember things forever after. But what really scares me is how all the things you forget to put down get lost.

"Sifting through the past," Mama used to call it, when I'd catch her sometimes hunched over the big photograph album. I'd study her face, the shadows fighting over her mouth, her eyes, coming finally to a kind of peace as she grabbed on for dear life to the parts of the past—the parts of us and my daddy, even herself—that she meant to keep. And letting the rest go.

I am as old now as Mama was when she got to be a widow. But I am not striking the same bargain with life—with hers or my own—that my mama did. I am trying to hold on to everything.

And so when Wim looks at me now, this near-old man whose eyes are crowded with so much best left forgotten, I do not look away.

"Tell me," I say. "Wim, tell me everything."

"It's fading," he says. He is looking at the sky. In the east the darkness is chalky now. But he is not talking about the night, nor looking toward the day.

"The edges, of course," he says, "are long gone."

"No," I tell him. "Not gone."

There is a peculiar stillness that comes to the earth just before the first touch of dawn. The night creatures seem to have vanished, and daylight life isn't ready to take over or show itself yet. Even the river is stilled, waiting. Wim's soft sigh is like the only sound in God's mute world.

"Not gone," he agrees. "But they don't cut anymore."

"They cut," I say.

"Then I don't bleed."

"Ten years," I say.

"Are you giving me an alibi?" Wim smiles. "It's not just the grief I'm losing," he says.

"I know that," I say. "Don't you think I know?"

"Exactly," Wim says. "You are the only one who knows."

He thinks he is explaining everything.

—∞—

The parts I remember of my sister are not the parts I would choose to keep. In the years that she has been gone, she has returned to me in body. But her spirit, her soul, seems to have left no trace in me. I remember a scar, a smooth red ridge low across her belly, and it is so real to me that it could be under my fingers this very minute.

And when I stand or stretch, when I bend low to retrieve something that has slipped through my fingers, I can feel where the tearing was, how skin-deep the mending. These are the keepsakes my sister left to me. . . .

These, and maybe Wim.

ii

I AM THE LEAST EXTRAORDINARY of men. I have always known it. That is why, at twenty-five, I lost the cheek, the essential bravado, to call myself a poet. Of course, with the lapse of the calling, the practice was bound to dwindle and die. Without hope, Dante says, we are doomed to live in desire. I have found it a cramped and surprisingly frigid realm.

I became, without poetry, an amputee, each day, each deed, treacherous with my own lacks and the world's thoughtless obstacles. I did nothing without calculating, first, the risks. My expectations were checked at every door. Pamela understood this, I think. It may, all along, have been her grasp of me that I found so bewitching.

My vacated soul, naturally, was more than willing to be bewitched. I should have been more chary of Pamela's eagerness to occupy the vacuum in me. That the doubling of destitution would result in famine should hardly have surprised me.

But how misleading to speak this way, pinning and mounting

complexities to some flat surface of comprehension as if they were butterflies—exotic, ephemeral, and utterly harmless. These few specimens of insight have taken me years to capture and identify. No doubt many others have eluded me utterly.

I once engaged a psychiatrist to guide my expeditions into memory and desire. It was not a successful venture. This physician of the spirit attempted to ransack my history, showing neither delicacy nor discrimination. His name (too good to be true, of course, but true nonetheless) was Messenger. He was a short young man, Yale-educated, with oversized hands and ears, thinning hair, eyes too avid to suit me. Dr. Messenger found it "curious," he allowed, that the two women I had managed to love were . . . "less than mature" was how he put it.

Once when, garrulous with self-pity, I alluded to a memory of Pamela's young body, its touchy finespun flesh, I heard the doctor's breath quicken. His eyes had taken on the hard dark glaze of a quattrocento saint. Visions unto unseemly rapture, I thought. He could not see me at all. It was Pamela he wanted, my late child bride. I permitted him to detain me there, Pamela's memory a decoy. The tactic enabled me to keep Leandra to myself.

Dr. Messenger, ensconced behind an olivewood desk with scalloped edges and curvaceous legs, had removed his suit coat and was leaning toward me, elbows on the desktop. His upper chest, under the crumpled broadcloth of a white dress shirt, had the soft amplitude of a woman's. I imagined an irresolute erection cradled between his pudgy thighs, concealed behind costly veneer.

"And you found that appealing?" he suggested. "The rather . . . *childlike* quality of your wife's body?"

It did not occur to me to reply. I retrieved my coat from an ornate hall tree by the door and departed. Driving through the chill dusk toward a scarlet sky, I imagined Messenger, alone in his overheated office, bringing to ignominious completion the arousal for which I would be billed.

The following weekend I first visited Clio's bed. My performance was adequate, if uninspired. My stay, that first time, was brief. But the occasion was nonetheless momentous. Clio had been my desultory Saturday evening dinner companion for some months. Her well-cushioned body invited neither remembrance nor comparison. I assumed my embrace of it marked a resumption of life. High time. Pamela had been gone nearly four years.

I did not, that first night, stay, as Clio suggested. My heart grew fonder at her lack of distress when I declined. I was back at her door early Sunday morning, a sack of sourdough bagels and the *New York Times* in my gloved hands.

"Look at you." Her sturdy blunt fingers kneaded feeling back into my cheeks. The January wind had whipped vibrancy into my face. Her failure to claim credit for my improved color reassured me. She produced a clever little device for splitting bagels without jeopardy. Her coffee, brewed in a French filtre pot, was robust. She is a woman of impeccable competence, my current wife.

If Dr. Messenger was surprised by my return that next Thursday, he was sufficiently professional not to show it. Before he could allude to the previous week's debacle, I plunged ahead to inform him of the latest developments with Clio.

"It's like a last-minute pardon," I told him. "A reprieve."

"Last-minute?" His pale lunar face was impassive.

"Solitary confinement." I smiled at my own melodrama. "Failure to thrive."

He nodded, noncommittal. "So you see yourself as having been incarcerated?"

"By the past," I said.

"And you were sentenced by . . . ?"

"Myself? Is that what you want me to say?"

Messenger smiled.

"Even if that's true, dwelling in the past can be lethal eventually. Surely you agree?"

The psychiatrist shrugged. He looked slightly bored, I thought. "Isn't there something else we need to discuss?" he said.

Slighted by his nonchalance, perhaps, I said, "I may marry this woman."

The claim was hopelessly diverting, of course. Messenger's martinet face betrayed a moment's mild fluster. "This seems—forgive me—rather precipitous," he said.

"I should think the inclination to impulse might be seen as some progress in my case." I lounged back in my well-padded hot seat, striving to look devil-may-care.

"Marriage is a big step." We both smiled at the obligatory nature of the remark. "If you want to cultivate impulsiveness," Dr. Messenger said, "I'd advise you to start with something that can be exchanged. Perhaps a new tie?"

We batted back and forth some speculations on marriage then, two men of the world—a widower and a bachelor.

I waited until the forty-eighth minute of our fifty-minute hour to indicate I would not be coming back. I thanked the doctor for his time and wrote a check to close out my account.

"This really *is* impulsive, William." Messenger had never before addressed me by name. "So much of your history we haven't begun to delve into."

I smiled as if he'd made another witty remark. "It's time I looked ahead," I said.

"You'll call if you find yourself . . . reconsidering?" he said.

I thrust out my hand for a manly shake. Dr. Messenger got hastily to his feet, his swivel chair nodding, manic, behind him. His hand's clasp, if not quite limp, seemed unwholesome. Below the slight soft swell of his belly, the fine charcoal wool of his trousers looked deflated.

The following spring, Clio and I were married by a superior court judge vacationing in Wellfleet. Our weekend honeymoon on the Cape gave Clio the opportunity to deliver that winter's crop of hand-loomed textiles to the specialty shops that sold her wares to the spendthrift summer crowd. Clio was only beginning then to make a name for herself. Now the bulk of her work is shipped to galleries in Marin County, SoHo, and Santa Fe. Several larger pieces have been commissioned by museums.

My sister-in-law was informed *ex post facto* of the marriage.

My letter to her was cordial but brief. Leandra sent a sampler in a thin gold frame. The alphabet, finely worked in rose-colored thread, was wreathed in dainty blue flowers that I take to be forget-me-nots. This was our only wedding gift. I, knowing Leandra, found it endearing. Clio, however, given her contemporary tastes, cared nothing for the sampler. It was stashed, for a year or two, in the back of a closet, behind the winter coats. Later, in a frenzied campaign to scale down our existence, my wife sent Leandra's homely gift off with other discards to a white elephant sale at Jack Magnuson's church, where for twenty dollars I quietly ransomed it.

I have never removed the sampler from the scarred pine cabinet in my office at the school. Still, it has been a small comfort, keeping possession of something wrought by her hands.

Pale moonlight sifts down like flour on the baked meadows that surround Leandra's rude little home. I arrived before sunset, exhausted. The elderly proprietor of the general store at the crossroads that constitutes Leandra's town was surprisingly forthcoming with directions. I said, with a husband's weary indifference, that I was delivering a consignment of dolls. "They hardly look worth saving to me," I said, "but my wife . . ."

The old man grinned. "It's Miss Leandra you want, then, to be sure," he said. "Give that girl a hank of hair and a glue pot, she'll make a critter walk out to meet you on two legs."

"So I hear," I said.

"A regular little miracle worker," the old fellow said.

Only moments from Leandra's door, one last turn to go, I stopped once more. Sitting in the car, I sized up the land. The Great Dismal's twilight, so close by, already seemed chimerical. An unusually hot summer, followed by an autumn without rain, has left the landscape cracked and dry, like the complexion of a beautiful woman whose lifelong indulgence has been the sun. Still, much remains green here, and the air is mild, even well past darkness.

In New England it is already cold, and the wild outbursts of color that seduce a million noisy disoriented strangers to our hills each fall are finished. We who live there have the place mostly to ourselves again, its garbless trees, stern town squares, and desolate roads. The fabled white spires of our churches look slightly soiled by November's light.

Busy getting my affairs in order, I failed to pay homage to the season this year. I neglected to pick apples or buy cider. Even the annual allotment of fresh schoolboys, lost and raucous, received no more than my passing attention. Yet I know the specifics of climate here, the poor yield of crops, the annual rainfall. For more than ten years I have kept close watch on the coastal Carolina weather, my unobtrusive way of keeping an eye on Leandra, a habit cultivated before I had learned how altogether capable she is of looking after herself.

My habitual scrutiny of the national weather map greatly amused Clio, who caught me at it now and then. "But, darling, you never *go* anywhere," she'd say.

"I like to see what I am missing," I would tell her.

My wife's smile remained indulgent. My eccentricity has seemed harmless to her, and likely has been. I merely wished to know what Leandra had to contend with as she went on about the business of her life—heat waves, cold snaps, approaching storms.

So now, at last, at least I shall know.

—∞—

The moon, given my sporadic attention, seems to have plummeted. There is no light yet from the east, but the dark there is losing its vehemence.

Craving the amicable silence Leandra and I long ago learned to share, I feign sleep. My chin rests on my chest. I hold my breaths steady and slow. Occasionally I force my eyelids up a fraction. I expect to see Leandra struggling against sleep, but her back, against the unforgiving slats of a bony chair, holds its own. Alert as a famished bird, she waits for me to tell her the nature of my errand here.

And surely, one would think, I'd have decided by now, settled on some version of truth or its selected parts. At least come up with a plausible alibi for my sudden presence in Leandra's world.

At dusk, beside the crackling mud of a shrunken stream, where the remains of lily pads clogged the thick green water, I slouched in my car trying to concoct a serviceable fiction. I have even gone so far as to imagine a simple surrender of the truth: I have come here to die, if Leandra will permit it. But one glimpse of her face under the flood of topaz porch light, and I knew I could not hand this burdensome knowledge to her. Not anytime soon. Not willingly. Talk is highly overrated as a cure.

There is so much that, even now, we have never mentioned. A history we both know perfectly well. It is my childish hope that my death may come to be as scrupulously understood and accepted as the rest that is unspoken.

Leandra's face keeps its composure. I have witnessed that composure through horror and grief—and, once, even in passion. Her gaze rests firmly on the unutterable. It is vain of me, perhaps, to imagine my death notice might hazard that sweet serenity. But I depend on it and cannot chance its loss.

The dampness has stiffened my neck. I turn my head just slightly, gauging the prospect of ever again lifting it. My rocking chair creaks. I try to cover the sound with a sleeping geezer's sigh.

"Never been a thing but awake," Leandra says, "have you?"

The pain, when I try to straighten my bent body, is a groan only my bones can hear. I must laugh. "And you," I say, "haven't you been sleeping with your eyes wide open?"

A night bird cries out once, a sound of pure disdain.

"How long do you mean to stay here, Wim?"

Here: a stiff porch chair, her house, this earth? I can't afford to leave the choice of meaning to her. I have no plans.

"You'd best tell me," Leandra says, "what it is you got in mind."

"I don't expect to be given your bed, Leandra."

"What then?"

"Perhaps a blanket? A six-foot fragment of your floor?"

It is as if I have not spoken. Leandra keeps full occupancy of her chair, her unyielding posture. Her meaning is clear:

We are going to sit right here, Leandra and I, until I offer a confession that satisfies.

"That bench might make a suitable berth," I suggest. "I have much to recant."

Leandra says nothing.

"I am tired," I say.

"You think I can't see that?" She waits.

The fact that her questions are largely unvoiced does not exempt me from answering them. The sun could come up to burn the flesh from our bones. The river might rise and engulf us or a hard frost freeze us in place. *Hell or high water,* Leandra might say, *until the cows come home:* we are going to sit right here.

In the first inklings of a dim gray light, from within a lifetime's obstinate silence, I begin to hammer out the terms of my heart's last will and testament, having always known that everything, in the end, would go to Leandra.

—w—

I hadn't thought of Dr. Messenger in years. But this evening, sitting in my car, stalled beside a retiring stream, I recalled the psychiatrist and was forced to reconsider his question, to admit it remains on the table:

What need, what flaw or sickness, can account for the unfitting loves I have allowed myself, for the stingy formulae by which I have attended to them? Is it too late, now, to ask?

The sun was hardening like a scab on the tender pink sky, Leandra so close now I could almost have called out to her with some hope of being heard.

I imagined my car like the needle of a compass, finding true north on its own, and for one moment I even imagined summoning the will to leave Leandra in peace, to boot my cravings back up the Atlantic coast, unexpressed, unexplored.

But now, when so little is left to me, I've lost the flair for self-denial, and shame barely makes a dent in desire. Letting Leandra be is beyond me.

The new doctor—his name is Kaplan, my ultimate messenger, and he shows small regard for my psyche—suggests I may feel fine for several months, merely tired. And after this serene phase of false fine fettle, Kaplan augurs, my decline is apt to be swift and otherwise merciless.

The locus of the trouble residing in my brain, however, I have some chance of growing insensible to my own suffering. I try to conceive of that as something to look forward to. Surely by then I shall have gathered the gracious resolve, the savoir faire of the soul, to remove myself from Leandra's sight?

Night spreads slowly across the land, a soft dark blanket moth-eaten with stars. . . .

Astrocytomas: tiny star-shaped cells aglitter in my brain, fanning out, burrowing into the dark folds . . . *countless,* Dr. Kaplan said. Seizures of light. Black lapses.

Were we to cut away . . . the attempt . . .

The moon is scalpel sharp.

What would be left . . .

By a cold invasive light, I made my way, at last, to Leandra's door.

—∾—

When dawn is a pastel smudge along the lower edge of the eastern horizon, Leandra cries uncle without a word. She rises from her chair to meet the dawn, a spare and bleary-eyed Venus. Adamant hand braceleting my wrist. Fingers frigid and faintly rough.

I permit Leandra to move me. Limping on benumbed feet, I follow her inside the house, a blind man led through alien streets by a guide he has no choice but to trust. I might as well learn. My eyes have every intention of failing me.

Just inside the door Leandra abandons me. I stand beside the bench but do not sit down. Without looking back, Leandra moves to the narrow bed and turns down the patched coverlet.

Two pillows, less than voluptuous, in thready white slips, lie at the head of the bed. Leandra claims one, leaves the other.

"You take it," I say. But she has already moved from the bed to a cedar chest. She drops the pillow, lifts the lid of the chest, removes two folded quilts, and spreads them over a crude rag rug.

"I won't have you sleeping on the floor, Leandra."

"This is my house," she says. "I'll thank you to remember that."

Keeping her back to me, she unfolds a dark wool blanket and lays it out, doubled, over the quilts. I recognize the throw Clio made years ago. Did I send it to Leandra for Christmas? A birthday, perhaps. I recall only that I took it without asking. If Clio noticed a discrepancy in her inventory, she never mentioned it.

All Clio's weaving that year was a seamless subterfuge of grays and browns. Her winter's accomplishment, rolled and folded, tightly packed into the workroom shelves, resembled a rock collection.

What an absurd gift for Leandra, this shady spread, heavy and rough and dour. In a snap, a whisper of cloth, a water-stained rose quilt covers the unsympathetic wool.

"Leandra?"

The last quilt, a crimson starburst on a balding blue background, flashes through the air, then sinks to the floor.

"Leandra, be good enough to look at me for a moment." My severe courtesy is a teacher's weapon.

Leandra hesitates, then turns around. She has picked up the pillow again and is hugging it to her chest with both thin arms. Tears seep from the corners of her eyes. She pays them no heed, just stares. "I am looking," she says.

"Why are you crying?"

She shakes her head. "Don't, Wim," she says. "Not now."

My dying, it is there between us. As fast as that. Even if she hasn't quite put her finger on it yet, Leandra knows.

If I could live long enough, would living with Leandra eventually free me of the need to say anything at all? For one moment I allow myself to imagine confession, absolution, passing between us over her small table as unremarkably as butter and salt.

A piece of twine is strung between two nails above the scarred deal table. She must work and eat here. There is nowhere else. The limbs of dismembered dolls dangle above the table in no discernible sequence. Fist-sized wigs are heaped beside the table in a willow basket. Severed heads and limbless torsos crowd the shelves of a corner cabinet. To live so long amid such breakage, alone, such loss . . .

"I see you are no stranger to hopeless cases," I say.

"That used to scare me, Wim, how I could barely finish thinking a thought before I'd hear the words to it coming out of your mouth."

Even when she weeps, Leandra's face does not surrender repose. She bends down to place the pillow on the bed she has fashioned on the floor. Then she crosses to a chipped oval table, its Victorian pretensions mortified by hard use, and switches off the punched tin lamp that has lent the room its stingy light.

I turn and stare at the window above the soapstone sink, where dawn is contained in a rough-hewn rectangle. The sun is just edging up over the selvages of a distant low hill. *"How pure the motion of the rising day . . ."* and Leandra a stillness behind me.

"I had to teach myself to stop dreaming it," I say. "Before I woke, that last instant, I was always here."

"Hush," Leandra says.

"You'd send me away," I tell her. "If I hadn't learned to stop dreaming, I'd have had to watch myself, over and over, leaving."

When Leandra crosses the room, I do not feel her behind me. She comes out of nowhere to grasp my waist, to turn me around.

"Well, you are here now," she says, "and you are not leaving."

Her fingers are slow and insistent at the artless work of unbuttoning my shirt, pulling it free of my trousers. The stale smell of me rises as Leandra parts the cloth, then lifts my shirttails to dry her own face.

I try, gently, to push her back, but her hands have hold of my belt. "I should tell you—"

She shakes her head. "We are both so tired, Wim."

She unfastens my belt. Then, one piece at a time, my soiled clothing is peeled away, and my stillness is the sole act of disclosure possible.

Leandra does not touch me again. When her own clothes have fallen beside mine on the floor, she does not lead me to the bed. She lays herself down on the blankets she's spread on the floor. As if I am not there.

I don't know where to go.

After a moment Leandra raises her arms, beckoning. *Come. Stay. Here.* But still she does not touch me.

Clumsy, meek, I lie down at last beside her.

Leandra touches my throat with one finger, then traces a line down my chest. I imagine an incision, without blood, without pain.

"You are here now," she says again.

I close my eyes.

"I thought I could stay away forever," I whisper.

Her finger is on my throat again. It trails lightly up to my chin, then presses down on my lips. "You don't know everything," she says. "And me? I know almost nothing."

I smile. She is lying. Lying the way she always does, meaning every word.

"Be still," she says.

It seems as if a very long time must pass before my hands and mouth and all the frayed parts of me are able to take what Leandra is intent on giving.

—~—

"You always sound smarter," Pamela used to tell me, "than you really are." She saw my cursory erudition as a pose, my cautious logic as a bully's tactic. Marriage often comes to this, I think: the very qualities that ignite attraction can flame into consuming resentment overnight. To marry is to burn.

Pamela was only a girl, of course, when we married. I was the one who might have been expected to know better. But I was, at thirty-five, still possessed of an uncommon innocence.

I think a war might have done me good, though that is nothing to wish on anyone, even oneself. It was the accident of my birth to fall neatly between Pearl Harbor and the Gulf of Tonkin, the wars that really mattered. Even Korea missed me, if only by a fraction of a generation.

I have made it a point to tutor my youngsters in war. A boy of fourteen, sixteen, is a savage, and battle is his heart's desire. The poetry of war, Wilfred Owen said, is in the pity. But youth knows nothing of pity. I aim literature at these children, if only to give them some notion what they could be in for, or what they might, with luck, just miss. I do not delude myself that pity is something one can teach.

Still, I send these would-be braves into the bloodier passages of Virgil and Homer, Hugo and Crane. Tolstoy has a thing or two to say about warfare. But Napoleon, breakfasting at the Borodino front, merely amuses these schoolboys. They find him a figure of fun, implausible as a terrier in gold epaulets. Hemingway is the one they inevitably fall for. It is a seductive conviction: that combat, like everything else, is largely a matter of style.

I had a premonition—no, more a conviction, in fact—that my son would fall in battle. Oh, I never for an instant doubted the child was male. The months Pamela carried him were a reign of terror for us both. My young wife, fighting her body's encroachments, resenting its betrayals, went mute with shock. While I, blinded by visions of my son's slaughter, could only grope and flail.

My retreat to the campaign bed in my study did not strike me as ungallant at the time. My wife, turned to stone, seemed monumental then, her need for capaciousness vital and boundless. If I chose to cede the territory of our bed to her, I'd have called it, then, consideration. Hadn't I already intruded upon her enough?

Terrors and night sweats afflicted me those months I slept alone. I entered the whirlpool. I could not close my eyes without seeing my son, on the very cusp of manhood, facedown in foreign mud. Or worse. Before my eyes he tripped wires, tumbled from sleek aircraft in flames. He removed the pins from countless grenades that adhered to his palm. He stared out from a blazing gunner's periscope. He lay behind bunkers in frothing red rapids. Even when the flesh of his fine-boned face had turned to ash, my son's eyes always sought and found me, asking a question whose answer I lacked, his mother's son in that.

I met these horrors in silence. But rather than chance disturbance to my sleeping wife, my gestating son, I elected to remove myself to a distance from which, I believed, I could do them no harm. I am prone, as Pamela said, to sound smarter than I am.

She had never intended to be a mother, and I knew it. Indeed, hadn't she most effectively explicated the matter when she was still my student? Her disinclination could not have been plainer, I admit.

I'd grown restive by then, my fourth year of teaching at a small women's college. My students, drawn mostly from the mezzanine of privilege and accomplishment, were far too eager to please. It was 1974 and feminism was well on its feisty rise. I liked to think my own interests were feminist at heart. I was teaching young women to think, and speak, for themselves. It frustrated me to discover how many of them aspired to no more than my good opinion. And to grades reflecting that, of course.

It was the spring term, a particularly raw and gloomy March, as I recall. Midterm papers had appalled me, not only with their lack of originality, but often with undertones of prim moral judgment. Ibsen's Nora, Tolstoy's Anna, Flaubert's Emma, had all been neatly consigned, by implication or nuance, to lying abed in narrow bunks they themselves had made. One student for whom I had entertained hopes had delighted me by departing from the syllabus and finding her solitary way to George Eliot. Her conclusions, however, reduced me to despair. The paper was a huffy defense of Rosamond Vincy. A woman can be expected to put up with only so much, seemed to be its major thesis. Dorothea was mentioned, disparagingly, in one footnote, I believe.

Well, that *was* original, actually. I should have been amused. Hearing the tidy mores of provincial grandmothers from these young mouths had canted my perspective, I'm afraid.

In vexation, I gave the class this assignment: "Write a ten-page essay in cogent and passionate defense of a position you personally hold that you believe runs counter to prevailing societal attitudes. *Be as opinionated as possible.* Try to draw upon personal experiences." Capital punishment was, as I recall, an extremely popular subject, pro and con. Safe terrain, I suppose, for being so eminently debatable. A person could hardly be *blamed* for having strong feelings on the matter.

One junior from Savannah, a Madonna-faced creature with a strawberry-blond halo, clutched at the safe-familiar term "societal" and ventured out onto a low limb, asserting that wedding costs should be shared fully by the family of the groom. The paper's charmingly earnest tone hinted at the author's expectation that such a notion would shake society to its very roots. Which perhaps in Savannah it would.

The only paper that met my crotchety terms was Pamela's. From the start of the term I'd been somewhat intrigued by this scholarship girl from one of the Carolinas. Her writing was only a bit beyond adequate. Her beauty was mitigated by a hardness about the eyes, a cynical cast to her rare smiles. She was a small, slender girl with coppery hair that fell straight down her back to a point indecently well below her narrow waist. Her clothes, too bright for the prevailing season or fashion then, marked her as something of an outlander. She was given to hair ornaments of questionable taste. Her eyes were the darkest blue I have ever seen, their oddness exaggerated by pale brows and lashes.

Pamela spoke up in class rarely, but always with clear intent to challenge me, to pinpoint some small chink in my competence. And though she did not rebut me outright, her midnight-blue eyes made plain that my answers were often found wanting.

I still recall the opening sentence of her essay: "The supposedly simple and 'natural' act of childbearing, that every society seems to feel is its right to demand of a woman, often amounts to the ruination of the body and smothering of the spirit."

The awkward syntax, the failure to distinguish the dependent from the independent clause, seemed forgivable weaknesses in so forceful a statement. The word *ruination* conveyed an almost biblical resonance, I thought.

The day I handed back the papers, I asked Pamela to read hers aloud to the class. She did so in a desultory voice that seemed to disclaim authorship. Her softened Southern vowels and melting consonants did nothing to dulcify the hard notions she was revealing. Her anatomical vocabulary was more than serviceable. In one concise paragraph she described an episiotomy with such precision that several of her classmates turned alarmingly pale.

Her grandmother had been a midwife, Pamela explained. The details and vignettes she plucked from childhood memories of accompanying the old lady on her rounds of mercy were harrowing and indelible.

I'd aired her paper to spark debate, of course. Naively, as it turned out. Pamela had not reached the bottom of the second page when I saw my misconjecture. My sedate students lowered their eyes. Their fastidious hands were warped in tight configurations upon their notebooks. A few blushed. Pamela seemed to be the only person at the seminar table not suffering.

I yearned, naturally, to stop her, to call a halt to the whole misguided venture. Reading the paper with the sensibility of a man of middle years, I'd failed to calculate its effects on the romantic and sheltered ingenues given over to my care. I could hardly blame Pamela. It was I, after all, who had coaxed forth this assault on delicacy and cherished ideals. To stop the performance *in medias res,* however, would only have added Pamela's humiliation to the accrued misery. What choice but to let her finish?

I had, in my discomfort, forgotten the essay's final sentence, its marvelous simplicity, its sheer nakedness. Pamela's uninflected voice assailed the clenched silence:

"There is no mother in me."

No one, though it was clear she was done, looked up.

"Thank you," I said.

I imagined the air in the room, a collective breath held too long, turning blue. Pamela reassembled her pages, slapping them against the marbleized Formica tabletop. Several young women flinched. Then the stifled room began to breathe again.

"That is a powerful, even disturbing piece of writing," I said. "Can you see that?"

Not one of the other young women was looking at me, only Pamela. Her delicate oval face withheld comment.

"Language as provocation, you might say. . . ." Then I could not think how to go on.

Pamela kept staring up at me, something mocking and mutinous trapped beneath the ice of her gaze.

"Perhaps we should begin, then, by looking at just that," I said. "The language."

I cannot recall how we got through the rest of the hour. I may have dismissed the class early. I really don't know.

What I do recall with clarity is how the other students seemed to regard Pamela after that day. Their glances turned sidelong and skittish. If before they'd ignored her, now they were stiffly polite. I saw that by exploiting her dark gift, I'd exposed the girl to something far more stringent than censure. She had, through my offices, been marked for exile.

Denied belonging, I would learn, deprived Pamela of her bearings. It was a loss for which I would never be able to make restitution.

—~—

A week or so later, I ran into Pamela on the library steps early one morning. I remember she was wearing a green raincoat of some silky iridescent material that appeared to be several sizes too large for her. Her hello was diffident, almost as if she couldn't quite place me.

"I've been hoping to run into you," I said.

"Oh?" she said.

"I hold office hours this afternoon," I said. "I wondered if you could stop in?"

"What for? " she said.

"I'd like to talk a bit more with you about your paper."

"That's all right." She spoke in a flat soft voice. "You don't need to."

"Actually, I want to," I said. "Very much."

Pamela shook her head. Her arms were full of philosophy books—Kierkegaard, Hegel, Kant.

I scanned the books' spines. "You're not skipping Spinoza, I hope?"

"I've checked him out." She shrugged. "Mighty optimistic, don't you think?"

"Optimistic?"

"Reckon if Will and Intellect were the same thing, you'd see a lot more genius around here."

I smiled. "Are you writing another paper?"

"Not if I can help it." Her voice was wry. "Look, I already know what you think you need to tell me."

"I don't—"

Pamela shook her head again, and a barrette, a rhinestone starburst, slipped from her hair and fell to the marble step. I stooped quickly to retrieve it and handed it to her. She dropped it into her pocket before looking up at me.

"That paper don't amount to much. You think I don't know

it?" The pale planes of her face were formal. Only the lapse in grammar signaled any distress.

"Pamela, it's extraordinary work," I said.

"No, sir," she said. "It is not."

She started to turn away, then changed her mind and took a step closer to me. The green raincoat gave her face a sickly cast. The March wind whipped its tawdry fabric against her legs.

"You wanted me to help you get a rise out of them," she said. "I was pleased to try."

"There's more to it than that," I said. But Pamela had already reached the bottom of the steps and I could not even be certain she heard me.

"Just stop in," I called out after her. "Will you?"

She was walking in long, quick strides, facing into the wind. Her bright hair sailed out behind her like a pennant. Suddenly she turned around again. She did not seem to raise her voice, but I could hear her perfectly.

"Forget it," Pamela said. "I mostly made it up anyhow."

Pamela's class attendance became sporadic, her attentions indifferent when she was there. I intended to speak with her again, but she managed to elude me, arriving at the last possible moment and slipping out again at the first opportunity. She always sat near the door.

The class had quickly settled back into its natural inert state. And if my students seemed warier of me, more standoffish to Pamela, I tried to reassure myself the difference was only a matter of degree. I gave conventional assignments, which the young women, Pamela included, fulfilled conventionally. I allowed my students to please me with their seemly efforts. But the complacency I struggled to cultivate in myself was both dangerous and false, and I knew it.

I began to make discreet inquiries concerning positions at other schools.

It had been my good fortune that year to win, by lottery, occupancy of one of the on-campus faculty houses. These places were few and far between, and not in the best repair, but they had nominal rents to commend them—and few obligations attached. The college maintenance crew saw to mowing the grass, keeping the outmoded plumbing operative. Faculty members residing on campus were asked only to make themselves available in emergencies (few enough in such a well-regulated institution) and to help entertain the rare trustee or generous alum stopping by to nose around en route to somewhere else. Command performance dinners at the president's house yielded, more often than not, an excellent meal and a change of company. They had the added attraction of being concluded strictly by nine o'clock, the hour at which, faculty lore had it, our rotund president routinely turned into a pumpkin.

The dusty-blue shingled cottage I luckily occupied was inaccessible by car, but the regular faculty lot was a mere ten-minute walk. I rarely left the campus anyway. My little house huddled at the end of an overgrown path concealed by the former barn that now served as the college music building.

My private, out-of-the-way quarters delighted me. The cottage had been built early in the century for a caretaker. I cherished its warped doors and crooked shake roof and listing chimney. Its two small rooms (plus bath and kitchen), never touched by paint, were adequate for my needs. Lamplight and, in winter, a glow from the fireplace were as becoming to the paneling and wide-planked floors as candlelight to an aging charmer. I loved the bashful way the cottage hunkered down among the trees, on the edge of things, like a child skirting a boisterous party.

I did not own up, that spring, to how perfectly the cottage suited me. It was the season of my discontent. And is anyone of intelligence—that is to say, anyone with aspirations—ever really content? I was at least secure, or believed I was.

I was working at my desk past the end of a long Saturday in early April, I recall, when the thought first struck me that the ideal of perfect contentment might constitute an affliction. That being so, I wondered, would it not be possible to cure oneself? A man, once recovered, surely ought to stand a better chance of attaining some inner poise, escape the exhausting habit of living at odds with himself.

After a dull rainy morning, the afternoon had brightened and the temperature had shot past seventy. The trees were just starting to bud. Sunshine and a peacock-blue sky had forced them into the limelight.

More than a month remained before finals, and midterm grades, for better or worse, were indelibly recorded. It being a Saturday, the campus was crawling with boys up to no good. All afternoon and well into sunset, I could hear through the open windows that flanked my desk the shouts and laughter that infuse those past a certain age with a pervasive and nameless sorrow.

I was grading junior papers on Porter's Miranda stories. I imagined the woods encroaching on my house writhing with naked young bodies joyously observing spring's pagan rites. I thought, amused, that I might listen to Stravinsky over dinner. No, Mendelssohn, I amended, and laughed aloud. I did not permit myself to leave my desk until the last paper was marked, the sky deprived of its last caress of rosy light.

In the next thing to darkness, I groped my way to the kitchen and switched on the austere overhead light. I opened the small window above the sink with some difficulty—it had been shut perhaps since mid-October. The protesting whine of the arthritic sash seemed to stifle birdsong. What sounded like a nightingale may merely have been a mockingbird keeping fast company.

In a cold and sterile light, I crouched to survey the contents of my doddering refrigerator. I'd forgotten the veal, an indulgence of the morning's quick foray into town for provisions. The small package was sole occupant of the bottom shelf. The white butcher paper was faintly stained with traces of anemic-looking blood.

The meat, tender slices already pounded thin, had looked irresistible to me. A special order, the butcher had confided, not picked up the previous day. The lady was having some kind of bash, he said, but she maybe got sick or something.

Now the veal—"scallopeen," he called it—was there for the taking, reduced, for anyone with the wit to snap it up. "Half price," the butcher said, biting the fringes of his graying mustache. "What am I saying? A third, max. This is your lucky day."

"Is it difficult to make?" I asked him. "Scallopini? I'm not much of a cook."

"A snap." He rattled off an impromptu recipe, even told me the best brand of cooking sherry and where I'd find it, aisle four, halfway down and on the left.

I thanked him and took the tidy white parcel tied up in frail white string, "$5.83" marked in black crayon and emphatically circled. It weighed next to nothing in my hand.

"You want the mushrooms fresh," the butcher said. "Don't skimp."

The mushrooms, corpse white, with bits of black soil clinging to them, crowded a clear plastic basket sealed in cellophane. I set them on the counter beside the meat, the bottle of sherry. I melted butter in a scratched nonstick skillet some previous tenant had providently left behind. I measured rice into one measuring cup, guessed at water in another, whose markings had been scoured away. The fragrance of the melting butter reminded me that I had not eaten since breakfast.

I peeled two pearly cloves of garlic, like bloodless ovaries, and crushed them with the flat of a wide butcher knife. I unwrapped the parcel of meat. As I lifted the fillets of pallid flesh from the paper, dredging each lightly in flour, some subtle foulness in their odor assaulted my appetite.

The garlic began to brown in the butter. The tube of fluorescent light above the stove was buzzing, a minor long-standing irritation that suddenly seemed ruinous. My tongue was grainy and dry.

Handling the floured meat as little as possible, I tucked it back inside its wrapping and returned it to the refrigerator. I shut off the stove. The gas flame under the sizzling skillet went out with a small huff of resentment. I switched off the kitchen light and, in darkness now matured, found my way out the back door.

The evening air was still balmy. I gulped it down greedily. When the queasiness passed, I looked up at the sky. A waxing moon dug a sharp white gouge into a blue-black sky just beginning to spot with stars.

The path meandering through the trees was still spongy from the morning's rain, the air heavy with smells of loam and greening. I tried to recall, taunting my senses, the odors of butter and garlic and meat, the feel of chilled flesh on my fingers, the familiar sensation of my teeth shredding animal tissue, my throat coated with its juices. But my bout of squeamishness had taken on the lurid illogic of a nightmare. I wondered if my mouth would ever water again.

As I drew closer to the music building, I glimpsed winking lights through the trees. A girl's voice called out somewhere, flirtatious. A car started up. A squirrel or some other harmless animal skidded across a soggy carpet of long-fallen leaves. And below all these sounds, giving them precedence, the notes of a piano drifted toward me.

I neared the edge of the wood. The back of the barn loomed like the hull of a cargo ship. As I emerged from the trees I could see one lighted window up under the ribs of the roof. Every note was clear now. I recognized the Chopin nocturne. The music was sentimental, unabashedly so, and yet no less heartbreaking for that. I stood, leaning against a surviving fragment of stone wall, and looked up at the lighted window, trying to smile at my adolescent longing to weep and to howl at a moon I could no longer see.

The playing was not expert and stumbled over the more complex fingerings. Its passions were squandered, at times, by a lack of rigor, and the piano was in less than perfect tune. Still, there was something terribly poignant in the music, as if a lonely voice were crying out with scant hope of being heard.

I am starving, I thought.

I tested the barn's disfavored back door and found it unlatched. I went in and started up through the treacherous dark of the rear stairs.

A doorway at the end of a narrow corridor on the top floor spilled out a frugal pathway of light. The floorboards creaked under me, but if the pianist heard, the music did not falter.

When I moved into the light and looked through the door's scrimping frame, it seemed to me that from the moment the music had first called out to me in the dark I had known I would find her here.

Pamela was playing with her eyes closed. A rusting iron fixture on the wall behind her backlit her fiery hair. She was wearing an oddly fussy white blouse, its low neck fastened by a painted brooch of the kind old ladies used to wear. The blouse's ruffles drew inordinate attention to her fragile bones, wrist and clavicle and shoulder. Her mouth, without the habitual slash of loud lipstick, was small with melancholy concentration.

The notes, in E minor, dwindled away like the last drops poured from a small glass pitcher. Pamela's hands rose slowly from the yellowed keyboard, hovered above it for a moment, then settled on her knees. She was wearing blue jeans.

"What are you doing here?" She did not open her eyes.

"I heard the music."

She nodded.

"You play quite well."

She opened her eyes. Her serene expression hardened into disdain. "How are we supposed to learn anything in this place, with y'all lying every chance you get?" she said.

"I wasn't lying."

"Exaggerating, then. Why bother?"

"To make a point, I suppose."

"What point was that?"

I smiled. "That you could be worse."

I did not know until she laughed that I had never heard her laugh before. I could not, in fact, have imagined it. The sound was low and throaty, resigned but not reserved. Pamela laughed like a woman who had seen enough of life to know a good laugh was about the most she could hope for.

"Reckon you've made your point, then," she said, still smiling.

"Where did you learn to play?"

"I didn't, yet," she said. "But my grandma got me started."

"The midwife?"

"Oh, Lord." She laughed again. "You New England folks do surely hold tight to a tale. I reckon it's the noble suffering you're so fond of." She looked up at me coyly. "I still got you believin' that bull-dinky?"

"I am a trusting man," I said, then immediately regretted what seemed too candid a remark. "I'm not in the habit of expecting my students to lie to me."

"Trust's nothing to count on," she said. "A body could hardly pick worse, in fact."

"You become quite the country girl when it suits you." I smiled.

"The way I talk?" She shook her head. "You seemed right smitten when it was Miss Flannery O'Connor messin' up your syntax."

"I suspect it wasn't a pose Miss O'Connor assumed when she was scared."

She gave me a scornful look. "You think I'm scared? Of what, Yankees?"

I stepped through the doorway into the room. "I think maybe it feels dangerous, sometimes, to be so smart."

"Reckon that's will passing for genius." Pamela picked up a plaid muffler and wound it around her neck. "I got no shortage of will."

"Dangerous and damn lonely, would be my guess."

She sniffed. "Only thing is, I'm so smart, couldn't I do better than B-minus on that last paper?"

"You didn't give Porter's stories more than cursory thought."

Pamela, her mouth concealed behind her hand, was laughing again.

"There's something funny about that?"

She couldn't seem to stop laughing. "Good guess?" she said.

"Oh," I said.

"Oh." She was mocking me.

"I just finished grading those papers an hour ago," I said. "How would you know your grade?"

"B-minus is what I got, though?"

"You did," I admitted.

She nodded, strangely satisfied. "Reckon I could have thought more about 'em," she said. "Just seems to me I didn' come all the way up here to read about diggin' up old baby rabbit bones."

She stood, pushing away from the piano bench with the backs of her knees. "I expect I'll do better by Miss Carson McCullers." She stuffed sheet music into a canvas book bag. "You may have to part with a precious A-plus when I get started on that one with the jockey in the dining room."

"You like that story?"

She nodded. "Don't you?"

"To tell the truth," I said, "I've never been quite sure I understood it."

Pamela moved closer to me, smaller than I'd remembered, younger, less tough. "Me neither," she said. "That's likely why I'm so partial to it."

She slipped past me then, clicked off the light, picked up her book bag. I followed her out into the dark hallway.

"Aren't you afraid," I said, "all alone in an empty building at night?"

"Wait." There was a fumbling sound, the rustle of cloth and paper. Suddenly a beam of strong white light streaked through the darkness before us and found the top of the stairs. "Best stick close." Pamela was holding a cheap plastic flashlight. "It's steep going down," she said.

At the bottom of the stairs she motioned me ahead of her out into the night, then stopped to lock the door behind us. "I got special permission to come in at night," she said. "My own key and all." Then she laughed a dry, jaded laugh. "You reckon they'll make note of that distinction under my yearbook picture?"

"I didn't even get my picture in mine," I said. "Missed a deadline or something. I can't say it's a wound I carry through life."

She smiled.

The air had grown chilly. The campus was silent. Everybody who was going anywhere was gone. The high library windows laid a mosaic of light across our path as we walked around to the front of the music building.

"You don't have a coat?" I said.

"Beg pardon, I thought this was April."

"It's also New England."

"Been trying to overlook that." Pamela inclined her head toward the woods. "Don't you live back thataway?"

I hadn't given a thought to where I was going. "I'll see you safely back to your dorm," I said.

She stopped and looked up at me. "Saturday night," she said. "What makes you think I'd be heading in so early?"

"I didn't—" My face felt hot in the damp cold air. "May I take it back?" I said.

"Even the part where you got me being lonesome and scared?"

"If you say so."

"I say so." Her gaze was grave and steady for a moment. Then she smiled and we started walking again. "I got to go scrounge around the union, see if I can find something worth eating in those cussed machines," she said. "I missed supper."

"So did I," I said.

She gave me a skeptical look. "I'm talkin' Fresca and Fritos," she said. "Reckon even a old bachelor professor's pantry got better than that."

"Somewhat better," I admitted.

I would like to say my next words came out before I'd had time to consider them. But the truth is there came an instant, distinct and isolate, when, like a man poised on the edge of a precipice, I paused and saw the whole dangerous panorama below. It simply did not occur to me not to jump.

"Why don't you come have dinner with me?" I said.

"At your house?" Pamela looked at me as if I might be joking, and cruelly.

"I'm no cook," I said. "But I can fix us something."

"Okay." She sounded surprised but hardly apprehensive.

"Your feet may get a little wet," I warned her.

Pamela followed me into the woods, the beam of her flashlight casting loops of light up ahead of us both.

I became, for that single meal, a charmed provider. My cramped cupboard revealed provender I didn't know I had—a tin of fat white asparagus, bottled peaches in brandy, the latter half of a still presentable baguette. The veal was tender enough to finger-feed a baby, and when, after the prescribed time, not a moment sooner, I raised the lid of the rice pot, jasmine-scented steam lapped my face.

Some prized early Horowitz recordings (rigor isn't everything) played on my decrepit stereo as I cooked. I left Pamela in the front room with the music and a glass of ginger ale while I pulled things together in the kitchen. She offered to help, but I was too much the novice to want a witness to my efforts.

A while later, when I went to call her to the table, I found Pamela rummaging through my overcrowded bookshelves. If Horowitz made an impression, she did not mention it.

I ate with more awe than appetite, incredulous that I'd managed to bring off such an exemplary meal. And it was sweet, I confess, to have company.

Pamela appeared to pay more attention to her table manners than to the food. Each mouthful was thoroughly chewed and swallowed before she answered the questions I could not seem to stop asking her. She also seemed to be trying out a new, less regional variety of diction, enunciating final consonants with particular care. There was something touchingly vulnerable in her posture as she ate, slightly hunched over her plate as if accustomed to asserting her claims over sustenance. She was, it seemed, quite hungry.

I suppose I should not have been surprised by Pamela's volubility on the subject of the college, or by the slightly bitter aftertaste of her delicious wit. Her gift for verbal caricature was equitably distributed between student body and faculty. She was particularly hard on those in whom she spotted artistic pretensions. The modern-dance department, she suggested, was a secret sisterhood of baton twirlers from Macon, Georgia, attempting to disguise themselves in black leotards, long scraggly hair, and "big old jewelry makes you want to take the silver polish to it." A particularly boring philosophy instructor, she confided, was actually a rogue scientist on the payroll of some unspecified foreign power scheming to overthrow the United States by drowsiness, thereby avoiding bloodshed. I never, after that evening, encountered our formidable dean of women without seeing "Miss Piggy in a Talbot's tweed blazer." I smiled so helplessly when I saw the dean, in fact, that the poor woman may have come to suspect I was sweet on her.

If Pamela was amusingly outspoken about the here and now, however, she proved reticent and balky on the subject of her earlier life. She did talk at some length about one high school counselor, a Ms. Basnight, who had piloted her through the college admissions and scholarship maze while extolling New England's *cultural superiority,* a phrase Pamela recounted in the wry and throaty voice of disillusion. She then made a conversational hairpin turn to review a recent college drama club production, an unintentionally hilarious musical based on the life of Emily Dickinson, called "Life, Love, Nature, Time, and Eternity." Written (for obvious reasons) for an all-female cast, the production featured a chorus line of Muses in prissy white dresses whose primary purpose was evidently the frenzied enactment of a rather bovine Emily's suppressed passions. As Dickinson's poems were sung in an operetta style reminiscent of Sigmund Romberg, garish color slides of illustrative images were beamed at the proscenium:

moor, sea, heather, frigate, and so on. I seem to recall brief appearances by a great variety of birds.

The grand finale, performed by a grieving Muse chorale over Emily's chaste corpse, set "Lay this laurel on the one / Too intrinsic for renown" to a melody that to my ear owed more than passing tribute to the "Merry Widow Waltz." Pamela's references, naturally, were more contemporary, less arcane. She observed that the senior cast as Emily, a phys ed major from Morristown, New Jersey, bore a striking resemblance, both visually and vocally, to Elton John.

Mouthwatering as I found Pamela's iconoclastic assaults upon the college, however, I was left starved for morsels of her history. The notable absence of parents and siblings from her patchwork narrative warned me off direct questions in that sector. I tried to steer her instead back toward the grandmother whose eclectic mastery of classical music and midwifery had already enlarged her to legendary stature in my mind. The moment I alluded to her, however, Pamela turned skittish and opaque, seeming to derive some feverish pleasure from keeping me guessing whether this remarkable woman had even in fact existed. It was as if Pamela were beckoning me one moment, barring me the next from some imaginative realm of which she both feared and desired to share occupancy. While I, in my eagerness to gain admittance to her history and her confidence, perhaps neglected to examine what I should have recognized as a rather frenzied flight from truth.

A sizable swatch of time seemed to have been snipped out of the evening. Suddenly I became aware of Pamela's clean plate, of the pale pellicle of fat congealing over the meat remaining on my own. I jumped up to clear the table and serve dessert.

Later, after we'd dawdled over the peaches and vanilla ice cream and I was carrying the dishes to the sink, I noticed thick brandied syrup pooled in the bottom of one of the small glass bowls. It was the only thing Pamela had not consumed. The amber liquid, richly veined with cream, looked like a rare marble found in the altarpiece of some ornate Italian church. I let the syrup run over my fingers as I poured it into the sink. When I put one finger into my mouth, the juice still held the alcohol's heat and was sweeter than I remembered from my own portion.

It was quite late by the time we finished. Pamela wanted to wash the dishes, but I would not allow it. "I'll do them later," I said.

I caught her studying me for a moment, making some calculation of motive or character. "If you like," she said at last.

"Would you care for some coffee?"

She shook her head, her mouth cramped with loathing.

"An acquired taste." I smiled.

"That's a thing I used to wonder mightily about," Pamela said.

"What's that?"

"Why a body'd trouble to acquire a taste for something she didn't care for in the first place."

"You no longer wonder about that?"

After a moment she laughed, a bit uneasily, I thought. "I still do," she admitted, "every now and again. Mostly, though, I try to keep my mind on . . . well, it's more a matter of rearing your tastes, don't you think, than acquiring them?"

"I'm not sure I understand."

"Looks to me like what we're born with, if we stuck with that, wouldn't let us in for much of a life," she said. "We intend to amount to anything, our tastes got to be brought up right, same as with manners. It's up to some of us to teach ourselves, is all. It can take some doing."

"I assume you're speaking from experience?"

Pamela seemed to glance inward for a moment. "You reckon I'm of an age where I have enough experience I ought to be speaking from it?"

"Flannery O'Connor says childhood provides enough experience to last us a lifetime."

" 'Anybody who's *survived* childhood has enough information about life,' is what she said, I believe." Pamela smiled. "While you're nosing around trying to dig up some of that *grotesque* y'all up here seem so taken with, you might want to remember Southern folks also got a little tendency to exaggerate."

"And here I've been taking Miss Flannery for gospel. . . ."

"She just tells more interesting lies than most of us." Pamela had stopped smiling. "Don't anyhow go looking for your Miss Flannery in me. You're apt to get disappointed something awful."

"You do like to tell stories, though."

"How else would I stand the least chance of becoming a hero?"

"That's what you want to be, a hero?"

"In case you didn't notice, I'm a woman. Where I come from, that mostly means getting stuck away in a corner of somebody else's story, some man's."

"Surely that's not all you intend for yourself?"

She looked around my kitchen, eyes lighting on a battered eighteenth-century pine hutch, where the few old family things I'd kept from my parents' house were gathered. "Not all," she said, her eyes roving through the shelves. "I didn't say that."

After a minute Pamela got up from the table, drawn, apparently, to a rock maple salad bowl on the lowest shelf. Her small pale hands circled the bowl's sides, probing meticulously, as if seeking out flaws. "I like it here." She stood at an angle, her back half turned on me. "I like you here," Pamela said.

"Thank you." My voice sounded hollow.

She turned to face me then, her hands relinquishing the bowl. "Sometimes in class you're so . . . you act like you been caught someplace you don't belong. But here . . ." She turned back to the shelves, hands reaching higher now, approaching, then withdrawing from, the roundness of a yellow Quimper creamer. With one finger she traced the slender neck of a Steuben bud vase, never quite touching it. Then, her lips pursing over the splayed orchid petals that formed the lid of an oval cloisonné box, she began to blow away the dust I only now saw I'd allowed to settle over everything.

"I'm not much of a housekeeper."

Pamela looked steadily at me. My face felt full of heat. "You have beautiful things," she said.

"They're just—"

"Acquired tastes?" she said.

"Inherited. A few old family belongings." No longer looking at Pamela, I rose and went to stand beside her. I stared into the shelves at the things I so rarely touched or even noticed. "Fairly useless, on the whole," I said. "I'm not sure why I keep them."

"Your parents are dead," Pamela said, "aren't they?"

I nodded absently. "If you want to know the truth," I said, "I probably keep them because they are beautiful."

"I know," she said. "Did you think I wouldn't know that?" Her eyes glittered with some intensity I could not interpret. Suddenly it dawned on me that I was afraid of her, and that I had been for some time. "It's late," I said.

"It's probably time I started learning to like coffee." Pamela's voice was tremulous. I watched her eyes fill with tears.

Timid and futile, my hand started toward her arm, then pulled back.

"I imagine you're better off without it," I said.

"All I want is to belong in a place the way you do," she said. "Like this."

"I know," I said softly. And I believed that I did.

Pamela rubbed her eyes with the backs of her hands. "I don't even know your damn name," she said.

It took me a moment to grasp what she meant. "It's William," I said.

"Given," she said. "But what are you called?"

I smiled. "William," I said. "As given."

She shook her head. "I'd be right sorry if that suited you."

"What do you think would?" I said. "Suit me."

She shook her head again, sadly. "I'll let you know when it comes to me, Professor," she said.

The kitchen had grown stifling. I realized I'd left the oven on. Avoiding her eyes, I went to turn it off. "Are you ready to go back?" I said.

"No," Pamela said. "I am not."

Behind me I heard her crossing the floor. Then I felt her hand on my back, a small hot thing like a live coal.

"What I am ready to do is stay right here," she said. "For a good long time."

I closed my eyes. "It's late," I said.

"William?"

I knew that if I looked at her something terrible would happen. Her hand pressed harder, hotter, into my spine. I shuddered. Something terrible is going to happen anyway, I thought. I turned around.

Her face was so white that her cheekbones seemed an indecency. Her chin and the bridge of her nose looked drained of blood. Her hands moved around my waist, up over my ribs, as they'd felt their way around the sides of the wooden bowl, their touch careful and covetous. I understood such wanting.

Because she so badly wanted me to, I held her for a moment. *"The awful daring of a moment's surrender . . ."* I could no longer hold up my head. She was so small. I bent lower, my face longing to lose its way in her fragrant hair. *"By this, and this only, we have existed."*

I tried to step back, telling myself it was too late only for caution, not yet for decency. "This is not what you want," I said.

But Pamela's frail arms detained me where I was. "Don't tell me what I want," she said.

I believe I did try to pull back. I'm sure I did. But Pamela would not let go.

"You need to go now, Pamela."

"Not on your life," she whispered. And: "Where do you think I would go?"

—w—

"No more seizures?"

I shook my head. "Not with the medication."

The doctor smiled, looking slightly smug. "There are also ways to manage the pain," he said. "When it comes to that."

I nodded. "Without one becoming . . . insensible?"

He hesitated for a moment, then shrugged. "There are inevitably trade-offs," he said.

A green marble Art Deco clock on his desk, a sylphlike woman balancing a globe, was running a few minutes fast, I noticed.

"There may eventually be some changes in temperament." The doctor stared at the face of the clock. "Those close to you probably ought to be prepared," he said. "It can be . . . disconcerting."

"I should imagine," I said.

When he looked up, his gaze hovered somewhere just above my head. "Is there someone you'd like me to talk with?"

"No one," I said.

iii

BEEN TIMES THEY TRIED to make me believe they was real, all them broke-down bodies and torn-off limbs and blind faces.

The baby dolls being the worst, of course, so pitiful with their little puckered mouths and cheeks, the tiny tucks of grievance around their eyes and across their foreheads.

I don't much care for the ones get noisy about their distress. You tip them this way or that, they'll whine and wail . . . makes my work harder, to be sure. "You are spoiled," I tell them. "Now just pipe down. Can't you see I'm trying to fix you up here, you?"

I also had a few that laughed, took on fits of giggles like my serious fingers made them ticklish. But those, the ones that laugh, ain't so common. Mostly they either squall or don't make a peep.

Anyhow, they are only dolls and not much company. And I would be in sorry trouble if I let myself lose sight of that. Never did concoct lives for them. Even as a youngster, I hadn't much use for dolls. Pammy was the one, Mama used to tell, who so prized the endless changing of clothes and combing of hair, fancy-dress balls and tea parties. My wildest dream was a pogo stick, a hope my mama was not prone to encourage. Done quite enough jumping around on my own, she said. Reckon she'd have been pleased to see me give a doll a second look. But I never had the smallest soft spot for them, not until I was a grown woman, or nearly so. And even then, the dolls had to get dropped in my lap before I paid them any mind.

And that is just how it happened. The dolls more or less befell me. A whole carton of them, in fact, old dolls in lace bonnets and ball gowns and pinafores the starch gone out of. Poor things was sore afflicted, all kind of maladies and wounds, but mostly old age and hard use was what it come down to.

Miss Mildred Brothers give me the dolls, that first batch, one Saturday when I was trooping around with Carol Jean, collecting things for the PTA rummage sale. I could see right away it pained that sweet old lady to part with what she been loving since a girl and all. But Miss Mildred had no kin, not even a niece to pass what she cared for on to. "Ain't doing me a bit of good up there in the attic," she said, "now are they?"

"Right kind of you," I said.

"You might not think me so largehearted, darlin'," the old lady said, "when you see the sorry state some of these gals got into."

"I'm sure they are lovely," I said. Carol Jean been waiting a quarter hour out there in the hot car already, and two babies strapped in them car seats.

"Reckon they'd bring a better price, somebody'd do a little fixer-uppering." Miss Mildred give me a sly look. "Somebody with time on her hands," she said.

What I had on my hands back then was one job toting up bills for the water company, another helping Johnnie Mae Jenks with her slipcover and upholstery business in the evenings, plus a good bit of baby-sitting for the Goodlin babies—only two of them then, Kyle James just a newborn. I knew what Miss Mildred meant, though: twenty-five years old, not yet married, and Branch no longer waiting on me.

"I'll see what I can do," I said.

"I know you will, sugar," Miss Mildred said.

What I could do turned out to be a far sight beyond what I'd have dreamed. By the time the rummage sale came around, the first week in December, those dolls were something to behold. All nine snapped up the first half hour . . . and not a one for less than twenty-five dollars.

I didn't rightly know how to fix dolls then, apart from mending their clothes. I worked out disguises, though, for what was wrong, or missing. Made a fancy mask, black velvet, for one lady in a red satin hoop skirt because she had an eye gone and a chip out of her cheek. Stitched tiny felt mitts for a waif lost half her fingers. The one with no legs came within a breath of the trash can. But her face was the loveliest thing. I made her a forked satin tail with green sequin scales, covered her bald head with dried seaweed and tiny shells. Miranda the Mermaid bring in the top price—fifty dollars—and wound up living in Atlanta, Georgia, with Mrs. Burdy Tompkins's little granddaughter, Tess.

Yessir, them dolls caused some little stir. Miss Mildred was tickled pink. And I hoped my mama was somewhere watching, feeling proud, because who was it nagged my stitches so itty-bitty till they all but disappeared?

Next I know, all kind of folks come toting their ailing dolls to me, believing I can salvage about anything, which I can't but figure I best start learning to.

Some people outright give me dolls too. I'd practice my fixing on those. By the time a year's gone by, I got two dozen dolls to give for the rummage sale, including a couple of the babies I made from scratch, and that's when Mrs. Duncan comes along from up in Virginia and sees how I do and says I am an artist and ought to be in business and she's just the one to set me up and get me started. . . .

Well, it was surely nothing I could have planned on, was it?

But ain't it just a part of the queerness of life, how so many of us land in what we do by pure accident? Imagine me doctoring dolls, who never cared a thing for them as a child. But maybe it would be too hard then, would pain me seeing them torn to pieces, if I loved them like I ought to.

Wim is like me in that, I'd say. I never heard a word out of his mouth nor saw his eyes shine in a way to tell he loves those children he teaches. He said one time that the young ladies at that college he was at before (his words, now) "came as a terrible mystery" to him. No, Wim being a teacher's an unlikely thing, if the heart is used for measuring.

Books are what Wim loves. Books and words. Seems like he just got too discouraged to write them . . . and too learned to go work in a library, like I maybe would do if I was him.

For all his careful decisions about his life, I don't think Wim ever once stopped and asked himself what he might like. He was just opposite of Pammy in that way, always looking to please somebody else. His daddy, already old by the time Wim, his only child, came along, was a stern and tightfisted old party, I think. He'd passed on, and Wim's mama did too, years before I turned up. But I saw their pictures by Wim's desk, and I could tell from their faces like you can sometimes that neither one must have been easy to please.

Wim's daddy was besides being a businessman some kind of inventor, and the things he made brought him a great lot of money that he hardly spent a bit of. When he died he left the most of it to some college in Virginia, where a building got named for him, Wim says. The legacy he left his son was just enough for building Wim and Pammy's house, not a thing that brought much ease or pleasure, from what I could see.

The accidents that make something or other of us don't always turn out bad, of course. I been mostly happy at my doll work these years. I'm grateful I could find a way to earn my keep without leaving home. Because I can scarcely imagine being who I am anywhere but here. I like how things grow here, kind of wild and careless even on tended acres, and that wherever you are you can smell the salt water you maybe can't see. I like knowing just enough and not too many folks and knowing they remember my mama and daddy and the child I was and Pammy. I even like, I got to say, living now and then on the edge of a hurricane, how it makes you see the mightiness of nature when the Lord turns it loose. Reckon I don't need to live in another place to know I'd be just lost there.

And I've grown right handy at this work I do, even been listed as an "expert" in a couple collectors' magazines the past few years, and people sending me dolls to save from all over the country now. I surely don't think myself the "artist" Mrs. Duncan, who got me started and still keeps me in work, says I am. It's just dumb luck I stumbled onto ground where I could learn to see what I was doing.

Well, Wim might have done worse too. If being a teacher hasn't made him exactly happy, I daresay it's made him a bit more patient, a little more kind. And it's surely a comfort having somewhere to go each day and knowing what wears you out is necessary and honorable work.

My own daddy could have been a right fit teacher. I reckon he had the character, though life never offered him the learning, and that was a disappointment to him. Daddy's accidental work came to be the death of him, of course, and some way my mama's too.

And poor Pammy, seems like, took after them. My sister becoming Wim's wife was, you might say, a fatal accident. If I'd been a bystander, there on the scene, would I have seen what was coming? Even if I'd been more than a youngster, I can scarcely imagine being anybody Pammy would listen to. My sister's ears were deaf to the Lord's own voice if it happened to be denying what her heart was set on. On the fierceness of that heart's setting, Mama used to say, our Pammy would breeze through life.

But it didn't turn out that way, of course, and I won't likely ever understand just how my sister's life went so awry. Wanting Wim in the first place—was that the turn sent her skidding? Could her baby, born right, have saved her? Could any of us—I older or Mama softer or Wim clearer of sight?

I asked him outright one time, just why did he marry my sister.

What did I expect him to say? I could think of a hundred reasons: because he would never find anyone so beautiful, so smart . . . because of the perfect motion of her hands and the perfect stillness of her face over the piano keys . . . because when she allowed her light to fall on you, you'd feel a kind of hopefulness about yourself that could make you believe you had everything to give her . . . *Why?* I asked him.

Wim thought a good while before answering. "Because she wanted me to," he said.

"What about what *you* wanted?"

Wim tried to smile. "At the time, I'd have been the last person to know."

I look at him now, his sleeping face like a shadow floating across the splash of midmorning light we're lying in. Something has sickened inside him. Before, it was simple sorrow made him look old. Now I know it's something different.

I wonder what accident brings him here. I wonder if he knows now just what it is he wants, and what it will take to get him to tell.

I know this much: Wim thinks, has always thought, I can take up the broken parts of him and fit them back together.

I know this just as surely as I know that he is wrong.

—∞—

I have never much cared for a closed door. But what with Pammy in the hospital, I started shutting myself inside the room where I slept at night. It seemed more proper, that's all, just me and Wim alone in the house.

From the time I first got there and Wim showed me to the "guest room," I kept wondering did he and Pammy intend on letting me keep sleeping there after the baby came. The room was long, its ceiling aslant. And while it was white like the rest of the house, it seemed warmer because of the old lace curtains that gentled the light through the windows and a wedding ring quilt on the wide spool bed. A weather-bitten steamer trunk with brass fittings hunkered at the bed's foot, and a flowered hooked rug sprawled across the floor. Violets were bunched on the lamp's glass shade. Mama would have prized these old things, belongings of Wim's grandmother that he just couldn't be talked into getting rid of, Pammy said.

I grew right fond of that room. It was the one place in the house felt like I halfway belonged in it, and I hoped they wouldn't put me somewhere else when the baby came along. Plenty of room in there for the both of us. A crib was already tucked under the slope of the ceiling, as well as a bassinet with bright jungle-bird cutouts dangling over it.

I pictured a white wicker rocking chair in the room's one empty corner, a little yellow night-light plugged into the wall behind it. I saw how Pammy would come in late at night and sit there nursing her baby. I would hitch myself up on the ruffled pillows, and we'd talk if she felt like it. "Lannie," I could hear my sister saying, "it does my heart good you are here." And: "What in the world would we ever do without you?"

The way things came to be, of course, it got hard to sleep there. Even after I took down the parrots and toucans and put them in a drawer, after me and Josie folded up the crib and bassinet and wrestled them out to the garage, I could scarcely abide being closed up in a room so all of a sudden empty. The corner where the rocking chair had never been seemed emptiest of all.

And then Josie stopped coming for a while. Called up and said she got a stripped throat or something, but I knew it was more a case of that house, the lot of us, just making her too sad. A month of Fridays, I missed her something dreadful. And when she finally came back, what with so much we couldn't say and didn't want to dwell on, seemed like we hardly talked at all.

Meanwhile, my sister's husband went on sleeping, or trying to, in a cramped room behind the wall at the head of my bed. And I'd lie awake through everlasting nights listening for sounds that could not likely have been heard anyway through two closed doors. For Wim, like me, would shut himself in at night.

It wasn't my business, of course—so much right under my nose in that house was no business of mine—but it surprised me Wim didn't go back to sleeping in the big white bed in the glass room once Pammy was in the hospital.

After our pitiful little suppers, neither of us with stomach or heart for what I cooked, Wim would go into his study. He'd leave the door ajar then, so I couldn't hardly pass by in the narrow hallway without seeing him. Mostly he'd be hunched over his desk, a stack of papers crowding under the lamplight. Or occasionally, late, he'd be slumped in the worn leather armchair, a book propped on his chest. Wim wouldn't look up when I passed by, but somehow it didn't look as if a book was what he was lost in.

Those walls crawled with books, though, they climbed right up to the ceiling. A little cot with a wood railing around three sides of it was pushed in under the one small window. There was hardly room for a man Wim's size in there.

Sometimes, when Wim was off somewhere, I'd loiter just outside the study door, looking in. From above the desk the tight pious eyes of his daddy and mama stared out from sharp-cornered black frames. The books' damp and dusty smell made the room seem like it was in a different country from the rest of the house.

One night, very late, I got out of bed to use the bathroom. I'd made peace with the house by then and didn't need a light. My bare feet went feeling their way down the hall, when a strange sound brought them to a sudden halt.

At first I couldn't place it. Then I heard the sound a second time. It was—just one low note, repeated—the piano in the living room. My steps carried me toward it in the thoughtless way of a dream. I could only think it was Pammy in there, my sister had come home now. And she would need me.

The trees around the house cut slats of moonlight that canted in through the glass, angled off the piano. Wim, bare but for a pair of loose cotton undershorts, sat on the piano bench. His head was tilted back, almost like he'd fallen asleep there. His finger, gone still, was a shadow on the silvery keys.

His near nakedness would have made it untoward to so much as whisper his name. I knew in some deep, fast way that I should turn around, creep back to my bed, allow us both to pretend I never saw him there. But the truth is, I wanted to be there myself, with him, and I waited for him to know it.

The piano sat askance to the room's strict straight lines. He scarcely had to turn to face me.

"Wim?" An indecency.

His head was still tipped back. Moonlight carved the lines on his face deeper, dug out the hollows. Even though it was me standing, it seemed he looked down at me from a sharp drop.

"Ssh," I whispered. And then, though he showed no intention to speak, I said it again: "Ssh."

Wim nodded.

I went over and sat down, my hip nudging his to make room for me on the piano bench.

"Pammy always craved a big piano," I said. "Had to work so hard to pay for those lessons, then nothing to practice on but that old rattletrap in the school gym and us little kids playing Red Rover and kickball all around her."

"Pay?" Wim said. "Your grandmother?"

I thought he was talking in his sleep.

"I must have misunderstood." Wim smiled sadly. "She hasn't played at all in several years."

"Maybe now—" I couldn't finish. I tried to retrieve a picture of Pammy's face above the piano, the joy that came over it when she didn't know I was looking. Music seemed like a thing she was born carrying inside her, Mama said, both the love and the gift of it unheard of in either side of the family. From the day Pammy's first teacher, Miss Garland Stokes, sat down on a rickety bench and plunked out "Skip to My Lou," Pammy was under a spell, seemed like. Miss Garland, who by the time I went to school was married and Mrs. Russell Burrus and had been moved up to third grade, still liked near ten years later to tell how she never before or since saw a child so take to the piano as our Pammy Jo.

So much I can't know, of course, but I wonder if the music wasn't like a place to her, somewhere Pammy could rest from the hard job she made of being Pammy, and could go there to recover when she was sick or sore. I tried to hope it might be a place she could go back to now, the music, finding comfort there. It was a hope I wanted to offer Wim. But pleasure or solace, even simple healing, suddenly seemed beyond what I could imagine for my sister, for either of them.

After what felt like a long time, I reached over and pulled Wim's hand from the keys. His fingers, chilly and stiff, made me remember how I'd touched my daddy's hand when he was in his coffin at the funeral home, the lifeless shock of it, and how that stopped me crying.

Pammy, watching from across the room, gave me a terrible look, like I done something to shame her. A good while later, though, she told me how it made her jealous, that touch. "You were so brave," she said.

"Brave?" I said.

"Don't know how you could bring yourself to touch a dead person, Lannie . . . and you just a little thing."

"I thought it was only Daddy," I told her.

She just couldn't get over it.

I flattened Wim's cold hand against his bare thigh now, held it there, weighed down by my own. His fingers warmed soon enough, but the rest of him kept on shivering.

"Ought to get back in bed," I said.

"Yes." Wim didn't move.

I waited some. Then I lifted my hand from his and stood up.

"Don't go, Leandra."

"I'm not."

I was standing by him, my hands hanging down useless, just like I'd pictured Wim's hands in the hospital when his baby son was dying. My arms felt paralyzed, or just too heavy to lift, and the rest of me lost without them.

It was like Wim knew then that I couldn't move, however much I might want to. He leaned back into me in a way made my body his sufficiency, and I have forever held that moment as the time when I grew into myself, no more than I needed to be, just enough.

The back of his head rested between my breasts. His shoulders pressed into my stomach. I felt how he was giving himself up into me and I understood that I didn't have to move to provide for him, didn't have to touch him, no need to move at all. My hands and my mouth would forever go begging.

I heard myself make a heartbroken sound. But to Wim it would seem no more than a breath with frayed edges.

I waited for him to tell me I could take myself back again. But he never did.

After a while I gave him breakfast like usual, though it was still dark. We acted like nothing was different that morning, or after. But I reckon we both knew it was.

—w—

My sister came home from the hospital bereft and blameful and mute. Which sounds, I guess, not so different from how she was before. But Pammy, too, was changed. I felt, beneath the willfulness of her withdrawal, something stronger, more dire.

It seemed to me that all through her life up to now, Pammy Jo had been the creature of her own will. And that will was a fearsome thing, full of hunger and spite. My sister had no liking for the world she'd been given. She had to set herself against it, to alter it in ways to suit her. Mama said that even as a baby Pammy Jo had this willful streak, it near about bent a body that resisted it in half.

Even a strong woman like Mama. Years after Pammy Jo had taken herself off from us, my mama still seemed worn to a nub by the near eighteen years of living with Pammy's ways. And Mama could, I promise you, be right mettlesome herself.

If Pammy Jo was balkish with the rest of us, though, it was nothing next to how strong-minded she'd be with herself. I was only nine years old, remember, when she left us. Still, I have no trouble recollecting the ways she changed herself, the merciless tasks she took on by way of turning into the various girls she thought she needed to be to get where she meant to go.

As a child, I idolized my sister, like little girls will. Besides that she was beautiful, and smart, seemed like wasn't nothing she couldn't do, nobody she couldn't get to love her. But it was a grief to love her. Because it was clear to me from the time I was small that where Pammy Jo meant to go was clear away. And I never doubted for one minute that I was to be left behind along with everything else.

I was in third grade when she left, and having a terrible time with school. I was too bashful to speak up when I knew something, and what I knew was little enough. I was smaller than everybody else, except for Randolph Prouty, who, because he was a dwarf, Mama said you weren't supposed to mention it.

My daddy was gone then almost three years. Mama must have been crippled with sorrow yet. But a child wouldn't see that plain, of course. I only knew our house had gone cold and dark and would be just that much less homey once my sister was gone.

For she was still all light to me then, Pammy. Those last months she was with us, I used to wait, keeping myself awake, until she'd fall asleep. Then I'd crawl into her bed and lie next to her for a while. I never wanted to fall asleep. I was sure if I did, she'd be gone for good when I woke up.

She was hell-bent on leaving, talked about it all the time and didn't seem to mind the least how her talk got under Mama's skin. Mama blamed Daddy's daydreaming, how he'd always say nobody could hope to build a decent life in a place had all the opportunity squeezed out of it years ago.

And how about having a piece of land of your own to build from? Mama'd say. You don't think having a roof over your head and walls around you is opportunity? She'd talk over these old

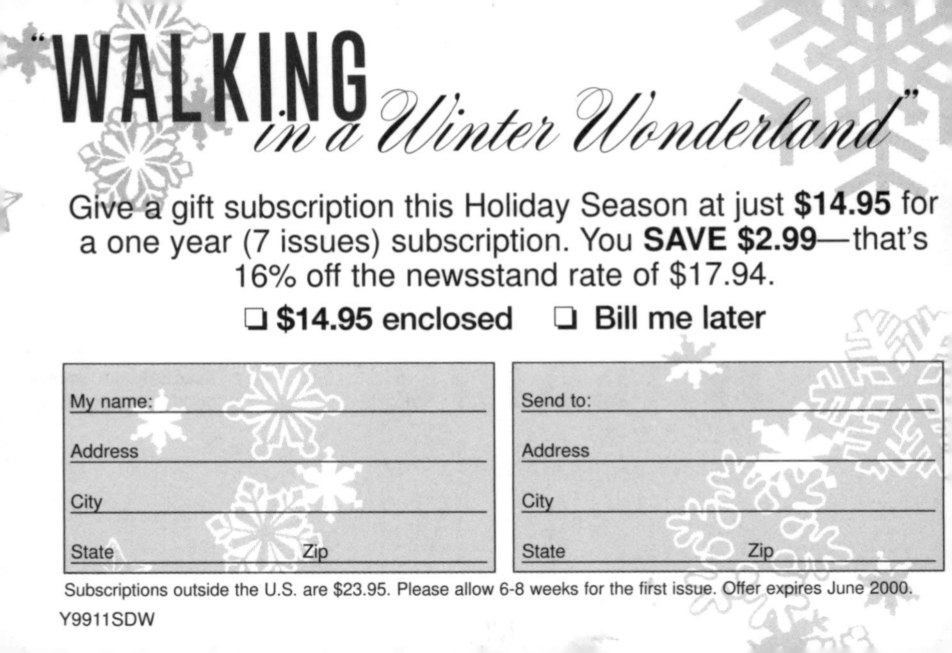
"WALKING in a Winter Wonderland"
Give a gift subscription this Holiday Season at just $14.95 for a one year (7 issues) subscription. You SAVE $2.99—that's 16% off the newsstand rate of $17.94.
❑ $14.95 enclosed ❑ Bill me later
My name:
Address
City
State Zip
Send to:
Address
City
State Zip
Subscriptions outside the U.S. are $23.95. Please allow 6-8 weeks for the first issue. Offer expires June 2000.
Y9911SDW

arguments with me years later, like I'd been there for the fireworks. And I maybe was, but just too small to take it all in.

My sister, though, took in plenty. She is your daddy's child and was from the second they clipped the cord kept her tied to me, Mama said. Won't hear of nothing but traipsing off to some city where she won't know a soul and don't think twice about how Daddy wound up when he left home, does she now? Life fell apart for this family then, and far as Pammy Jo's concerned, it's like it never happened. . . .

Then Mama would add her sayings about charity beginning at home and where the heart is and little frogs in big ponds and blood thicker than water. Oh, I can just hear her sometimes and for a second forget how sad things turned out and just wish Wim would have known Mama. . . . The wish alone can make me smile.

But Mama's mouth was full of bitterness then, and I spent the nights trying to keep awake, to keep my sister there. Pammy Jo would be graduating, valedictorian of her class, on the twelfth of June. She'd leave the following week: the college had helped find a summer job for her up north. Her scholarship would cover everything, she told me, even her books. But she'd be needing money for clothes, for tickets to the concerts she meant to attend in Boston. One day when I was older I'd come visit and she'd take me to the symphony, she said. Then she laughed and asked would I mind too bad if I wound up having to sit by myself, because she might be guest soloist up on the stage in a long black velvet dress and . . .

I'd surely be scared, I told her, but I would be there.

"I'll make sure you're in the front row," Pammy said. "That way, when I take my bow at the end, if I fall off the stage I can land right in your lap."

She was all high spirits then, of course. Her bags was already more than half packed. She carried her Norfolk-to-Boston bus ticket to school in her purse every day . . . no telling what Mama, mad as she was, might do.

I near expected Mama to stay away from commencement, to

keep me from going too. But we were there, Mama flouting the heat in the dark-flowered, long-sleeved dress she wore for Daddy's funeral, and a shiny black straw hat.

Mama was only just at the start of growing stout then. It was maybe Pammy's leaving brought on all that soft white flesh . . . like my sister filched the last bit of willpower from the house when she left, leaving Mama nothing to fight with.

At the commencement exercises, nobody could take their eyes off her. It makes me feel, even now, like a traitor to say it, but my sister never looked more beautiful, nor stood so clearly apart from everybody around her.

All that winter and spring, despite the bad feeling between them, Mama had been working on Pammy's commencement dress. It was made of layers and layers of white organdy, with cunning lace edges sewn by hand on every layer of the full skirt. Chains of white daisies were embroidered around the fitted waist, the slightly scooped neck, the little cap sleeves.

Mama stayed up late nights, working on that dress after we were asleep. She meant for it to be a surprise. Which was maybe a mistake. Because right when she was getting ready to finish, commencement just two weeks off, Pammy Jo came home from Norfolk on a Saturday afternoon with the dress she'd bought out of her baby-sitting money and tips from Jolie's Pizza Kitchen.

Mama's face looked about the color of canned tuna, and I couldn't have looked a lot better myself. But my sister was waltzing in her own world, her face shimmering like it had candlelight on it.

"There's this shop, secondhand—but they call it consignment—that only carries things with designer labels? And you couldn't believe . . . "

Pammy was near about as pleased with herself as Pammy was likely to get. "Everything dry-cleaned," she said. "Professionally. Still got the plastic bag and all."

Through the cloudy wrap billowing out from her arms I could

see something dark and silky, no fullness or body to it. Pammy slithered the plastic up over the dress, then held it out in front of her.

"Seventy-five dollars." Her voice was hushed, like she was praying.

"For a dress a stranger wore already?" Mama shook her head.

"Cost six hundred new, the lady said."

The dress, on a padded pink satin hanger that must have cost five dollars by its own self, looked like nothing to me, I got to say. And I wasn't just taking Mama's side. It was silk, I guess, and a dark purplish blue, no color for summertime. It sagged from the hanger on ribbony little straps, and the hem slumped over Pammy's sneakers when she held it up close to herself.

Mama was standing stiff behind the ironing board, the iron still in her hand. Her face was stony, almost like at Daddy's funeral. Shock, I reckon. You could tell she wasn't going to say another word.

The iron hissed and let loose a puff of steam. Mama jumped a bit. Then she set the iron upright on the board. She snatched the plug out of the wall socket by the cord, just like she was always telling me and Pammy not to.

Pammy, of course, was unmindful of Mama. In fact she was so wrought up she took off everything but her underpants right there in the front room, with me and Mama watching. Her breasts, which I'd never really got a good look at since she got them, looked like little yeast rolls on her chest that weren't half risen yet, and her nipples were the shade of Mama's summer face powder.

Pammy was slipping the dress over her head then, her face lost in a silky snarl. And I told myself it was a good thing, a blessing and a grace, that the beautiful white cloud of organdy was waiting hid somewhere, because it would grieve me to see my sister stand up to make a proud speech in this pitiful limp dark thing she'd dragged down from Norfolk after throwing away a fortune.

But that house felt dangerous to me, like something was getting ready to explode, and I wanted to tell my sister to keep her head down, her face covered, and not come out of the dark-blue dark until I told her it was safe to.

Pammy's head emerged, a golden thing, shining, and next I saw was how the color of that secondhand dress matched my sister's cobalt eyes and made them look electrified. The slick cloth slipped down past Pammy's breasts and she just caught it there. Smiling, she held it close to her middle, like an embrace. Then she raised it up and slid her pale thin arms through the stringy straps, and I could see her nipples pressing like tiny snaps against the thin cloth when she reached around behind her to zip up the dress.

"Oh," I said, a small helpless sigh like the breath squeezed right out of me. And something happened to Mama's breathing too then, cutting and painful and deep.

Pammy Jo was chattering: an admiral's wife . . . worn just one time, a ball on the deck of a ship . . . put on weight in the hips, and the lady in the shop didn't even charge a penny for the alterations. "You were *born* for this dress, darlin'," Miss Frechette said.

Back then an oval pier glass stood in the corner of the front room, a fancier thing than we had call for. Its frame was bird's-eye maple (at least that's what the dealer said who bought it from me after Mama passed on), carved with lilies at the top in a cluster. A leafy vine belonging to no lily I ever seen run down the sides to meet at the bottom in two leaves folded together like hands in prayer. Daddy found the mirror, ruined, at a tag sale, pieced it back together, and refinished it. A wedding gift to Mama, he said. She used to tease him, in fact, how he didn't get the mirror respectable until a few months after Pammy Jo was born, by when Mama's pleasure in studying her own figure was considerably reduced. Birthing wreaks havoc on a body, she liked to say. And any woman who hoped to hold a man's interest would do well to avoid the whole business of babies.

Daddy would get to looking sheepish then, and Mama'd wink at me and Pammy like she didn't half mean what she said. But she said it too often and too forceful for it to be anything as flighty as teasing, and pure teasing wouldn't have left my daddy's face looking like that. Got so I didn't have much fondness for that mirror, seeing what it provoked. But Pammy was right partial to the old thing and what she saw in it.

I can still picture how precise she centered herself in the glass. Her small fine hands smoothed the flighty fabric down over a body still begging for belly and hips. Then my sister just stared and stared until me and Mama had to turn away from a self-pleasure that, even to the child I was then, was unseemly.

Pammy didn't seem to notice, let alone mind, that nobody had a thing to say.

Mama drifted back to the kitchen, the cooling iron ticking in her hand. I thought I ought to leave too, but I could not seem to tear myself away from the sight of my sister taking stock of herself in that looking glass.

Pammy Jo lifted up her long heavy hair and twisted it around her head like a crown. She narrowed her eyes, tilted her head. The crown slipped, and she let it. Her hair tumbled down her back. She narrowed her eyes again. Then she nodded.

She lifted one foot, held it out in front of her and studied her pointed toes. Shiny pink polish the color of faded peonies glistened on her toenails.

"Sandals dyed to match." Her voice was dreamy. "Silk, with just the tiniest heel." She was not talking to me.

The midnight dress hung on the outside of the closet door in our bedroom all those two weeks. The afternoon of the day before commencement, I came home and saw the white dress hung there too, just slightly overlapping it. The full layered skirt made our room seem crowded.

A pair of white patent-leather pumps and a matching clutch purse with a pearl clasp were laid at the foot of Pammy's bed. I knew Mama'd sent off for them months before from the JCPenney catalogue, using the gift certificate she'd got at Christmas from one of the ladies she cleaned for.

I wasn't there when Pammy Jo first saw the dress. It hung on that door overnight and all the next day, but for all the attention it got from my sister, it might just as well have been a pipe dream that existed nowhere but in my mind. Strawberries had just come in, and Mama was busy putting up preserves. Seemed like the only one expecting anything out of the ordinary to happen was me.

Commencement was to be at seven o'clock. I was helping Mama clean up after supper when Pammy came out of the bedroom wearing the midnight dress. The thick fire-colored braids wound around her head were woven through with lilies-of-the-valley. Little crystal teardrops dangled from her ears. Her face, pale and set and smooth, reminded me of a damask tablecloth.

"T.J.'s daddy's giving me a ride," Pammy said. "I'll see y'all there, I guess."

Mama nodded and turned back to the sink. Her lips looked glued together.

As my sister stepped out onto the porch, I glimpsed the small satin wedge of one heel, midnight blue. The door closed softly. After a minute a car pulled up outside, the sound of voices happy and excited. Then a car door slammed and the car pulled away.

"We best be getting cleaned up." When Mama walked into the bathroom, wasn't nothing showing on her face, nothing at all.

Never a word was spoken in our house about the white dress, not anyhow in my hearing. When I went to bed that evening it was gone, the shiny shoes and bag along with it. I always kind of hoped Pammy Jo somehow took it all with her when she went up north. I'd imagine her, those first few years she was away, wearing the white dress at a college dance, where she would be the homecoming queen. She might even decide, I thought, to save the dress for her wedding.

Reckon all little girls dream about weddings. It strikes me odd only now to recall how the wedding of my dreams was always my sister's, not my own. I would be her maid of honor, in a ruffled lilac dress. My stubby hands would hide behind openmouthed irises with golden tongues.

By the time that white dress turned up again, though, Pammy Jo was already married. And I, of course, was not there.

I found the big flat box beneath the bed Mama died in, maybe a week after we buried her. Sheets of tissue, like new and barely creased, lay between layers of the skirt. The shoes and purse were there too, inside a grocery bag. The box had been sealed against dampness in plastic sheeting and cellophane packing tape. The years hadn't laid a finger on what was inside.

My mama was never much a one to save things. I reckon she figured she couldn't afford to be. Still, finding Pammy Jo's commencement dress didn't surprise me so much as the two other dresses I found along with it. One was a shell-pink sheath of polished cotton, with a little short jacket to match. The label said it came from Belk's and was a size six. I'd seen it in pictures, of course: the dress Mama was married in.

The third dress was just one of my first-grade school outfits, a red plaid flannel jumper. The shiny plastic buttons that ran up the front of it were cherries. Unlike Mama's and Pammy's dresses, mine had seen a good bit of wear and tear. Its colors were washed out, and a button was missing.

For the longest time I could not make sense of that box. It reminded me of one of those test problems in school, where they'll show you a row of little drawings—an apple, an orange, a banana, a pear, and maybe a carrot. And you're supposed to pick the one that doesn't belong with the others.

I could never have figured out the answer so long as I let the sorrow wafting off those two unspoiled dresses distract me. What did my raggedy little school dress have to do with such as those? It was a question, like Wim says, of finding the common denominator, discovering a kind of logic behind things.

Well, it came to me one day—Mama's logic. My mama, in spite

of everything, never stopped believing. She believed with all her weary heart in a Hereafter where our bodies would rise up perfect to meet our finally cleaned and mended souls. She kept a vision all her own, Mama, of who we each should be and how we should properly be turned out to meet our Maker.

Me, I prefer the notion we go to Him naked, pink and perfect and identical each to the other as new baby dolls. I did not keep that box. I did not want its weight on me, nor all the room it took up.

I might have sent those dresses off to the Goodwill, along with Mama's Samsonite and waffle iron and all else I couldn't hope to make room for in my own little house. But I reckon there is something of Mama in me. I found my way to making use of what was left.

My jumper, small as it was, made shirts for three Raggedy Andys. Mama's pink polished cotton was perfect for the shiny smooth skin of baby dolls. And after the fat little limbs were stuffed and shaped and sewn, after the cobalt glass eyes were set into the pudgy blind faces, I dressed those half-dozen babies in the loveliest christening gowns, layers and layers of sheer white skirts with little lace edges.

I still wear the pumps for dress-up, weddings mostly. And now and then, if I'm of a mind to go to church on a summer Sunday, the clutch purse is something to carry my offering in.

Lying abed with a man beside me while the day melts to nothing is not an experience I had before, nor ever especially hoped to.

We are not, strictly speaking, in a bed, of course. But that, like Mama was fond of saying, is splitting hairs.

And Wim, while I have tended his body when I saw the need to be extreme, is hardly my lover. What would a person call such little as has passed between us when we lie together? Solace, perhaps. A giving and a taking of small comfort.

Or maybe not so small—by my lights, true comfort's never a

thing of small consequence. I know what my mama, what lots of folks I know, would call it: *sin*. An abomination before the Lord. A scandal . . .

I can just imagine the talk. And imagining, I can't help but smile. If I had the slightest leaning toward debauchment, couldn't even such as I find bawdier and more abandoned things to do with these arms and legs than wrap them around a withering and dolorous old man?

I have known, though Wim might be the one scandalized now to hear it, a lover's touch. Branch Goodlin, who owns this very land I live on and the leaky roof over my head, had been waiting since eighth grade to step in and fill any gap I might admit to. And the months after my sister and her child died, my mama and daddy both gone and the one real granddaddy, who I barely knew, I could hardly deny the emptiness gaping all around me. Especially when it seemed like I'd lost Wim as well.

Branch is as fine a man as a woman could hope to attach herself to. I think as much to this day, and so, I don't doubt, do his wife, Carol Jean, and their four handsome sons. But Branch was not spoken for then, ten years ago, and I was given the right of first refusal, like Branch, who's done right well in real estate, says.

He will stop in for coffee now and then on a slow day. Even now he asks, "Leandra, is there anything you need?" And sometimes I will bring myself to say, "Now that you mention it," and Branch will carry in the toolbox from his big white car and tighten up the hinges on a sagging cupboard door or fix a dripping faucet. In spring he'll send a man around to try for the tenth or twentieth time to find that sneaky chink up there by the rafters where a water stain has inched into a shape that looks more like a boot than Italy ever did.

Branch still has the cornsilk hair and nut-brown eyes he had as a bashful little boy. But he's grown into a man I could easily have pictured as my sister's bridegroom—tall and straight and strong and honorable. He wanted, he said, to be a husband to me. But I had something else in mind.

Branch accepted the task I gave him, and when we were twenty-two, he taught me what I thought I needed to learn of a lover's ardor and the body's secrets. So much of what we learned of life we started out learning together, Branch and me. He sat out the worst of my grieving with me, gauging its deeps without discovering its causes. Sometimes, during the year or so we kept company after I came back home, I'd catch him studying me, his eyes taking in more than I was giving away. I will always be grateful for all he didn't demand, when he had every right, to know.

Branch waited until I seemed back to myself again; then he asked me once more to be his wife. I told him, once more and finally, that I could not. He didn't ask why and I still didn't say. What need? Knowing my heart like he did, Branch was bound to have noticed so much of it being gone.

We both knew, anyhow, that Carol Jean Medford had been waiting her turn with Branch. When he left my bed, I believe I even gave him a nudge in her direction. Now I'm godmother to their youngest boy, Fowler, the one takes most after his daddy.

Sweating in the midday heat beside me, Wim falls short, as he always has, of the man I'd see fit to marry my sister. In a few months' time I'll be as old as Pammy, who will never be anything but young. She didn't need to die. She could, beside this husband, have been young for as long as she lived.

Wim, flat on his back, sleeps like an old gent, his face raised up like a human sacrifice. His mouth is set to catch flies. Each breath makes a small effortful sound. His nose is getting beakish, like an old man's will.

I lie, just slightly apart from him, on my side. I watch him sleep with an attention that makes it hard for me to swallow. The stubble on his chin and cheeks has turned silver. He is sore in need of a bath.

I still, after everything, cannot imagine my sister married to this man . . . or explain how, even now, he is all I ever wanted to keep for my everlasting own.

—∿—

"As simple as that?" I asked him. "Because she wanted you to?"

"I thought she needed me," Wim said.

I shook my head.

"She needed someone," he said.

"Reckon she did. But what about you?"

He looked at me like the question was outlandish.

"You must have needed something too?"

Wim rubbed his eyes. "I can't remember," he said.

—∿—

We lie here in a hot misery of tangled sheet, the floor, for all the quilts, hard beneath us. Both playing possum while we try to figure out how to face what is left of the day.

Of ourselves.

Of each other.

There are people, I know, in the habit of waking up this way with strangers. It's a horror I am thankful I can't imagine. This is bad enough, and this is just Wim. And me.

I imagine myself out in the spiteful heat of the tin shed, digging through the boxes of battered and dismembered dolls I've promised to make ready for Christmas. I've given my word; who will keep it if I can't get back to myself?

I remember a movie I saw once on Vietnam. Boys with holes in their chests, with legs blown off, with most of their faces missing, were carried off of helicopters while the blades were still spinning. An older doctor with kind eyes and a crusty disposition explained to the younger doctor, who only just got there and looked right sick at the sights, how they had to make hard quick judgments. "Every godforsaken day," he said, "you have to decide on saving a few who can maybe be saved and leave the rest to die." *Triage,* he called it. I am going to have to learn to practice that now.

This warm dry weather we been having since before Halloween

is good for the more complicated repairs—the porcelains and resins and bisques, the paints and papier-mâché, the quicker they harden, the smoother things mostly turn out. And it seems like my hands do their best when there's not much time for thinking.

But now, ten days to Thanksgiving, I'll be obliged to concentrate on the simpler things—restringing arms and legs, resetting eyes and wigs, plus all the needlework. I need to be tough-minded. I can't dawdle and distress myself with what's liable to turn out hopeless in the end.

And Wim shouldn't be here at all.

But perhaps he is only lying here next to me long enough to study how he might get clean away. Might be if I'd send him out for milk and butter he'd jump in his car and keep on driving, only stopping to send a postcard from Virginia or Maryland somewhere. "It was a mistake," he'd say. "Forgive me, Leandra. . . ." And after a while, I would.

"Leandra?" His voice, low and froggy and uncertain, is such a sorry thing that for a moment it gets mislaid in my daydream and I don't answer him, he's too far away.

"Did you get any sleep?" Wim says.

"Truth is, I didn't." I smile, so as not to seem blameful. "Did you?"

He doesn't answer. His bony brown wrist falls on the pillow near my head as he rolls over. I pick up his hand like something that belongs to me and look at the face of his watch. At first I think one of the hands has fallen off . . . but no, it is noon, worse than I thought. "Lord have mercy," I say.

Wim smiles. "Were you supposed to be somewhere?"

"On my feet," I say. "About six hours ago."

"We were up all night," he says.

"So I heard."

I toss back the sheet and stand up. Until I see the way Wim is looking at me, I forget he would never have seen my body before, not all at once like this, naked and in such squanderous light.

His eyes look shocked, almost stricken. But even so, it's only my face I want to hide, to cover my hair. If I could keep those out of sight, I reckon I could pass for my sister . . . my body her body before the surplus of flesh so small a frame wasn't made to carry, before the milk filling her breasts, the knife splitting her belly. Is that what Wim sees in my nakedness, the body of his true wife? Is that what I want him to see? Were there whole years when they were happy?

My own scars are all inside and need never be seen. Still, I duck out of the sunlight, into the shadowy corner where my chifforobe stands, and pull out my old flowered blue wrapper. I keep my back to Wim. But when I raise my arms to slip on the robe, he whispers, like something urgent, "Leandra, don't."

I turn around very slowly. It is not by intention that the faded blue cloth drops to the floor. He frightens me. I stand stock-still, my hands at my sides, so still.

Wim lies there for a moment looking at me. Then, stiffly, he raises himself, peels back the rumpled sheet, stands. He looks so frail. Even the band of softened flesh around his middle appears smaller, as if the long night has whittled away at him. Only his eyes keep steady as he comes to me.

His hands, moving up and down my body, tremble. He measures the span of my shoulders, my waist, my hips. He gauges the scant weight of my breasts in cupped palms.

Then his arms wrap around and pull me into himself. His skin, bound to mine, feels hot and smooth as a feverish child's.

When he lifts me off my feet and carries me to the bed, it seems like a miracle of strength, a desperate act like you'll hear about when an ordinary woman lifts a car off the body of her injured child.

Then his body on my body has no weight to it at all and his flesh within my flesh is as pure intention, his mouth at my breast no mere hunger but a wresting of something more immediate, more dire.

My body becomes my sister's body then, opening, straining to give back all it has taken. The part of me that aches with this ill use, this displacement, cries out once, wordless, then, unwanted, moves away.

But I hear Wim calling me back. "Leandra." I am not free to go. And I am sucked back inside the helplessness of being only myself, here, with him, who I could surely never save and can scarcely console.

"Don't leave me, Leandra," Wim says. "I won't let you leave me again."

Surely I did not leave him, could not have done. But Wim has set down the words now, and so I know he will remember it that way. Me leaving. I never.

iv

I HADN'T BEEN in love before. Oh, I thought I had, of course. But my passions had always kept their distance, something I'd dreamed up, contrived from scraps of vapid fantasy and stock lust.

I'd had the misfortune, my first year in college, to fall under Goethe's spell. It never occurred to me, after *The Sorrows of Young Werther,* to distinguish love from angst—hardly an uncommon adolescent disorder. I simply suffered from it for an uncommonly long time.

I was stunned by Pamela's desire for me. My previous affairs, all too few, had been with aloof, cerebral women, often older than myself. If ever I had been pursued, it was only as the sexual equivalent of the extra man, available to balance the table at a dinner party. Such passion as I was accustomed to expired of ennui . . . or inconvenience: a Fulbright year in Reykjavik, a husband returning from sabbatical in Greece.

But Pamela was not, she made clear from the start, going anywhere. Nor was anyone likely to come after her. We'd been married for months before she admitted to the widowed mother, the sister still a child—and then only after I'd come upon a snapshot of a stout and rather censorious-looking woman in a florid dress crowding a frail girl against an oleander. The girl wore a straw hat whose brim layered her face in shadows. The woman's smile was martyred. My question, evidently, caught Pamela unprepared. Her mother and sister, yes. Her summation utterly chilled me: "They've got nothing do with me. Not now." I was to be her history, she said.

There had been earlier versions of her autobiography, of course: Pamela raised by her maternal grandmother—not really a midwife, no, but a primitive painter of some regional renown. The old lady had been afflicted with religious visions, vivid and terrible, since the day her daughter had died in premature childbirth on the hay-strewn floor of a derelict barn, where the girl, just sixteen, had been confined to wait out the consequence of her disgrace.

"That was me," Pamela said. "The consequence." She was speaking suddenly in the voice she'd been trying so hard to leave behind, the voice that gave away both her origins and her feelings. "Wasn't a full hour old when my grandma found me. Came out to the barn to see was the milking done, and there I am dropped between my dead mama and a cow fit to bursting. I looked so like a blood clot in the dirty hay it was pure luck I didn't get swept up and out, Grandma said."

She first told me this bit of the family saga the summer before our marriage. We were in my bed, in the dark, and I could not see Pamela's face. I could scarcely speak, of course. She was between my legs, I still inside her but going soft. The summer night was hot. We were uncovered. I was sweating, but Pamela's skin was cool and dry.

"She was this old Pentecostal woman," she said. "Near fifty when my mama got born, and all her other children growed and gone, my granddaddy gone too then, dead.

" 'And when I saw my girl there, stone cold of my righteousness,' Gran told me, 'and felt you breathing on me like the bloody wrath of God, was when the visions started. Hadn't of turned them into pictures like I done these years hence, I reckon they'd torn my insides to ribbons,' she said."

Pamela's voice, in the dark, was contrite and venerable. I felt as if, had I turned on a lamp, I'd have found myself held fast in the stringy arms of an old woman with eyes that looked right through me.

Then, returning to herself, Pamela sighed, and with that slight movement I slipped out of her.

"No," she said. "No, Wim." Her hands reached down and clasped the wet, limp, shrinking flesh of me, trying to gather it back inside her, but it was no use.

She moved against me then, somehow frantic.

I was shivering. "Don't," I said, though I didn't mean to. The mattress beneath us felt blood-soaked, and I couldn't stop hearing the old woman's voice.

Pamela's head dropped to my chest. "I shouldn't have told you, should never . . . " I realized, after a moment, that she was crying. Her tears were the only part of her that felt warm.

"It's all right," I said. "It will be all right." I stayed there, holding her, though I ached to let go, get up, leave the room. Or at least turn on a light.

She did not cry for long. Her breathing soon slowed and evened, and I hoped she was asleep.

"The pictures are all of women birthing," she whispered. "But what's borning is never a baby, Wim. And it's always stuck there, halfway out—"

"There's no need to tell me," I said. "Not now."

"Don't I need to tell *somebody*?" Pamela said.

A light summer rain began pelting the rhododendrons below the window. Water ticked on the roof above our heads. The air was stifling and still.

"Sometimes it's just animals being born, dogs and pigs and even birds. And if it's the head coming out, you'll see sharp teeth or a beak. But sometimes it's hooves and claws, and you can't scarcely imagine what the critter means to be."

My arms tightened around her. *Don't.* I could not breathe.

"But there was worse things," Pamela said. "Worse than the animals . . . just awful things, Wim."

The rain was falling harder now, straight down. No need to close the windows, though I longed to.

"The last one I saw, it was Jesus," Pamela said. "The full-grown man, you know, and his head wrapped in thorns." She was moving against me again, chilled flesh burrowing between my thighs. Her words, sounding disembodied, wafted like an odor through the room.

"Reckon you'd expect them in a crown," she said. "The thorns. But this was more like a helmet, His whole head sharp and cutting."

I felt myself hardening, my body, against its will, beginning to move with hers.

"His eyes drowning in blood." Pamela's arms entwined my neck, choking off air. *Don't.* She was on top of me. I thrust up inside her and she rose on her knees, bone grinding bone, as she pressed down. My pushing upward felt like plummeting.

Then I was deep inside her, in the dark. Her face, a pale shadow, loomed over me in the blackness, then lowered.

"She's probably some kind of genius." Pamela's breath came quick and hot against my face. "That's what the newspaper in Charlotte said."

—∞—

My initial symptoms, oddly, resemble the early stages of pregnancy: brief bouts of morning nausea, a whimsical appetite, sleeplessness, lethargy. There are the headaches too, naturally, but I've had headaches all my life, and these, so far, are hardly different. The occasional spots before my eyes might be the rightful repercussion of too many books devoured by too little light.

The strong coffee Leandra brewed at noon did not agree with

me. I tamped it down with soft white bread, managed to keep it down until she'd left the house.

"I got to work," Leandra said. "You think you can look after yourself?" She smiled. "For a while anyhow."

She was standing in the doorway, a blue stoneware mug in her hands. She wore ancient bib overalls, faded nearly white, and a frayed gray work shirt of the sort repairmen wear. A pair of rubber gloves hung from the hammer loop of the overalls. Her feet were bare.

"Where on earth are you going?" I asked her.

"Not far." She looked distracted. "The shed out back is where I work."

Arriving at night, I'd seen no shed, of course.

"I'll be here," I said.

Her smile faded. "I expect so," she said.

I waited until she had time to get out the door and move around to the back of the house. Then I walked to the sink and looked out the window above it. Leandra was picking her way through the scrappy yard, her toes scuffing up pine needles as she moved through streamers of light and shade.

The shed was a long low building of rusting corrugated metal, something like a squared Quonset hut. It had no windows. A door, fashioned from a pair of cast-off shutters, hung on loose hinges, curls of maroon paint peeling from its warped slats.

Leandra set her coffee mug down in a patch of sandy soil and wrestled the door open. Then she retrieved her coffee and disappeared inside without glancing back at the house.

The noonday heat, even with the door and all the windows open, was staggering. I thought of Leandra working inside that hot metal box and wondered if my intrusive presence exiled her there.

The wave of sickness hit hard and sudden. I leaned over the sink, grasping its edge, spewing out a foul rush that seemed to have oddly little to do with me. When it was finished, I rinsed out my mouth. I let the tepid tap water flow into the sink for a long time. It must be suffocating, I thought. She cannot last out there.

But it is after three now. Leandra's been gone for hours. Surely she knows I will outwait her.

And she will also know—just as surely and with as little fluster—what I've been doing, left to my own devices here. I have searched her premises, rifled through her cabinets and drawers, made free with her belongings.

Her clothes are few and unfashionable, her underclothes, cotton, white, and plain, are scented, bringing to mind an ancient great-aunt. Olivia Fitch was her name, and I barely knew her. But she left me a "tidy sum," as they used to say, and a rather handsome cottage on the edge of Lake Geneva. When I went out to Wisconsin to clear it out a few years back, pursuant to its sale, I found in each drawer a tiny hand-stitched sachet. "Lemon verbena," I was informed by the fussy antiques dealer who accompanied me. Her nose twitched delightfully. "Ladylike, very old school," she approved. The linens alone fetched four thousand dollars. I should have saved the doll collection for Leandra. I simply didn't realize . . .

The dolls are everywhere, out in the open. I make my way past them, interested only in what is concealed.

The food in Leandra's cupboard is sparse and wholesome, largely beans and grains. A bin of root vegetables snugs under the sink, smelling of loam. A yam and two onions are sprouting roots. Leandra harbors few spices or condiments, no cosmetics apart from one pinkish-red lipstick worn to a nub, a jar of Pond's cold cream.

A single small bookshelf is bracketed to the wall above the bed—three cookbooks, a dictionary, a Bible, and perhaps a dozen books about dolls.

An old-fashioned family photograph album with a violet plush cover, a nosegay of pansies embroidered on it, is wrapped in plastic and stashed in an inconvenient cupboard above the refrigerator. I pull it down, rocked slightly as its full weight drops into my hands. My heart quickens and I glance uneasily around the room. The ruined dolls and I have largely ignored one another until now, but suddenly the eyes of blue and green and amber glass accuse me. Painted irises of brown and gray with huge black pupils flatten with disapproval. From a corner a fat infant with livid cheeks, fisted hands, and no eyes at all appears to be screaming.

The album is fastened shut with a tarnished brass lock. Its key is missing. I find myself relieved. I have never seen Pamela as a child. Now I discover I no longer care to. I see the child in Leandra every time I look at her.

I replace the album on the high shelf, its shroud intact, and the cabinet door clicks shut. I feel as if I have been spared something.

"Wim?" Leandra's distant voice sails through the window.

"I'm here," I say, my damp forehead touching the screen.

"I know." Her smile is wry. She stands shaded in the shed doorway, wiping her cheeks with the backs of her hands. She has taken off the gray shirt, wears nothing under the overalls. Her arms and chest drip and shine as she takes a step into the sunlight.

"Calling it quits?" I say.

"Indeed not." The air between us is flecked with gold. I can't read the expression on her face.

"It's just there's soup and such as that," she says. "In the cabinet. You must be famished."

"Yes," I say. "All right." And for a moment I think I will confess, turn myself in: *You will have nothing here that I don't know about if you are not more vigilant. . . . Come back, Leandra. Hurry back. . . .*

"Can I fix you something?" I say. But she is gone.

I keep listening, leaning into the window frame. Leandra's afterimage shimmers in front of the wavy silver lines of the shed, a mirage, and even the birds are still.

When finally I turn from the window, the room goes black. That tends to happen now, when I neglect to shade my eyes from brightness. I grip the edge of the deal table, waiting for balance. Sight, soon enough, will return.

The doctor waxes, in turn, prosaic and poetical. "Radiation," he says. "An inexact science at best." And: "Time?" He shrugs. "It's all guesswork." His language for impairment is crude, halting, but then these marvelous Latinate lapses will loosen his tongue:

Glioma . . . Glioblastoma . . . Medulla oblongata . . . Cisterna magna . . .

Chamber music.

Subarachnoid . . . Papilledema . . .

My head is a chamber filled with the scherzi of spiders and butterflies.

"And the nausea, of course," the doctor says. "But you are already familiar with that."

My losses, by the time Pamela and I married, were prodigious. The professional setbacks did not alarm me. I had never intended to stay at the college any longer than necessary, and I couldn't imagine that leaving under a slight shadow would have far-reaching consequences. The subtle imposition of social quarantine, once word of my involvement with Pamela leaked out, was almost welcome. Communal life on the campus, such as it was, had never included me more than superficially, nor had I desired its embrace. All the less now, when I wanted nothing more than to keep Pamela to myself.

Pamela, on the other hand, had evidently been entertaining some naive hope of social acceptance. I was amazed and disconcerted to find her suddenly weeping and railing at me as I explained why it would be impossible for her to accompany me to a faculty banquet. I must, she charged, be ashamed of her.

"It's myself I ought to be ashamed of," I said, hoping to humor her toward reason or perspective. I'd come to realize, of course, the gravity of treating lightly Pamela's slightest whim. But calculation of any sort must hibernate through the first season of infatuation.

Perhaps the one bit of good sense I managed to keep active was my determination that Pamela finish school before we married.

Her campaign to defeat me was ferocious and exhausting. Indeed, this disagreement might well have driven us apart but for the fact that Pamela chose to stage most of its battles in bed. It seemed, that first year, that there was no end to our passion, nor bounds. Pamela's will wasn't always convenient, but at least it left no room for ennui.

"I hate it here anyway," she'd tell me. "If you'd get a job in New York, I could go to Juilliard, Wim. Here I can't even major in music."

"I thought you were taking your degree in literature," I said.

"That's yours," Pamela said. "I mean, you got there first, didn't you?"

"You're joking," I said. "Aren't you?"

I must have looked horrified, for Pamela's smile looked automatic, placating. "Of course, silly," she said. "But neither of us needs to stay in this no-count place, do we? You ought to be somewhere big and famous. Columbia's in New York, right? And maybe I couldn't get right into Juilliard first thing, but with some lessons from a really great teacher, somebody with a reputation . . ."

"Sweetheart," I said, "Columbia's hardly champing at the bit for a junior instructor from a school like this, a dropout poet with one mediocre little chapbook published by a small press that's gone belly-up. And Juilliard—"

Pamela's face looked small and still and dangerous.

"Even if I could find a teaching job in New York," I said, "the pay wouldn't keep the two of us alive there, let alone cover piano lessons or any kind of tuition for you to finish school."

"I hate it here." Her voice was sullen and clipped.

"I rather hate it here myself." I offered her a cautious smile. "But we're only talking a matter of months. And your scholarship—"

"They don't have a music major."

"Surely you realized that before you came?"

"There's not even a decent piano teacher on the faculty."

"Well, maybe we can find somebody in Boston."

"Boston." I might as well have said Lisbon or Istanbul. "How's a person with no car supposed to get into Boston from out here in the backwoods?" Pamela said. "I was going to hear concerts, look at paintings and statues all Sunday afternoon. . . ." All the huffiness seemed to leave her in one long tremulous breath. "Never been to a single museum in my whole life," she whispered. "Wim, I'm scared."

"Scared?" I reached for her. "I don't . . ."

Her eyes had filled with tears. "How am I supposed to grow into somebody you'd stay with? A man like you can't love a person's never seen inside a museum."

"But I do love you," I said. "You know that."

After a moment Pamela shrugged out of my arms. "It's just I keep wondering how soon you're liable to stop."

"Not in my lifetime," I said softly. "Nor yours."

"You mean it, about us getting married?"

"As soon as you've finished school."

"I could maybe switch majors," Pamela said. "To philosophy."

" 'Adversity's sweet milk, philosophy,' " I said.

" 'Unless philosophy can make a Juliet.' " Pamela hooked an index finger through one of my belt loops, pulling me toward her. " 'Romeo, come forth; come forth, thou fearful man.' " Her fingers easily defeated buckle, button, fly. " 'Affliction is enamour'd of thy parts,' " she said.

She edged me to the bed and tipped me backward. Then, laughing, she collapsed on top of me, breath hot and moist at my ear.

" 'And thou art wedded to calamity,' " she said.

She kept, like a prisoner, a running account of time served. "Two hundred and thirty-eight days," she'd inform me. The calendar, featuring trite New England scenery in colors nature never came up with, was tacked to the wall above the head of my bed. One at a time, Pamela fully blacked out the days. Still, she threatened every few weeks to break out.

"Your scholarship . . ." I'd remind her.

"As if I give a hoot." The concentration on philosophy was a poor choice, of course. Pamela had the kind of intelligence quickly made bored and irritable by abstractions. By the time she gauged her error, though, it was far too late for another change.

"This will be over soon," I'd promise her. "You have a whole future to think about."

"Which is you," she told me. "You are my future, Wim." It was a heady claim for a man such as I to hear. And all the while her hands would be taking possession of me with such bawdy hunger. I barely remember teaching. That whole last year at the college has vanished from my memory like perfunctory dinner table conversation over a sumptuous meal ravenously and blissfully devoured.

We were married on the Saturday following Pamela's graduation, a ceremony she declined to attend. Regrettably, however, I was obligated. Begowned, I assumed my place at the tail of the academic procession. The Elgar, the gladioli and counterfeit prayer . . . the college seemed to take pride in not missing a single cliché.

Yes, I was present, as required. But I was already gone, my position at the college but one of the forfeitures of that deviable time.

I had not, in fact, been fired. I had simply been advised that my future at Runyon College no longer reeked of promise.

"You just might survive, William. But I won't mislead you. You're not likely to thrive."

The dean, Bob Fetterman, was an affable fellow, given to double-knit suits, wide ties, and longish hair. No prude, he said, but the "grooves of academe" being what they were . . . He shrugged, for regret, and smiled, for camaraderie.

"Can't say I entirely blame you, either," he confided. "She's a lovely girl. And hell, she was already twenty-one, right?" His tight smile loosened into a gamy grin. "I'd call you a lucky cuss, Bill.

But the president calls you 'indiscreet,' and he's the one calling the shots. The trustees get wind of something like this . . . " His hands pantomimed helplessness. "You know what I'm saying?"

"In at least four languages." My smile was gamy too.

The dean appreciated my lack of flap. "Your references . . . there won't be a breath of negativity," he said.

Nor was there, insofar as I could tell. Unfortunately, neither were there any jobs, it being late in a year of glut. I was fortunate when the prep school position opened up—another's misfortune, in fact. An aging housemaster, having fractured a hip during a fire drill, had acquiesced to early retirement. I accepted the position, on a nonresidential basis, for one year. I have remained in it since 1976.

But when Pamela and I married, in late May of that year, I had neither employment nor prospects. My salary checks from the college would stop in August. My health insurance would lapse a year after that. I dreaded the probability of dipping into the modest inheritance left me by my parents. It was the only security I—we—could expect to have.

I had hoped, as a married man, to buy a house. Pamela had dreamed of going to Paris as a bride. As it was, we rented a two-room apartment near Porter Square. Cambridge, I assured my wife, bore many similarities to the Left Bank. Pamela found a piano teacher in Brookline, an elderly Ukrainian émigrée who affected snoods and flowered shawls. I managed to pick up some freelance editing work for the M.I.T. Press.

Our wedding, witnessed by two passing strangers in a musty little courthouse in the Berkshires, seemed faintly tragic to me. We both lacked family (or so I believed then), and our situation at the college had stifled any slight inclination we might have had to cultivate friends.

A sullen drizzle was falling. We stepped out of the courthouse, into a chill. We had reservations, that night and the next, at a picturesque inn in Stockbridge. Our Cambridge apartment would not be available until Monday.

Pamela took my hand as we neared my pocked Skylark. "We should go somewhere," she said.

I turned to her. She looked exquisite, even exotic, in a slightly yellowed ivory silk suit from the twenties and a lace cloche hat that entirely covered her hair. She had found her wedding ensemble in a vintage clothing shop in Great Barrington, even the ivory kid boots that buttoned snugly around her ankles.

A gardenia, its edges beginning to brown and curl, was pinned to my bride's lapel. I'd never so much as thought of flowers. "Go somewhere?" I was stupefied with sudden sorrow. "Love, where would we go?"

Pamela threw back her head and let the soft rain fall on her face for a moment. Her ebullience startled me. Her beauty was terrifying.

"Oh, Wim," she said. "Don't you see? Now we can go anywhere."

I forgot entirely where I was then, a small town square busy with Saturday afternoon traffic. I pulled her—my wife—into my arms, pressing myself against her. I tore the lace cap from her head and buried my face in her fragrant hair. I was dangerously close to weeping.

Pamela's small hands, proprietary, worked under my suit coat, wormed their way inside my shirt, kneading the flesh at my waist, digging into my skin with her blunt polished nails.

"I'll take you anywhere you say," I whispered.

"I know." Pamela lifted her head, pulled back slightly. Her fingers, slipping down inside the waistband of my trousers, were warm and unruly. She was laughing. Her eyes shone. "I know that, Wim."

I gently pulled her hands away and tried not to be too obvious about straightening my clothes. "Just tell me where," I said.

"I want to do something I never did before."

"Be careful," I said. "You don't want to frighten me."

Laughing, she reached toward my belt again. I caught her hand and drew it away, kept hold of it.

"Tell me," I said.

Her face was grave now. "I always wanted to go to a Chinese restaurant," she said.

"You haven't . . . ?" I tried not to sound shocked.

"Never," she said.

My throat constricted.

"I have a lot to learn," Pamela said. "I never pretended I didn't."

I took her face between my hands. It was raining harder now, the rain darkening her hair. "I do too," I said. "Forgive me."

We had to drive all the way to Pittsfield to find a Chinese restaurant that was open in midafternoon. I ordered improvidently. Pamela devoured everything but the bamboo shoots. "Reckon these must be an acquired taste," she said.

Pamela declined the silverware, struggling to master chopsticks. After we'd finished she asked the waiter, a slight and sober middle-aged mandarin, if she might take the chopsticks home. "I need to practice," she said.

The waiter, informed of the wedding, presented her with two new pairs—not the splintery bamboo version, but plastic ones fashioned to look like ivory, their sides embossed with Chinese characters in red and green.

Pamela held the chopsticks as if they were fragile. "A real wedding gift," she said. She wrapped them in a paper place mat and tucked them inside her purse.

As I waited for the check, she shattered six fortune cookies before finding one that suited her. *You are about to embark on a long journey,* it said.

Just when I think I have thoroughly ransacked the place, set everything back to rights, covered the tracks of my prying, my eye falls on the small footlocker edged into a corner, behind a woebegone armchair.

The chest is embossed tin, its black lacquer scratched and chipped. Rotting leather straps, their buckles broken, fasten its lid.

I inch the heavy armchair out of the way, hunker down before the chest. It opens without a fight, as if it has nothing to hide.

Here, at last, is that evidence of a secret life, that strain of rife indulgence, I've always suspected in Leandra. The compartments of the trunk, lined with water-stained flowered paper, are stuffed with extravagance: satin and silk, velvet and lace, gold braid and bright ribbon, slip through my fingers as I go digging. A tin pillbox is filled with seed pearls, brilliants, jet beads. Silk rosebuds tumble from the mouth of a small drawstring bag.

I picture Leandra adorned, gussied up, her soft features sharpened by sure-handed strokes of paint. She is Pamela's sister, after all. Her lids the iridescent blue of an exotic butterfly, her lashes hard black spikes, her eyes have a startled look. Her wide sensuous mouth, rose madder and glossy, is shameless.

I dig deeper. Beneath the trunk's removable shelf is more decadence—tapestry, moiré. The bottom of the chest is lined with the slight remains, muslin wrapped, of slain animals—a collar of mink, a cuff of Persian lamb. Snippets of kid and chamois, bits of ermine and fox, unroll from inside a slick pelt of what may be sealskin.

It is all for the dolls, of course. A fool would have recognized it. There is not so much as a full yard of anything. Still, the image persists, sickening and fascinating—Leandra tricked out, transformed. For a moment, forgetting I imagined her, I feel utterly betrayed.

And so I am prepared, almost resigned, when the trunk's false bottom reveals actual perfidy.

I raise the lace cloche to my face and could swear the scent of rotting gardenia clings to it. When I drop it, the hat, still shaped to the head of the woman who last wore it, falls soundlessly onto a swath of black velvet, where my dappled vision transmutes it into a skull.

The last object in the trunk, wedged into a back corner of the hidden compartment, is a small flat parcel, perhaps six inches square, wrapped in tissue. The paper has grown fragile with age. It falls to shreds between my fingers as I part it.

Pamela took the photograph of me a year or so after we were married, not long after we moved into the house. It was late summer, at the height of a heat spell that seemed to last forever at the time.

I know that I am naked and that I am standing in water up to my knees—a slightly brackish pond on a then neglected property at the end of our new road. We had climbed a cyclone fence to reach it, had made love in the water because the ground there was hard and rugged and we hadn't thought to bring a blanket. The pond was surrounded by stunted trees, and the sun, in late afternoon, was still high in a fish-belly sky.

But you can't see any of that, of course—the sky or the trees, my nakedness or the algae-colored water. There is only myself, in black and white, from the waist up. My chest glistens with drops of water or sweat. My skin is dark, my hair already graying. My eyes and my smile look so uncertain that for an instant, gazing at this slightly familiar man, I yearn to befriend him, to urge him to unburden himself and confide in me.

Pamela, also bare but for a towel draped across her sunburned shoulders, stood close to me, too close, when taking this photograph. My nose and mouth lack definition. A shadow, like a birthmark, darkens my right shoulder. It is Pamela's head, I believe.

I remember we'd quarreled that morning, for reasons I can no longer recall . . . something Pamela craved that I could not provide. She'd customarily stay close to me for a spell after we argued, as if she feared I might turn my back on her and stalk away. The lovemaking, of course, was temporary settlement, a retreat if not a truce. We had already fallen into something that resembled desperation more closely than desire.

Once the house was acquired—finished, furnished, occupied if not paid for—Pamela grew curiously passionless at home. I'd come home to find her beautifully groomed and dressed, nicely situated but looking somehow lost. It was as if she'd spent all her attention and ingenuity on sets and costumes, only to realize she was not conversant with the play being staged. Sometimes I found myself wondering if the design of the place—her choosing, her dream, her desire for order fully realized—may have accounted in part for the chill, for I surely felt it too. I have lived in that house for close to two decades now, first with Pamela, latest with Clio, and alone for an interim of several years. The only time its rooms ever felt quite real to me was during those few months when Leandra occupied and warmed their corners.

But if Pamela seemed lukewarm, at best, at home, she was capable of astonishing heat in less private places. She loved to seduce me in risky spots where just anyone might stumble upon our coupling. More than once she staged dalliances in my office at the school, at lunch hour or late in the day. My resistance would be token. It was not difficult to take panic for a kind of arousal.

As soon as we left Cambridge, I taught Pamela to drive. Eventually she'd start working and we'd need a second car. First, however, she needed to do some thinking, she said, about just what she intended to do. The occasional moonlighting I still did for M.I.T. would cover piano lessons, I told Pamela, perhaps a symphony ticket now and then. I pictured my wife nibbling a salad in the MFA cafeteria as she studied an exhibit catalogue, keeping up with seasonal changes abloom in the Gardner atrium. But Pamela possessed neither the bravado for driving into the city, she said, nor the patience public transportation required. I suspected that riding into Boston on the T was simply too great a violation of her fantasies of elegant urban life. In any case, from the moment we moved to the country, Boston might have been the center of a different solar system than the one we occupied.

This is not to say Pamela was inclined to remain at home during the week, when I was working. It became her habit to drop me off at school, then roam restlessly through the less populous reaches of mid–New England—scouting locations, as I came to think of it. Come Saturday, she'd tell me, "There's a place I need to show you, Wim." Or, more directly: "I'm taking you out for a treat." Her eyes would have a febrile glint. Her clothes, even in the coldest season, would be flimsy and loose.

I quickly learned to recognize the signs, of course, to make sure there was a blanket in the car. I would drive, and Pamela would navigate. Her directions would be elaborate, but purposely obscure, as if I could not see where she was taking me.

I certainly did nothing to thwart her plans. I soon came to thrive on the intrigue, in fact, warming myself on the fierce heat such ventures generated in her, thawing the weekdays' chill. Pamela would lead me over rough ground, inciting me to trespass, to risk limb if not life. And when she'd taken me to where she wanted me, I was invariably eager and edgy and combustible as an uninitiated boy.

Pamela would select the exact spot, always a bit too exposed for my comfort. She'd arrange the blanket just so. Often she'd have brought some coy diversion—sketchbook or camera, a picnic lunch. She'd acquired a cheap pair of binoculars and an Audubon guidebook, a kit to make gravestone rubbings. But such projects, even eating, hardly got under way before she was tearing at my clothes. I was never permitted to undress her until I myself was fully naked. And when I entered her I always had the feeling that it was Pamela who was entering me.

Time after time, just as I was on the verge of release, I'd hear her urgent whisper, feel her hot breath against my neck: "I think somebody's watching, Wim!" Or: "Oh, is someone coming?" Her body would quicken and pitch, and as if in obedience, mine would as well.

"Light listened when she sang."

—~—

I do not know she is there until, cramped, I try to stand and discover I cannot.

I am hunkered down, the lush fabrics a promiscuous snafu

around my ankles, a plummy nest. The ivory lace cap might be an egg between my feet. My fingers feel soldered to the plain silver frame around the photograph.

"What are you doing, Wim?" Then Leandra laughs softly. "Reckon that's one of what you call your rhetorical questions," she says.

My head, still lowered over the photograph, kowtows further. "I'm sorry," I say. "I couldn't resist."

For a second I entertain the absurd possibility that she may not have noticed or recognized the picture, and my hand ventures toward the open chest to drop it in, facedown. Then I pull back, hold up the photograph. "Leandra, where did you get this?"

"I made off with it." Her voice is mild.

I stare. "You pilfered it?"

The word makes her smile. "Like Robin Hood." She nods. "There it was, gone begging on the closet floor."

"In the guest room?"

"It's how I hoped to remember you," Leandra says. "At the time."

I study my own face—younger, out of focus, and faintly perplexed. Then I wrap it as best I can in what is left of the tissue and replace it in the trunk.

"You can leave it out," Leandra says.

"No, thank you." I exert considerable effort not to look down at the hat. "Did you take anything else?"

"Pilfer, you mean?" Her smile deepens.

"Perhaps 'salvage' would be a better word."

"No, sir." Her smile is gone. "Best I can recollect, I didn't salvage a thing," she says. "And that picture is all I made off with."

My gaze drops to the hat.

Leandra squats down beside me and begins scooping up scraps of finery, dropping them helter-skelter back into the little trunk. The hat is lifted carelessly with her third armload. I snatch it from the pile before it is buried.

"Pretty," I say.

Leandra is barely interested. "That come from Massachusetts," she says. "I paid fifty cents for it at a jumble sale Reverend Jack had down to his church."

My heart, for a moment, is accorded my full attention. When it fails to register a cramp or skipped beat, I let the hat drop back inside the trunk.

"Don't know why I bought it," Leandra says. "Makes me look right foolish, to be sure." She hoists up the shelf and fits it into its bracket, then closes the lid of the chest, fastens its straps as best she can, and shoves it back into the corner.

"I don't imagine it suits you," I say.

"Not one bit," she agrees. "I just got a weakness for old things."

She has dropped to her knees beside me, close enough that I can smell her sweat, a slight must in her hair.

"Lucky for me," I say.

Her face clouds. "Don't," she says. "I don't care for such talk."

I study her for a moment. "You don't usually mind the truth."

Leandra nods, then quickly stands up. She doesn't even need her hands to steady herself. "There are limits," she says.

I am unable to rise. Leandra, catching sight of my attempt, reaches down, grasps both my hands, and pulls me to my feet. I feel as if my legs will never straighten. The room reels.

I keep hold of her hands, waiting until the spare details of Leandra's existence fall into place around me.

"I shouldn't have been going through your things," I say.

"I don't mind," Leandra says. "Reckon it's some way what you came for."

"I've always wanted to know," I tell her.

"What?" she says.

"The other parts of you. There was just so little. And then you were gone."

"I wanted to stay, Wim."

"I know. And I . . . my God, I wanted you to."

"We did what was right," she says. "Except that one single time. After that we did what was needed."

"Ten years." I touch her cheek, feel the fine grit of dried salt. "I never wanted anything but to be here."

"I never doubted it." She looks into my eyes for a long moment. Then she gently removes my hand from her face. "There are other things you need to tell me now."

"Yes," I whisper. The heavy armchair is just behind me. I reach back and grasp its threadbare arms, lower myself into it. Leandra sits down on the floor, facing me.

"Do you want help with saying it, Wim?"

A man would know how to do this, I think.

"You are going to die," Leandra says. Her face is pale and cool and still.

"We are all going to die, Leandra."

"Don't run me off with words, Wim, not now."

"Too glib about eternal things . . ." My face floods with shame. "Yes," I tell her.

"Soon?" she says.

"Fairly." I try to smile. "Sooner than I'd like, in any case."

She lowers her head. "And me," she says.

When Leandra raises her face, a ghost of a smile haunts the corners of her mouth. Her eyes are clear and dry.

"And I get to keep you?" she says. "Here, until then?"

"If you want to."

"I do." She leans forward, resting her head on my knee.

"I shouldn't ask it," I say.

"You didn't," she says. "And you don't need to."

"It might be—"

"Don't." A sharp pain flares where her fingers dig into my thigh. "You just give me a while now, you hear?" she says. "Before you tell the rest."

"Yes," I say softly. "All right."

Leandra inches forward on the floor. Her arms enclose my waist. Her head centers itself on my lap. She is perfectly still then.

"Are you crying?" I ask her.

"I won't be long," she says.

I reach down to untie the damp gray shirt knotted around her waist. I wrap it around her bare shoulders. Then I hold it there, the only bit of warmth that I, from here, can offer her.

—~—

By the time we'd been married five years, Pamela's hair reached the backs of her knees. She washed it three times a week—Tuesday and Friday mornings and late on Sunday afternoons—with a thick chartreuse shampoo that smelled of green apples. Sometimes she would rinse with beer or vinegar, sometimes with chamomile tea.

When Pamela was twenty-five her hair began, just slightly, to darken. In the summer she squeezed the juice of fresh lemons on it and sat for hours out in the yard. But summers are stingy in New England, of course. By the time winter set in, Pamela's hair would have returned to its natural shade, somewhere between bronze and amber.

Provided that Saturday afternoon—that is to say, I—had fallen in with her plans, Pamela would allow me to shampoo her hair on Sunday, a ritual enacted by a strict set of formalities and accoutrements—a wide-toothed tortoiseshell comb, two oversized towels (white, Turkish), a rug of Haitian cotton under our feet to catch stray drops of water. This rug, the color of old parchment and fringed at the ends, was reserved for this single purpose. Though never really soiled, it was laundered each Monday. It hung, for the remainder of the week, on a wooden drying rack in a utility closet, where its fibers were warmed by the nearby hot-water heater.

I assumed, as one naturally might, that Pamela loved her hair. Her attentions to it (and mine) were both extravagant and tender. It would not occur to me until much later that my wife's hair may have represented a kind of tyranny, incarcerating her in a perpetual girlhood, and that she might have been seeking a kind of safety there. I wonder now if Pamela ever came to see, as I did, how that long silken spill of tarnished gold ruined her fine proportions, disguised her womanliness. But did she think that womanliness, come into its own, might mark the end of my desire for her? Did she never sense my discomfort at the spectacle her hair made of itself?

I would not have dreamed of mentioning it, of course.

By the seventh year of our marriage, when I became aware of Pamela's pregnancy before she'd had time to dispense with it, her hair had gone to freakish lengths and acquired a rather frazzled look. She, too, must have noticed the lackluster, though neither of us acknowledged it. The Sundays when, having failed to displease or disappoint her, I was permitted to tend her hair had grown occasional. Perhaps we were both relieved.

I loved my wife more now than I had ever loved her. Yet the more ardent my attentions to her, the more she seemed to doubt my devotion. She accused me of every sort of fraudulence and failure, calling me to account for each moment I was out of her sight, interpreting the small gifts I brought her as proofs of betrayal. Though we really couldn't afford it, I tried to take her out more. In restaurants and movie theaters and shopping malls, she'd charge me with staring lasciviously at women I hadn't so much as noticed.

"I can imagine how you act when I'm not there to see," she said.

"Where?" I asked, thinking with some amusement of the few women I saw on a daily basis at school, none with the slightest potential to drive a man to distraction.

But Pamela was not to be pinned down to the reality of my days. "Wherever it is you're always going," she said, her tone so aggrieved as to leave me, for the moment, speechless.

I was almost flattered, at first, to be found so roguish. Surely no one had ever before shown such acute interest in me. Pamela interrogated me relentlessly about my romantic life, admittedly limited, prior to our meeting. The hint of my slightest fondness for anyone I'd known before her seemed to render her inconsolable, yet she'd question me without letup, like someone compulsively probing a wound. We rarely touched anymore, apart from the risky and elaborate trysts Pamela still staged from time to time.

Moments of spontaneous affection, however, now seemed impossible. This wasn't altogether new, of course. For years now we'd already been, each to the other, a universe, complex and perilous. Our universe had simply turned out to be trickier than our first explorations had revealed. Still, we might have gone on this way forever, I suppose.

There came, however, the dawn of a day in early January—a revisionist conceit, perhaps, but my memory has always marked it as the Feast of the Epiphany—when a wide and irreparable fissure split the carefully maintained facade that housed our marriage.

It was not, actually, dawn but well before it—five-thirty, I think—when I pushed my way through a lather of dreams into the silent dark of our bedroom. Pamela was not in the bed beside me. For a second I felt paralyzed by an unaccountable dread. Then I heard from the bathroom the sound of retching.

I am not an impulsive man. My conclusions, such as they are, tend to be measured, based upon the empirical. This slightly abbreviated lifetime of mine has nonetheless presented moments when, given no more than a drop of evidence, I have been engulfed by certain knowledge as swiftly and ruinously as a flash flood.

In the autumn of my final year in high school, when the vice principal quietly intruded on my advanced calculus class toward the end of an unremarkable Tuesday, I knew the moment her blockish shoe crossed the threshold that the message she carried was dire and that it was meant for me.

No, let me be more direct: I knew that my father was dead.

The woman's eyes did not seek me out. I am not sure she would even have recognized me. She entered the room reluctantly, handed a folded note to my teacher, and departed. "William Cantwell, you are needed at home," would naturally set off alarms, for never had I had the slightest sense of being needed in my parents' house. Twenty-five minutes would pass before my mother seated me in a Morris chair and offered the particulars. By then I had already absorbed the salient fact, was making my adjustments.

And Dr. Kaplan, bless his practical heart, scarcely needed to call me into the office a few weeks ago. Giving it to me straight was both *pro forma* and *ex post facto*. I'd already read my poor prognosis in the obligatory vials of piss and blood extracted from me five days earlier in the cinder-block basement laboratory, heard my sentence announced in a blasé radiological hum. What emerged from the magnetic field that briefly surrounded my head hardly came as news.

And so it had been with Pamela, vomiting up her calamitous secret in the eclipsed bathroom. She had closed the door, but I heard enough.

I stayed in bed, reviewing the evidence I'd unwittingly compiled—her moody exhaustion and the sudden drabness of her hair, the swelling of her tender breasts, their nipples rougy and slightly distended. And hadn't she asked to keep the car tomorrow—today? Some vague doctor's appointment in Boston—just routine, she said. Except hadn't there been a check-up in July? Why Boston? All that way, when the drive so unnerved her . . .

Perhaps ten minutes passed before Pamela returned to the bed. I lay on my back, arms rigid at my sides, and listened to the rush of water, the splashing and draining. I thought I heard her, once, sigh.

She knew, in her witchy way, that I was awake. *I think I'm sick,* she said, her voice petulant, her breath minty and medicinal.

"Wim, I think I'm sick."

"I don't think you are," I said.

"I threw up." She was outraged.

"Yes," I said. "Are you feeling better?"

"Just don't ask me anything, all right?" I heard her fear.

She was close to me, not touching but close enough to cast a slight heat in my direction.

"Pamela . . ."

"Go back to sleep," she said. She rolled over onto her side, facing away from me. The water-filled mattress pitched. Slowly, arching her spine, she began to rub her backside against me. When I did not respond, she reached back and placed her palm low on my stomach. Her fingers inched down toward my groin.

"No," I said. "No, Pamela." I lifted her hand and placed it on top of the covers between us. "We need to talk."

She continued to rock.

I moved away. "Please," I said. "Pamela, please talk to me."

She rolled through the space I had created between us, moving with enough force to land half on top of me. She grasped my wrists and pinned them to the mattress hard, using the leverage to raise her upper body.

"You are hurting me." My voice was quiet and cold. My hands were going numb. I thought of snow.

"You like that, Wim," she said. "Don't you?" She was swaying now from side to side, her breasts in a playful sweep across my chest. Her hair fell over my face, a suffocation.

"I want you to stop, Pamela." *The snow would muffle every sound, conceal every trap and disfigurement in the landscape. . . .* "Stop," I said.

"No." Her pelvis ground into mine. The bed bucked. "You want to fuck me," she said.

The voice, low and rough, wasn't Pamela's. She had—perhaps we all have—a different voice for the bedroom. For lovemaking she became a little girl. Her vocabulary for sex, such as it was, was reticent, childish.

"I know you want to fuck me," she said.

I do not know her, I thought. *I have never really known her.*

"All I want," I said gently, "is to talk about this."

"About what?" She stared down at me, her eyes chilly and defiant, but I heard a tremble in her voice. "Since when do you feel like talking before you fuck me, Wim?" She was terrified.

I wanted to hold her then, to feel everything that held her body rigid over mine collapse: rage and terror, defiance and even desire.

I yearned to comfort her.

But she kept me pinned, flat on my back, and I could have freed myself only by toppling her.

"You're pregnant," I said softly. "Aren't you?"

"Even if I was," she said, "that would be *my* problem." She closed her eyes.

"Ours," I said. "But does it have to be a problem?"

"Anyway, I never said I was, did I?" She let me go then, pulling roughly away, from me, from our bed. "Just leave me alone," she said.

Then she ran, naked, from our room, stumbling into the dark hallway as if pursued by something huge and monstrous.

The last time I saw my father, he told me I was not likely to amount to much.

He sounded, when offering this prognostication, dispassionate and dead sure, as if it were something he'd pondered for a long time and been forced to conclude.

The early-acceptance letters from Harvard were out that week, a fact my father well knew. The daughter of his business partner, a cherub-faced girl with a genius for math, had received one. She had just turned sixteen.

I, soon to be eighteen (I'd started school a year late, due to a bout of scarlet fever), was the editor in chief of the school literary magazine. I hovered somewhere in the upper ten percent of my class, with an A-minus average. Trigonometry was largely responsible for the minus.

My mother sat across the breakfast table, in a powder-blue chenille wrapper, making small abstract sculptures of her hands. "But, Martin, don't you think . . ." she said.

Her being overlooked was not unprecedented. My father leaned toward me, his gaze speculative and bleak. "Of course, you might still get in by the common route," he said.

"I wouldn't count on it," I told him.

"And why is that?"

"I didn't apply."

"I see," he said.

And then he laid into me, without ever once raising his voice.

A teacher by the name of Tabitha Skelly, a sober young woman with ashen hair and a faintly bohemian wardrobe, had taken me under her wing in tenth grade. She served as adviser to the school literary magazine. My early poems aped the Beats, and badly. Miss Skelly had turned me gently toward Williams and Larkin, Auden and Yeats. She even made a rather valiant attempt to walk me through "The Waste Land."

Thus prized and attended, how could I fail to thrive? "You have a *voice,* William," she told me. "Do you know what a treasure that is?"

Miss Skelly had gone to Hampshire College. It was a place where individuality was nurtured, she said. So Hampshire it was, my heart's one true desire. I made Haverford my backup choice. I also applied to Dartmouth—and prayed I would be turned away.

My father, his voice dry and neutral as lint, detailed my shortcomings by rote. I tuned out most of the specifics as I tried to get through my bran flakes. I suspect that only my mother took his indictment of me to heart.

When my father had finished with me, he folded his white napkin in tight equilateral triangles, an accountant's etiquette, and rose from the table.

"I may be late this evening," he said. "Dinner can proceed without me."

My mother nodded. "You're sure?"

"By all means," my father said.

A familiar pleat pinched the center of my mother's brow. I felt far more remorse for her headache than for my father's disappointment. But it was all my doing, of course.

That afternoon, driving back from a luncheon meeting with a client in Framingham, my father veered his Chrysler into an abutment near Springfield. His aim was so true that intent was suspected before the autopsy disclosed a heart attack.

For years, however, I harbored a keen and unyielding belief in my own culpability. I did not imagine my defectiveness had driven my father to suicide. I simply assumed that it had goaded him to recklessness. My four miserable years at Dartmouth may have been, if not expiation, a rather fitting memorial tribute to the man who first calculated the wages of recklessness for me.

—∾—

Impending fatherhood, its sudden and unforeseen possibility, turned me rash in ways I had never been.

I had lain in bed awhile after Pamela stormed from the room. By the time the first rays of wintry light sliced through the shades, I was mad with wanting, a hunger all the more voracious for its long concealment, even—especially—from myself.

I found Pamela, still naked, huddled under an afghan on the living room sofa, a barricade of velvet throw pillows raised around her.

"What did you think you were going to do?" I asked, then immediately wished I had not, for I feared my love for my wife might not survive her reply.

"You know what I'm going to do," Pamela said.

The absolute failure of her attempts at carnal diversion had left her, left us both, skittish and spent. We were in unfamiliar territory now, bereft of our usual means of battle or reconciliation.

"It's not that hard to figure out," Pamela said.

"It should be hard," I told her. "It should at least be that."

"You act like it's my fault. Do you think I'd do this on purpose?"

"On the contrary," I said. "I realize you'd do anything to avoid it."

She stared up at me, her face yellowish and dull, like wax, against the white upholstery. "I will," she said.

"Pamela, did you ever once consider, even for a moment, that this is a child, *our* child?"

"It's not much of anything." Her voice was sullen. "Not yet."

"Convenient to think so anyway, isn't it?"

"No," she said. "There's nothing convenient about this."

"Pamela—"

"I told you I would never do this, Wim. You said it didn't matter."

My wife's eyes, dark with weariness, seemed as hard to catch as smoke.

"That was all . . . theoretical," I whispered. "Wasn't it?"

Pamela stared at me, but I could see her eyes were not taking me in. The room was freezing. Pamela pressed her lips together. When I released my own breath, it wafted between us like pale smoke.

—w—

She was, I would learn, just nearing the end of her second month then. We still had a month or two to fight it out. It was an unimaginably dreadful time. I, who had always prided myself on a sense of fair play, fought dirty. Never once, during those weeks, did I allow Pamela to have the car. I kept the checkbook locked in my desk, doled out cash in niggardly allotments. I called incessantly during the day to make sure she hadn't left the house. I resorted to theological arguments I didn't believe in myself.

But such carryings-on were largely superfluous, I think. For I had played my decisive card early, and I kept it on the table until she folded: I told Pamela I would leave her if she did not agree to bear this child. She believed that I meant it, and I had. It was as simple as that.

It does me no honor, I know, to recount all this, and I give myself away by speaking in terms of gamesmanship. But in some perverse and reprehensible way it was just that, a game. I bullied and badgered and cheated. I took a reprobate's pleasure in knowing, almost from the start, that Pamela could be no match for me once I adopted the strategy of withholding love.

I do not excuse myself. I never will. I stand condemned by my own retrospective grasp of the harm I did my wife. I quake in belated recognition of how little I understood what I was fighting for or why.

I knew I had won on the day I came home and saw that Pamela had cut her hair.

It was a cold afternoon, a scant hour of silvery daylight left in the goose-down sky. Pamela stood before the stove in the kitchen, stirring something in a smoked glass pot. The air smelled of apple liquor, cinnamon, and clove. She did not turn toward me but lifted her head and smiled slightly when I came through the door. When she lowered her head again, I saw that the lightest parts of her hair were gone. The loose coppery waves that remained just touched her shoulders. I saw in them graceful consent and in her newly composed face acquiescence.

"Did you do this yourself?" I was warily enchanted.

"There's this woman over in Southbridge . . . she makes house calls." Pamela, too, was chary. "It wasn't exactly cheap," she said. Then again she raised her head, smiled. "You left the desk open."

A strand of dark-gold hair had strayed across her cheek. I brushed it back with my fingertips, let my hand linger on her face. I had not touched her in weeks. "You are so beautiful," I said. And she was. She was breathtaking.

"I had a facial too," Pamela said. "And a manicure." She took hold of my wrist, moved my hand slowly down her cheek and neck to the hollow of her throat, then held it there, her nails indenting my skin.

After a moment I took my wife in my arms, but I held her gingerly. Then Pamela, no longer smiling, led me into the cold living room, a space gravely underfurnished. We were going without considerable comfort to accommodate the piano we could not afford.

Pamela had fashioned a bed of sorts on the floor in front of the broad glass wall facing the road. The front walk and driveway were powdered with snow. The late afternoon light, icy and blue now, was trapped in a large mirror and in the pieces of art glass sparsely lining an étagère opposite the window.

A school bus rumbled down the road and came to a cautious

stop near our mailbox. Three children got out and headed for the hydrangea-colored Cape across the way, where a woman in a yellow sweater stood waiting in the front doorway, hastening the children toward her with pale fluted hands.

Pamela, half facing me in front of the glass, did not wait until the children were inside and the bus had pulled away. Her white wool robe tumbled to the floor. Then, pulling me into the day's last blue glare with her, she unbuttoned my shirt, unfastened my trousers.

The pile of pillows and comforters so artfully arranged on the floor proved tepid. I tried to cover us both, but Pamela thwarted the attempt. Her breasts and the negligible swell of her belly felt tight and hard, and we were both covered in goose flesh.

I entered her easily but found no release, and a long time passed before Pamela cried out. I pulled away too quickly then, startled by the thump of the evening newspaper against the door.

"Do you think he saw us?" Pamela's eyes were shining

Unsettled, I turned my head, looking past her. The half-empty room suddenly seemed huge to me.

When I turned around, Pamela had risen to her knees before the window. I imagined how she would look from outside, her voluptuousness framed, lit, captured. Shivering, she wrapped her arms around herself, lifting her full breasts higher into the light. "He must have seen us," she said.

That I would risk anything for her, I thought, it's only that she wants to know. I got up and stood with her before the cold glass.

Pamela, still on her knees, laughed softly. Then she turned her head and I felt her mouth closing around me, her sharpened fingernails digging into the flesh of my thighs. A low choking sound was not quite stifled at the back of her throat. I shut my eyes against the room's bareness, its desolate light.

—∿∿—

"I want to tell you something I have figured out," Leandra tells me.

We are on the porch, eating dinner—Leandra calls it "supper," and six o'clock is far earlier than is my custom. The air is still full of heat, but it is already dark and I am surprised to discover that I am hungry.

"I am listening," I say.

Leandra nicks a wedge of boiled cabbage with a dull dinner knife, then sets down the knife. A hurricane lamp flickers on the small low table between us, and when she looks at me there are sparks in her eyes.

"The Lord don't hold us accountable for what we can't help," she says.

"Just what *us* might you be talking about?"

"The one takes in everybody. But for an example, let's say, you and me would serve."

"So God is the topic, and I am a sacrificial lamb on the altar of discussion?" I smile. "When did you take up theology?"

"About like everybody else," Leandra says. "When I needed to."

"And when was that?" I ask.

"You ought to know," she tells me.

The things I ought to know . . . *to have known:* bewilderment my boon companion, still, in this dark wood. I measure out my ignorance in coffee spoons. And I've begun to suspect there may be, in death, no end to it. How fitting, after all, for a benighted soul like mine to pass eternity in a heaven or hell it cannot name, without a clue how it got there.

Pregnancy was hell, Pamela said, a claim whose extravagance I, in my ignorance, chose not to dispute but simply to dismiss. I coddled her with small attentions that seemed only to infuriate her. Each of us, in an elaborate choreography of misery and mistrust, circled, parried, withdrew. I left her, finally, to herself.

Things might have gone better, I suppose, had the pregnancy run a more normal course. Pamela was just thirty, petite, but healthy and strong. The condition that made her such a poor candidate for childbearing was uncommon, unlucky. "Just one of those things," her obstetrician, Dr. Hathaway, said.

The required surgery was only a partial success. The anesthesia terrified Pamela, who had never experienced so much as Novocain.

"You won't feel a thing," I told her. "And it's only for a couple of hours."

"During which I am as good as dead," she said.

"I'll be right there, sweetheart."

"For what that's worth." She gave me a wintry smile. Her lips were chapped and bloodless.

Pamela's blood pressure dropped alarmingly during the surgery. "It was touch and go for a while there," Dr. Hathaway said. "And I've got to tell you, I'm a little stymied that it's taking her this long to come out of it."

Pamela had been in the recovery room for hours but was still showing no sign of regaining consciousness.

The doctor, who must have been at least sixty-five, was a sturdy and forthright woman. The fact that she spoke so little like a doctor greatly endeared her to me. Pamela, I think, was not so fond of her, for the sympathy the doctor dispensed was of the no-mollycoddling variety from a bygone era.

"I'd have expected her to be awake—wide awake—by now." Dr. Hathaway's small lapis-blue eyes looked faded with fatigue and worry.

"Can people stay under because . . . they want to?" I asked her.

She stared at me, startled, and didn't say a thing. My face felt hot, my eyes watery. "I think it might suit her to sleep through most of this," I said.

The doctor studied me for another interminable moment. Then she took me by the arm and led me into a quiet alcove in a deserted waiting area. She pointed to a chair. I sat down.

"Wait," she said.

She returned in a moment with two Styrofoam cups, handed me one, and sat down in the chair facing mine.

The tea, strong and bitter, scalded my tongue. "Thank you," I said.

Dr. Hathaway nodded. "I expect you'd best tell me what's going on here," she said.

I was not reluctant to confess. I simply could not puzzle out where, or how, to begin. "You'd need to be a psychiatrist," I said.

"You ever gone to one?" she asked.

I shook my head. "Not to say I'd rule it out." I waited for the doctor to smile, but she didn't.

"Do you know how long their training goes on? Some of them are darn near grandparents before they're fully certified."

A hefty nurse's aide in a pink nylon smock slouched into the room, took stock of us, and drifted out again.

"You won't catch me making light of psychiatry," the doctor said. "Psychiatrists save at least as many lives as the rest of us, and it looks to me like their job's a whole lot harder." She shrugged. "Certainly takes longer, anyhow," she said, "than mine."

She was quiet for a moment, and I wondered if she'd got lost in her own little digression, forgotten the point. Then she grinned at me. "Hold on," she said. "I know where I'm going." And I was startled by the sound of my own laugh.

"What I've figured out is, for all that training, the years of analysis, everything, the best psychiatrists are the ones born with common sense. That, and maybe a little extra dollop of compassion . . . and a whole lot of patience.

"What I'm telling you, Mr. Cantwell—"

"William," I said.

"William." She nodded as if we were just being introduced. "What I'm getting at here is that . . . pardon me tooting my own horn, but you could look around a good long time before finding somebody to put me in the shade on those."

She stared at me. Her eyes were bright now, a steady and startling blue. "Especially the common sense," she said.

And so I began, in a halting way, my version doubtless warped by a lack of perspective, to tell Dr. Hathaway what I could. It was, and remains to this day, my only full confession.

"I was wrong," I said, "wasn't I? I shouldn't have . . ."

"I've got no earthly idea," the doctor said.

"I won't be able to forgive myself if Pamela . . ."

"It's not up to you to forgive yourself, William," Dr. Hathaway said, and it was perhaps my first encounter with chastisement delivered in kindness. It made me want to weep.

"When you get right down to it, we are unforgivable." The doctor smiled. "It comes with the territory, don't you think?"

"Territory?"

"Humanity." She shrugged. "God's mess. But I've come to suspect His love for us is largely due to how we keep on shooting for the impossible—to forgive each other, Him, ourselves. Even He has got to be astonished by such pigheaded *hopefulness*."

My eyes were stinging and my throat felt clotted. I slanted my face from the brightness of hers. "I don't know what to do," I said.

"Loving her would be the best bet, I'd say. Can you?"

"I do."

"Even if she can't love you back as much?"

I recognized the question, instantly, as the center of everything.

"I don't know," I said.

"If I were you, I'd try like hell," Dr. Hathaway said.

"Accountable," I say to Leandra. "That's an interesting word. This Lord of yours, He's a bookkeeper?"

She picks up a sweet potato, baked whole in its jacket. She pinches one end from it, and the bright-orange meat slips intact from the skin. Leandra bites into it, her face beatific. "Sweeter than my mama's divinity fudge," she says.

"You are a pagan," I tell her.

"Only when you are around," she says. "A bookkeeper, huh? You think the Lord don't know you're making light of Him?"

"Any God worth His salt would know, of course. But would He *care*?"

"I always had a notion of bookkeepers as being picky. Don't reckon God has time for such as that."

"But He keeps accounts?"

"He knows what He knows." She gives me a fortune-teller's smile. Then sorrow steals over her face. "God knows I love you, Wim. Ain't never been able to help it."

"Finish your supper," I tell her gently. "We'll have time for this later."

She looks into my eyes. "How much?" she whispers.

"You have every right to ask, but . . ." I shrug.

Leandra wipes her hands on a faded square of calico. Then she leaves her chair and comes to stand behind mine. I feel her hands on my shoulders, heated and steady as a permanent intention.

"Sooner or later," she says, "you are going to tell me everything."

I start to nod, but she takes my head between her hands and holds it still.

"House rule," she says. "Every last thing."

"Yes," I say softly. "All right."

"I'm not finished," she says.

I wait.

"I will thank you not to snigger at God again. Because while it might be your freedom to do it, you are cutting it mighty close."

Leandra pauses, drawing in breath and holding it. When she lets it go, she pulls my head back hard, pressing it to her middle. "And because that scares me, Wim. And I will not be scared in my own house."

"Forgive me," I say.

"Ssh." Still holding me against her, Leandra leans down and rests her head on top of mine. "This last one got nothing in the world to do with God. It's just between you and me. But I need you to make me a promise now, before God, that you are not going to break. And if you think you can't make that promise, I want you to leave here. First thing in the morning, you hear?"

Her hold on me is fast. She makes me struggle against her. When I am free I stand, turn around, look into her eyes.

"Now I am afraid," I tell her. "If it's something I can't promise you, this is going to break my heart."

"And mine," she says. "I'm afraid we got to chance that."

"Tell me."

Leandra reaches out as if to hold me. Then her arms drop to her sides. Her eyes do not leave my face.

"However long it is going to be," she says, "however terrible, I want all of it."

Then I am shaking my head, helplessly, like someone in a melodrama refusing to believe calamitous news. "No, Leandra. I—"

"Hear me out, Wim." Her voice is steely.

"If you mean to stay here," Leandra says, "—and I want you to with all my heart, to stay—but if that is what you intend, I will not have you leaving early. No easy ways out, you hear me?"

"Leandra, I don't want—"

"I'm sorry," she says. "But we are talking now about what *I* want."

"You don't understand."

"I believe I do."

"A time is coming when I won't even know you, Leandra."

She studies my face for a moment. "But I will know you," she says.

"I don't intend to become a burden."

"And I don't intend on you leaving this world without me being there. Not if I can help it."

"A man should be allowed to choose how he'll die," I tell her.

"I expect you're right," Leandra says. "But I don't care. Do you understand me?"

She waits until I nod. "Now you just keep still for a while," she tells me. "I am going to wash up the dishes. I am going to mend a couple of lady dolls coming apart at the seams under their fancy clothes. When I get tired, which is apt to be soon, I am going to get to bed.

"I hope it will be before that when you'll come in and tell me you are ready to live by my rules in this house, Wim. But take all night if you need it. I won't pester you."

"You could at least hear my side." I am pleading with her. She knows it.

"No," she says, "I could not. My mind is made up so tight there's no room in it for your logical arguments. I'm sorry."

I am still on the porch three hours later, my eye stuck on a waning moon, when the lights go off inside.

I have decided this much: I will not lie to her.

Then again, I could change my mind.

This house is already more familiar to me than my own. I have little trouble working my way through the dark to the side of her bed.

"I'm awake," Leandra says. "Reckon you knew that."

"I will be here." I kneel down beside the bed and whisper into her ear. "I'll always be here, Leandra, with you."

"Are you splitting hairs?"

"I am not."

"You promise?"

"Yes."

"Are you certain?"

"No. But you have my word."

"All right, then," Leandra says.

I stand up slowly.

"All right." Leandra sighs.

When I have washed and undressed, I feel my way into the bed. Leandra is already asleep. But she has left just enough room for me there beside her.

PART
II

V

WIM SAYS MARCH up there in Massachusetts can be twice, maybe three times as long as any other month.

"Then I ain't got one whit of sorrow about missing it," I tell him, and we both smile a little too hard, what with trying not to think of the year we are talking about without mentioning it.

"Look here," I say, pointing out the window to where jonquils dot the patchy yard. The crocuses already come and gone, been such a mild early year. "This here's as likely a March as any," I tell him. "And it will be gone before we know it."

I want to bite my tongue off at the roots then. Wim sees and gives me a never-mind smile.

"I'll know it," he says. "You don't let me miss much."

"I'm sorry," I say.

"No," says Wim. "No, Leandra." He's laying where I put him after lunch, on that big wide bed I still can't get used to in front of the broad window that makes me feel like anybody of a mind to could see straight into the middle of my life.

And Wim's. He is so thin now that even bundled up he somehow looks naked, nowhere on him for anything to hide.

I edge a chair right up beside the bed. The room is warmed by the afternoon sun, but dampness comes creeping up through the floorboards this time of year. I raise up my bare feet and rest blue toes on the edge of the starburst quilt, where against the deeper blue Wim looks peaked and flimsy as a wafer moon in an afternoon sky.

"Seems like I always got my foot in my mouth," I say.

Wim looks at me with those big dark eyes that are always holding a smile these days, along with sickness and pain.

"What?" I say. "You see something to smile about?"

He takes hold of my right ankle, picks up my foot, and sinks his teeth right into the tender part, where it arches. When his teeth let go, he is laughing. "You thought that was *your* mouth?" he says.

I want to get on my high horse. He needs to be precautious now, to guard against dirt, against germs. Next to nothing could make him sick. And nothing could get him better. Death's in a big enough hurry like it is.

But Wim has no need of homilies and scolding, and neither do I. Ain't we both near worn out already with being so watchful of his poor body?

I reach down and rub the traces of his spit into the bottom of my foot. "That was *you*?" I say. "Seems like it's getting hard to tell the difference."

Wim nods. His hands reach out for the part of me that's nearest. A chill moves up my legs. My knees part slowly, then meet again, enclosing his hands between my thighs.

I no longer know where I end and you begin.

Wim's face is right pleased, like he thinks he has carried some news to me that my body did not already know.

—∞—

Been here four months a week ago Tuesday—I keep an accounting of the time, just as strict and sure as if it was written down, even though it's only my mind keeping track. One hundred and twenty-four days here with me, counting today. Give me a pencil and pad, a few minutes, I could break it down into hours. Which, someday, I know I will. I mean to remember every one with gratitude.

It's a puny portion of a life, of course, barely a sip from a full cup. But it's been time enough for Wim to take over, to alter everything, until I scarcely recognize my own life anymore and catch myself amazed that somehow it still seems to fit me.

Made no bones about it, either, did Wim. Just barged right in and got to rearranging things. Next I know, the walls aren't in the same place and light comes pouring in where I ain't used to it and even the roof has stopped leaking.

It was because of Branch, of course, that Wim was able to get away with so much—Branch Goodlin, my old friend who used to own this land that now is mine.

A body would never have dreamed, from the manner of their first meeting, Wim and Branch winding up in cahoots and even friends. Be hard to find two men less alike if you tried.

I could see right away where each came as something of a shock to the other, first time Branch stopped in. I hadn't seen him in a week or two. Wim been here three, maybe four days. They acted, as men are prone to, like a couple of coon hounds. You can get a good bit of understanding about men, I'd say, from watching how dogs behave. Mostly what it comes down to is two simple rules: If it moves, fight it or bite it. If it don't, lift your leg and pee on it. The minute Wim and Branch started sniffing around each other, going all bristly, it wasn't hard to figure out the direction things would likely take.

I set them both down on the porch and brought out some cold tea I made extra sweet the way Branch is partial to and Wim don't care for. I tried to usher them along to some conversation, but the job was hard enough to bring on a sweat.

It was already hot. I'd been working out back in the shed that afternoon. I was wearing my overhauls and had taken off my shirt, like I mostly do in such weather for working. And even though I was decently covered where I needed to be—my bosom is small and apt to stay put—I could see the both of them not liking me being seen by the other in that state. I ought to excused myself to slip on a shirt. But the fact is I was afraid to leave them two alone in case the fighting and biting and peeing got going without me there to pry them apart.

"Wim is my brother-in-law," I told Branch. "Pammy Jo's husband."

Branch nodded so somber I was afraid he might be getting ready to offer condolences at this late date.

"Come all the way down from Massachusetts," I said. "Just marches up to my door Tuesday evening and surprises the living daylights out of me."

Branch nodded again, his blond eyebrows pointing up toward his sunburnt forehead. Wim's eyes were moving from Branch to me and back again like we were playing badminton.

"Welcome, sir," Branch said, trying to regain sure footing by climbing up on good manners. "How do you like Columbine, North Carolina?" He sounded stiff and peppy, like that fella over in Greenville selling used cars on the radio.

"I've never seen anything quite like it." Wim's smile was wry.

"Plan on staying long?"

"A while," Wim said.

Branch's jaw was set, his silvery eyebrows looked knotty.

I turned to Wim. "Branch is my landlord. It's him I pay my rent to."

"Only because she's so mulish about it." The look Branch give me had a history in it meant for Wim to read.

"I gather you've known each other a long time?" Wim said.

Before I could open my mouth Branch jumped in. "Only forever," he said.

Then the two of them just stared at each other, not even trying to pretend friendliness.

It was mostly me doing the conversing after that, which I wasn't much good at. It felt like a rescue when Branch said he had some business to discuss, if Wim would kindly excuse us?

Wim looked at me. I hesitated just a moment before nodding.

"I could stand a walk anyway," Wim said.

"We won't be long."

I swear that, watching him walk away, I could see him growing old. I waited until he reached the road. His back looked humped, his color faded. Beside me, Branch loomed wide and golden, smelling of fresh sweat.

"It's hot," I said. "Let's go in out of the sun."

But we barely made it through the doorway. "Who *is* this guy? Leandra, what's going on?" Sounded just like a little boy, Branch did, angry and confused and hurt all tangled up together . . . and scared maybe too, the way men can scare over what they can't do a thing about.

"I told you, Wim's my brother-in-law."

"Wim?" Branch said. "What kind of name's that supposed to be?"

"William, just like your second littlest." I smiled. "Only it's shortened."

Branch grunted.

"It was Pammy's doing," I rattled on. "On account of how he'd sign *W-m* . . ."

Branch was staring at the single bed in the corner.

"Kind of like *M-r* for *Mister,*" I said.

"He's staying here? With you?"

"He is," I said.

A little ridge of muscle flexed itself along Branch's jaw. Otherwise his face might have been frozen.

"He's not just your brother-in-law, then," he said.

"No," I said softly. "He is not."

"Leandra." Branch looked at me for the first time since we came indoors. "This fella's old enough to be your daddy."

"Nearly so." I looked back at him steadily as I could. "But he is no such thing."

"I can see that," Branch said.

I sighed.

Branch stayed still as a grave marker, but the effort somehow showed in his body as he tried to get his feelings in hand. Then he sank down on the mourners' bench and I sat down beside him.

"You and me been knowing each other, like you said, forever," I told him.

"And I never did stop loving you," Branch said. "Never even minded all that much that I didn't. Not till now."

I touched his shoulder, felt him shaking. "I never stopped, either," I said. "And this—Wim—got nothing to do with that, Branch."

"Don't go humoring me," he said.

"I wouldn't dream of it."

We sat there in silence for a minute, like we've always been able to do since we were youngsters. But we were not quiet this time, not inside, and I didn't know what to do about it.

"You love him," Branch said finally.

I nodded. "I need you to honor that," I said.

"Leandra, have you thought about this?"

"For about ten years," I said. "But now there's no more time."

Branch waited then, as he has ever done when I have had some sorrow that needed saying and the job has come slow and hard.

"He's dying," I said.

Branch didn't say a thing, didn't touch me, seemed like he didn't even breathe. He just sat there beside me on that hard bench, a strength I could lean against when I had to, which wasn't quite yet but would come.

And he faltered only once, only for a second. "You don't need this, Leandra," he said.

"Yes," I told him. "I do."

—ʍ—

Branch had been gone more than an hour by the time Wim came back. The lowering sun was losing its heat, but Wim's blue shirt was dark with sweat and his face was streaming.

"You overdone it," I said. "I figured you would."

Wim smiled. "It's hard to overdo sitting under a tree," he said.

"You shouldn't stay out so long in the heat," I said. "Even with the shade."

"A new idea or two to get used to," Wim said. "It can take a while."

"What ideas you got exactly?"

"You and Mr. Goody."

"Goodlin," I said. "Branch. He is my friend."

"Yes, I could see that."

"You're jealous?" I said.

Wim thought for a moment. "It doesn't feel quite like that," he said. "But probably."

"What does it feel like?"

Wim sat down on the bed, his fingers digging into the edge of the mattress. "Surprised," he said. "Maybe a little embarrassed." His smile was rueful. "Of course I realize I was presumptuous to think I knew everything about you."

"You do," I said. "Everything that matters."

I sat down beside him, our shoulders just touching, but I didn't look at him. "Branch and me been friends since we were little ones," I said. "He's married and has four boys. Whatever went on between us was a mighty long time ago."

"He still loves you." Wim's voice was mild, like he was thinking out loud.

"Reckon he does," I said. Then I turned and smiled at him. "Surely you can't blame him for that," I said.

Wim was studying my face, like I'd asked a thorny question. And I guess maybe I had.

"You want to know about it?" I asked him.

"I don't know," Wim said.

I waited then for him to make up his mind, but if he did he didn't say so.

I put my arms around his waist and laid my head against his chest, nudging him backwards to lay on the bed. Then, still holding him, I settled down beside him. "Will you listen?" His shirt was wet and cool under my cheek.

"I suppose I'd better," Wim said.

I waited until his breathing slowed. "It was a while after . . . you know, when I came back here? I was in need of comforting, Wim. And sometimes there's a comforting in the body when a spirit can't hope to be consoled. I learned that with you."

Wim's chest, weighed down by my head, was scarcely moving. "Yes," he said quietly. "I know."

"It shames me to remember it this way," I said. "Not the loving with Branch so much, but the way I measured sorrow then."

I shut my eyes tight but felt tears leak through. I had to stop breathing for a minute.

Wim waited.

"My sister and her—and *Will*—Pammy and Will were in the ground, and I was grieving. But it was losing you, Wim, it was for that I could not be consoled."

"You didn't lose me, Leandra."

"You needn't say it."

His body drew me in closer.

"Branch was no little comfort," I said. "I owe it to him to tell you that. I couldn't accept enough what he tried to give. So it didn't keep very long, just a year and some. But the love ain't likely to wear away."

"I'm sorry," Wim said.

"No." I reached up and wiped the corners of my eyes. "There was right much gladness in it," I said. "He is a good man."

"Then I am thankful to him," Wim said.

"And there is another thing which I maybe ought to tell you," I said, "though it's a good way past mattering now."

Wim lifted his head and looked at me.

"I couldn't have babies—I can't, I mean."

"Leandra, I . . ." Wim's face went drawn and chalky.

"It's a lack I didn't want Branch tied to."

"He left you for that?"

"Said it didn't matter to him. He swore it." I closed my eyes again. "It mattered to me, though. It mattered *for him*."

Wim tightened his hold on me. "Is that why you wouldn't stay?" he whispered. "With me."

"Ssh." I pressed my fingers to his lips.

Wim's hand banded my wrist, pulled my fingers away. "Leandra, was it?"

"Don't know as my thinking ever got that far. I only knew I couldn't stay. I'm not sure I'd have been able to say why."

"And now?" he said.

"Now none of that matters," I told him. "None of it."

"I wouldn't have—"

"Hush," I said.

Beneath mine his body shifted, rose up. I could not open my eyes. I felt myself gently overturned. Then the weight of Wim's head settled on my belly.

My hands reached down and enclosed his face. "It's a good long way now," I said, "past mattering."

I felt a stiffness in him. I knew he was holding back tears. I knew he needed to, like I did. My hands slipped down to his neck. "Isn't it?" I waited until his shoulders eased.

"I've got the one thing in this world I couldn't live without," I said.

"And you—" His voice was papery.

"And now I will never not have it," I said.

—∾—

"Leandra?" When I opened my eyes, the room was growing dark.

I lifted my head and looked at him, his face all in shadows.

"You'll want to know about Clio," he said.

I nodded.

"It wasn't so different from you and"—it was hard for him still to say the name—"Branch. Some warmth, a bit of comfort. But I wasn't as wise as you. I believed I could get by on that indefinitely."

"Wim, where are you supposed to be?"

He looked at me with startled eyes.

"Where does she—Clio," I said, "—where does she think you are?"

"She knows where I am," he said. "I'm not expected back."

"I don't understand," I said.

"Someone like you probably couldn't." Wim's voice was sad and surprised. "When there is no . . . passion, things tend to be less complicated," he said.

A bird flew up against a window screen, a panic of beak and claw, wings shiny black against the dusk. Then, unharmed, it flew off again.

"She knows you are . . ."

"She knows," Wim said. "She would have seen me through it." He sighed. "And maybe that would have been best. My wife is a remarkably sturdy woman."

"Don't," I said.

"What?"

" '*My wife,*' " I said. "I know it, but the words are hard for me."

Wim nodded.

"She loves you?" I said.

"Clio is . . . fond of me. And loyal. But in some way she has always known there was you. Whatever else may have been missing between us, honesty was never lacking."

"You told her about me?"

"Not until recently, though I would have, had she wanted to know. I never made any secret of the fact that my heart was no longer . . . available."

"I don't understand," I said again.

"There are things more practical than love." He smiled sadly. "Nothing I could say would make you understand. I'm almost glad."

His eyes studied me for a moment. "Some of us can't survive solitude, Leandra. Clio and I were alike in that. We didn't go into marriage expecting more than companionship, so neither of us was disappointed."

"Until now," I said. "She is alone now."

Wim looked at me steadily. "Just a little sooner than she might have been. She told me she would be all right, and I believe her."

I tried to take comfort in that. But imagining so cold and stunted and ruly a life as Wim and this woman had shared chilled me, and I felt my heart shrinking.

Wim understood, maybe, because he didn't try to explain anymore what I couldn't grasp, what it hurt me to think about.

After a while he fell asleep again. I got up and covered him with an afghan. Then I laid back down beside him and closed my eyes. But I did not fall asleep.

I puzzled through the deepening twilight. By half past five the trees looked black against a fire-opal sky. All I could really comprehend was that there would never be enough time for us to understand the lives we had each bargained for during all the years we kept apart. There was only now, curt as it was, to make sense of. And we would both be among the blessed of the earth should we, in the remaining days, manage so much as that.

Things happened so fast I scarcely realized that what was being torn down and rebuilt around me was my whole earthly existence.

Now I catch myself looking around sometimes, not certain just where I am or if I even belong here. And I wonder—had there been more time, had things not moved so quick, might I have found in me the gumption to object?

Not to say objections would likely have had much sway once Wim and Branch got together, taking my "best interests" to their own bully-boy hearts. Like cowboy heroes in some old movie—*Stand back, little lady, we'll handle this*—those two been about looking after me to death. Next I know, seems like the house that's mine isn't . . . and the long-borrowed ground it stands on *is*. Been hard, lately, to keep my bearings.

There are two rooms now, instead of one. The passage that links them is wide and full of light. So easy is it to move from one to the other, I can sometimes forget where I am.

Reckon I should have known something was brewing the second I come up to the house from the shed that day and found the two of them, Wim and Branch, with their heads together, thick as thieves, no sniffing now.

Branch's first drop-in had been just two days before—when he first met Wim, I mean. I wasn't altogether surprised at seeing him back so soon. He didn't like the situation one bit. Just like Branch to take it on himself to keep an eye on me.

What I wasn't readied for, though, was how those two men got suddenly cordial as a pair of deacons at the same church. Seemed like I must have been woolgathering while they were climbing into each other's good graces.

From the porch I got wind of Branch, sounding right chummy. "Waterfront properties," I heard him say. And as I come up where they could see me, "balloon notes" it sounded like.

"Leandra, we have company": Wim, pleased as could be.

"I was just passing by." Branch, at least, looked sheepish.

"You know you're always welcome," I said.

"Branch was just telling me about his business," Wim said.

The both of them had jumped to their feet when I come in. Now they just stood there looking gawkish.

"Only ducked in for some water." I gave Branch an apologetic look. "Work's fallen way behind."

"You go right ahead, Leandra": Branch using that voice I reckon serves for business, certain and a bit too hearty. I only heard it twice before—when Branch was the Rotary Man of the Year and, just this past June, when he was commencement speaker at the high school. "William and I are striking up an acquaintance," he said.

Wim smiled a sneaky cat's smile. *William.*

I studied them two a minute. More than passing strange. But maybe they just got to finding out they liked one another—why ever not, after all?

"Reckon you'd best sit down, then," I said.

Branch nodded.

Wim smiled some more.

I took a plastic milk jug filled with water from the Frigidaire.

When I stepped outside, the two of them were still on their feet, looking bulky in that small room.

It was soon after that Wim started taking rides out through the county with Branch.

"He seems to get a kick out of showing me around," Wim said. He'd even seen the new community center and been inside the county courthouse, which I never had myself. One day they ate lunch at that restaurant has a wishing well in the parking lot, where the hush puppies is supposed to be so good.

"Overrated," Branch said. "Greasier than they need to be. Right glad of some company, though."

Well, it was the most unexpected thing, but I was grateful for it. Wim's spirit got brighter. And knowing he was occupied made it easier for me to try to catch up on my work, Christmas barreling down like it was.

Out in the shed, the dolls lining the wall shelves and covering the plywood tables were starting to resemble patients in a ward where everybody laid low by an epidemic took a turn for the better all at once. The bisque and porcelain repairs were finished now, all but the most ruinsome cases.

There were six dolls who'd have to wait past Christmas—*triage*—and I was sorry for it, having to disappoint anyone. But a body can do only so much in a month. I made a list of the ones weren't going to make it in time and sent it with my apologies to Mrs. Duncan up in Great Bridge.

"I never let her down so bad before," I told Wim. "Hope she won't be too put out with me."

"Leandra, you've been working day and night," he said.

I shrugged. "It's Miz Duncan will lose most money—her shop, I mean—me falling behind this way."

"You do the work, she makes the money?" Wim gave me a suspicious look.

"Well, we both do," I said. "Get paid."

"How much?"

"Me?"

Wim nodded.

"Depends," I told him. "I get six dollars an hour. She trusts me to keep track."

His face got dark, like a rainy sky. "You think that's fair?"

"Fair enough."

"You'd make more flipping hamburgers," he said.

"Well, I should hope so, for such nasty work."

Wim shook his head.

"Worked one time at this little barbecue stand used to be just up the road," I said. "I smelled like pork fat all summer long. And didn't make nowhere near six dollars, either."

"I'd like to have a talk with this Mrs. Duncan," Wim said. "She's taking advantage of you."

I steadied my eyes on him. "Did I give you the idea I was looking for a manager?"

He looked a tad huffy for a second. Then his face turned sad and old. "You need to look after yourself, Leandra."

"Seems like I been doing that for quite some time," I said.

Wim held up his hands, then let them drop to his sides.

I was letting near everybody down, seemed like: Wim who wanted to look after me and Mrs. Duncan who counted on me and a bunch of folks waiting on their Christmas dolls. At least it wasn't youngsters I'd likely be disappointing, is what I told myself, as I looked up at the shelf where the set-aside dolls rested. Such ancient, fragile, costly creatures weren't Santa's business. More likely they belonged to dealers or soon would—grown-ups who'd sell them at the first good offer. And what with the doll business booming like it was, they were apt to be worth more in February than in December.

"Don't hardly matter," I said to Wim, who nodded like somebody's not clear what it is being talked about.

In the shed, I restrung bodies now, touched up paint, reset eyes. I put stuffing back where it belonged and closed the wounds with tiny stitches. There is a satisfaction in making something whole again that shores up the heart. I replaced composition fingers and toes in nothing flat. Naked skulls were covered with curl and shine, and lashes sprouted, turning dull eyes curious.

One afternoon while Wim slept, I made from scratch five mohair wigs that come out the best I ever done. I'm getting right good at this, I thought, as I watched my own fingers lay flat the soft slippery wisps, stitching them fast at the center part, trimming the ends to one even, silky length. There are days when my hands don't know the first thing about doubt and I can only watch them in pure astonishment.

In the evenings, near giddy with the fumes of glue and paint and light-headed with lost humility, I'd leave the shed, one hand firmly shutting the door behind me. In my other arm I'd cradle one chosen doll, two at the most, to be carried inside for the night.

After supper, the dishes done, I'd hunch over in a pool of unsparing light—*proper* light, Wim said. He'd changed all the lightbulbs one afternoon. Now every lamp shone forth at one hundred watts. It was a wonder I hadn't ruined my eyes, he scolded me.

The finish work—the fine tucks and flounces, the tiny buttons and snaps, the stitches close together as snail tracks—came easier now. But I missed the light I was used to, the dim goldish glow that hid the cracks and smudges and cobwebs, the chips of missing veneer. There can be something downright easeful in the blemishes in your own house. Only you just might not want to look too close at them.

The nights were cooling at last, and hurricane season gone by. I pulled Mama's old rocker in off the porch and made a place for it near the woodstove. Wim would sit there reading while I worked. Branch had started bringing him by the library. When I hankered after the room's accustomed dimness, I reminded myself it would be a poor light for him to read by.

One day, coming back from one of his outings with Branch, Wim had a new radio in tow. It was black and very small, about the right size for an evening bag. I knew it must have been expensive, like small sleek things often are. It had more than a dozen buttons and dials on it and a silver wand of antenna that nearly touched the ceiling.

Wim set up the radio on the deal table Mama got out of Miss Melba Corliss's house when the old lady passed on. He fiddled with knobs and switches and wires for what seemed an unconscionable time. There was a puff of static now and then, a few shrieks that sounded like pigs being slaughtered. The station he wanted came all the way from Chapel Hill. The piano notes that poured from the small black box were so fast and complicated, I could scarcely believe it took only two hands to play them. The announcer was a woman, but she sounded like an undertaker anyhow.

Wim leaned back in the rocking chair and shut his eyes. The filigree of music made me hurt inside, but his face got so peaceful that I couldn't mind what I was feeling.

Music, Wim told me once, was his one temptation to believe in God.

I figured I'd get used to the sound.

Well, those were next to nothing, of course, the music and the stepped-up light. Only the beginning of what would change once Wim, with Branch to help him, started rearranging things. Some days I wonder if I oughtn't mind more . . . or if maybe, later, I will.

And Wim got him some conscience about it too, seems like. Because once a week he'll ask me should he have left well enough alone. He knows, does Wim, he took my life and turned it upside down, twisted it around, made it into something else.

But maybe he only keeps asking to find out can he run me out of the clichés I find to answer him with.

"What's done is done," I tell him. And:

"Don't cry over spilt milk. . . . Don't look a gift horse in the mouth when the cows are already out of the barn. . . ."

He'll look around the house then, these two patched-together rooms, and his smile is so deep-down satisfied, it would, in another man, seem brazen. He has made something whole, is how he feels, I think.

"You look like the cat swallowed the canary," I tell him.

"It is a considerable improvement," he'll say, running his hand around seamless new window sashes, smooth strips of caulking. "Better, isn't it?"

"Comparisons are odious," I say. It's one I learned from him.

The house I live in now *is* better, considerably so. The heat and cold and rain can be shut out now, if I've a mind to. I can work inside, plenty of light shed on what I am about. There are cabinets for the dolls and all they require, a spot for the kiln Wim wants to buy me so I can do my own glazing. Bathroom with a door on it, instead of just a curtain. And plenty of room for that ample new bed, of course. I could not ask for more.

It's just sometimes I catch myself wishing for *less*. This house I live in now, with Wim, reminds me of some of those dolls you'll see at shows and auctions, in fancy shops. Old, to be sure. Authentic, the dealer tells you. Only so many parts of them been replaced and gussied up, it's hardly the same doll anymore, no matter what anybody says.

But what's done *is* done, truly. Wim can make light of such wisdom all he wants.

And afterwards, when he's not here anymore, when this house comes to feel too big for just me, the whole world will be past recognizing anyhow. So what do a few changes matter now? Maybe I am, like Wim says, a fatalist.

—~—

Him and Carol Jean wanted Wim and me to come eat Thanksgiving with them and the boys, Branch said. I thought that would be fine indeed. But before I could get my mouth around *We'd love to,* I heard Wim saying *Thank you, but we've made plans.*

"We have?" I said.

Branch looked taken aback, Wim embarrassed. "*I've* made some plans," he said. "It's supposed to be a surprise."

Branch nodded like he'd just remembered something. "Rain check," he said.

My heart kind of sank, to tell the truth. I figured Wim's idea of a surprise must be eating Thanksgiving in a restaurant somewhere, and I never did expect there'd be much pleasure in leaving home on a holiday to spoon up dun-colored vegetables an elbow away from pure strangers. But I didn't say much about it; just once:

"I could cook."

Wim smiled. "Don't meddle," he said, a fine one to talk. "Too many cooks spoil the—"

"Surprise?" I said.

Branch had some business up to Norfolk Wednesday. Wim decided to ride along and was gone near about all day, then comes back hefting a whole heaped-up carton of things and carrying a shopping bag to boot. I saw a tall green bottle capped with foil and a little wire cage, poking up next to a bunch of celery.

Wim looked right wore out, his pale forehead glassy and knotted with pain, but Lord, how he was smiling.

I helped him set down the carton. He put the bag on the drainboard by the sink.

"You mean to tell me now what you are up to?" I said.

He tried to look modest. "Just the usual Thanksgiving," he said. "Did I ever happen to mention that I am a magnificent cook?"

"I believe I missed out on that detail," I said. "You know how to make collards and corn bread stuffing and—?"

"Thanksgiving originated in *New England,*" he said.

I sniffed. "*Cooking* was invented in the South," I said.

"It might behoove you to reserve judgment, my dear."

We liked to believe, the both of us, that he was still holding the sickness at bay then. But standing under a window in the late afternoon sun and Wim awash in its light beside me, I couldn't help but glimpse how far the sickness had already gone toward claiming him. The bones of his face poked out, a flimsy armature, and I fancied I could in light a fraction brighter have seen right through his skin. The wider he smiled, the smaller his face got, seemed like.

"Just leave everything to me," Wim said.

I nodded. I could not, just then, smile. I took his face between my hands like the precious thing it has ever been. "My God, you are a beautiful old man," I said.

Apart from the oyster stuffing (which I could have done without) and the absent collards (which I hardly missed), the meal wasn't all so different as what I am used to. I never drank champagne much before, just a taste at a wedding but mostly not then, either, as folks around here are apt to be hard-shell Baptists who don't countenance spirits. I liked it fine. I was also partial to the cranberries, which were chewy and tart and flavored with orange peel, not the usual jelly kind. A turkey being way too much for the two of us, Wim bought a small goose instead. He got up before the sun to put it in. It needed to cook about all day to let the fat drain off, he said.

The thing I remember most, though, is the dessert. No man I ever run into can make a decent pie. I offered to do that part, but Wim said no, he had something else in mind.

It didn't look like much, I got to say, a bowl of brownish lumpy stuff with cream poured over. My spoon started off kind of cautious. But Lord, one bite and I'll swan, if I hadn't been so already filled up I'd kept dipping into the baking dish till there wasn't a speck left in it.

"Indian pudding," Wim said. He scarcely touched it himself. "It's an honorable old tradition."

"As *should* it be." I helped myself to just a dab more.

It was cornmeal and molasses, he told me, mostly.

"Well, no wonder! Ain't much I wouldn't relish with some cornmeal wrapped around it and blackstrap molasses poured on." Raisins in it big as water bugs.

Wim was sipping champagne out of a jelly glass. He took another swallow, then set it down. He looked happy as could be, but I could see the meal, whether the cooking or the eating, had taken the starch out of him.

"You need a nap," I said. "I'll do up the dishes."

He shook his head. "Not done yet," he said.

"Good gravy, Wim, I couldn't eat another bite!"

Laughing, he got up from the table and went over to take something from the old gladstone bag in the corner, where he was still mostly keeping his things.

When he came back to the table and sat down across from me he was holding a plain white envelope. He reached over and handed it to me and I saw my name written on it in the spidery letters I know came from Wim's hand.

"A small gift," he said.

For some reason I was shaking. "I believe you may be flummoxed," I said. "In this part of the country it's Christmas you give out presents."

"Open it." He looked mighty sober for a man been laughing and pouring champagne a moment ago.

The envelope, a little fat, was unsealed. I took out the papers inside, about six long pages, I'd guess, all tiny print and stapled together. As I unfolded them, my own name—in full, even my middle initial, which is R for Ruth—and Wim's leaped out at me.

I knew it was a legal document, of course. I set it down to hide how bad my hands had got to trembling. All I could think was he'd made a will, and I didn't want to know.

Wim was looking at me, waiting.

"Maybe you'd best tell me what this is all about," I said. "Or I might be reading till doomsday."

I can't summon up, now, the words Wim used to tell it, but I recall they were simple and few. He'd bought my house, and the whole twelve acres it sat on, from Branch. This was the deed. It was in my name.

I can recollect parts of what I said back, though, and sometimes I wish I couldn't: *You had no right . . . I don't want . . . Wim, I do not need . . .* And: *Not your concern . . . no right at all.*

He was a fraction slumped forward in his chair. His face was drawn and white. His mouth cut a straight stubborn line across his face. Wim didn't look defeated, not even hurt—just like a tired man settling in for some hard bargaining and he knows he won't be able to quit until he wins.

"You ought to first talked this over with me," I said.

"You'd have tried to stop me."

"Indeed I would."

"What's done is done." He did not smile. "Cow's out of the barn."

"I don't have to accept it," I said.

Then I tried to squeeze the anger out of my voice by talking very soft. "Wim, don't you know it makes a body feel . . . *puny,* being so beholden? Sometimes it's not right to foist on a person what she's not able to get for herself."

Wim was nettled now. "I'd hoped you might be more generous," he said.

"Generous? I don't . . ."

"Yes, generous. You are talking about pride, Leandra. And it's not only false, it's selfish."

"Reckon that must be one of them things y'all learn at college," I said. "Sounds all inside out to me."

Wim sighed.

"I'm not so smart, and I know it," I told him. "But when it comes to my own life, I can decide things right well, thank you."

"I knew you would argue," Wim said. "I simply wasn't prepared for you to—"

"What? Prefer not to be treated like your idiot child?"

"That isn't fair, Leandra."

I hesitated. "No," I said. "Reckon it ain't."

Wim pressed down his palms on the edge of the table like he meant to get up, but he stayed where he was.

"I want to come hold you," he said in a low shaky voice. "But maybe that wouldn't be fair, either."

"No," I said. "Just now it would not be."

"Neither of us would want to be unfair," he said.

I nodded. His face was peaked with pain.

"Maybe this ain't the time," I said, "for settling this."

Wim looked at me with beggar's eyes. "Could you listen?" he said. "Just for a minute?"

I waited.

After a moment he took a deep breath. "You should have been my wife," he said. "I should be your husband."

I covered my face with my hands. "Don't," I said, but Wim went right on like he didn't hear me, and I stayed in the dark, listening to what I didn't want to think about.

"Maybe I didn't give enough thought to what you needed," he said. "This is what I need, Leandra . . . one small too-late chance to"—his voice caught—"to provide for you.

"And it may be less than fair to tell you. But I need you to allow me this now. It will bring me peace," he said.

I was far past refusing by then, of course. Seemed like I'd already forgot what we'd been arguing about.

Finally, I let my hands slip from my face. It was nearly dusk. The room had grown dim and cool. But my eyes, coming out of darkness, could not seem to adjust. The harder I stared at Wim's face, the more it resembled a mirage, something shimmery and vague far down a furrowed road.

"So you really mean to die, then?" I said.

Wim's features settled back into their proper place. He was smiling the smile of a man who knew he had won.

"I'm afraid I don't see any way around it," he said.

Some of the oldest ones got bodies made of kidskin. It's a thing that can, especially if it hasn't been dyed or painted, just last and last.

If the doll has been handled a good bit, better loved than protected, the skin will wear thin in spots. Its color will change in the handling. You can mostly get the dirt to come off if you're patient. You got to be careful, of course.

But there's this oil comes from human hands. That never comes off. It sinks into the hide, sort of shading it. If a kid-body doll has been touched right much, its skin will be mottled and thin and supple—sometimes, closing your eyes, you might almost believe it was human hide you were running your hands over.

I have one doll like this. Of my own, I mean, to keep. Mrs. Duncan give it to me because the head is gone. The doll is more than a hundred years old. The head, she says, would likeliest have been clay, unglazed. A thing not made to last.

Or it might have been soft wood, carved by some daddy for his little girl, and both of them a century dead.

The body is lumpy and blockish, and the clothes are long gone, of course. Chances are it was meant to be a girl or a lady. But it could have been a boy, I suppose.

"Find the right head for that doll, Leandra, you'll have a fortune on your hands," Mrs. Duncan told me. Only I knew that must be impossible, or why else would she give me the doll?

Still, I treasure this critter more than a businesswoman like Mrs. Evangeline Duncan could calculate. I keep it apart from the other dolls, swaddled in tissue inside a shoe box that's too big for it by half—I like to think that gives it room to breathe.

That doll is like a child to me—not my own child, I mean, but somebody's. Made, for love, by a man and a woman. He would have tanned the hide, molded or carved the head from something the land provided. She would have shaped the body, sewn tight the seams, clothed it. You can tell just by looking at what's left that their creation went on to a life not so different from the rest of us: some tenderness and some rough handling, a lot of loss, a little neglect.

"It is difficult to estimate," Mrs. Duncan told me, "with so much gone. But it wouldn't surprise me if this doll went back as far as 1840 or so."

I got no intention, I don't mind saying, of going off on some wild-goose chase, hoping to find a head. Not for love nor money. Not for this one, which is mine. I like that nobody else would have her, not the way she is.

Sometimes I take her out of the box, unwrap her, and just hold her in my hands. I am hoping the invisible oil from my fingers and palms is seeping in, softening, leaving my mark.

And I can't help hoping the Lord is taking this in, how a simple man and woman managed to make a creature that has already lasted near twice as long as most created and supposedly loved by Him.

I don't mean to blaspheme. I don't. But *Look,* I want to tell Him, *oughtn't You be able to do better?*

Branch came by Thanksgiving Saturday, just before noontime. I knew to be wary now. I saw that big blue boat he started driving a few weeks back, some kind of van with his company logo painted gold on both sides. It pulls in aslant by the mailbox. Then Branch comes high-stepping toward my door, and he's not near there yet when I see this grin to warn me that inch I already gave's about to turn into a mile.

Branch sees me on the porch and tries to tone down his face, but way too late.

"Leandra," he says.

I hold the screen door open. "Branch."

He shuffles his feet and palms back his hair. "How y'all?" he says. "Fine mornin'."

"Never you mind that, Branch Goodlin. You think I can't see whatever you swallowed's a far sight stouter than a canary?"

"Reckon it's all that stuffing." Branch goes to patting his belly, that is flat and narrow as an ironing board. "Where's Willy?"

"Willy?" I say.

Behind me, indoors, I hear Wim laugh.

"You got a caller, *Willy,*" I say.

"Come on in, Branch," says Wim. "You want some coffee?"

Branch's eyes give me wide berth as he steps inside. I pause before following him in and get there just in time to hear, "Need to talk." Branch tries not to move his lips, but what with that grin he can't lose, he looks more like the dummy.

"Reckon y'all'd deem it right considerate if I'd just grab my coffee mug and slip on out to the shed?"

Branch was blushing.

Wim just laughed. "It might be best if you'd stay," he said. "Considering."

Branch gave him a startled look.

Wim nodded at him.

"Considering," I said.

"Have a seat," Wim said.

The smile I give him was tight as one of Mama's home permanents. "Mighty thoughty of you," I said.

Somehow we all got ourselves set down at the table with coffee in front of us. Then we just sat there for a minute, like three world leaders with a big problem and no common language to work it out.

Finally, Branch squirmed in his chair, and I felt sorry to see him so itchy.

"I know," I told him. "About the land and all."

He nodded, not looking at me.

"The surprise approach didn't go over too well," Wim said to Branch. "So if there's something—"

"Y'all just pretend like I'm not here," I said.

Branch sighed.

"It's all right," Wim said. "Did you find something?"

Then Branch couldn't help himself. He got all smiles again. "About perfect," he said. "And just for the price of moving it. Which I figure's maybe five thousand."

"I take it back," I said. "Stop acting like I ain't here."

"It's only an idea," Wim said. "We haven't done anything."

"Five thousand," I said. "Meaning dollars?"

"Might do it for three," Branch said. "Not all that much to it."

Wim told me then how he'd got this notion the house ought to be bigger, the shed being no fit place for my work. Which I had to admit it wasn't.

"It's what I'm used to," I said.

Wim give me the sorriest smile then, and he didn't need to say a word. We both knew I'd already set my feet on a road lined on both sides with things I wasn't used to.

His eyes got a dreamy look, traveling around the room as he kept on talking, taking in the overcrowded shelves, the small lopsided windows and chinky walls, and the brownish map on the ceiling.

"I kept thinking about adding on," he said. "Along with some work to get this part in better shape, of course."

I stole a peek at Branch, to see if his feelings got hurt. This place belongs to him, after all. But Branch's eyes gone dreamy too by now.

"Anyway," Wim said, "anything I could picture I knew you would hate."

"I love this place," I told him. "Like it is."

He nodded.

The faucet in the kitchen sink was dripping. I got up and went to turn it off. The drip slowed some but kept on steady. I sat back down again.

"So I was trying out some various ideas on Branch," Wim said. "He's the one who came up with what I think may actually be the solution."

"Sound as a dollar." Branch had that canary look again.

The value of land around here shot up right fast this past few years—I could have told Wim that myself. Because of it, Branch said, a lot of folks been buying up run-down old places, having them torn down or carted off to make way for the fancier houses they got in mind.

"Just simple, sturdy old buildings." Branch gazed up at the webby beams overhead, like a man smitten. "Pretty much right like this one here."

"So he came up with this idea," Wim said, "that we could move one of these unwanted places here, adding on without violating—"

"You want me to have two houses?" I said.

"Two rooms," Wim said. "Maybe three, depending."

I looked at Wim. Then I looked at Branch. I wasn't even mad, just purely dumbfounded. "I think you both lost your good sense," I said.

"Leandra, will you please listen?"

"Wait till you see this place I found."

They were both talking at once. "A jewel," Branch said. "A breeze," said Wim. I folded my arms across my chest and kept still. But I had no intention of keeping an open mind.

The building, Branch said, was a net house—one big long room with windows all around and a high ceiling. Fishermen used it as a place to store their equipment. They hung their nets along the rafters to dry and met there in winter to mend them. The place was set on a little slope overlooking Currituck Sound, a spot where the new owners, who were from Richmond, meant to build their dream house.

"Nice folks." Branch hushed his voice like somebody might be eavesdropping. "But the beauty is, they just don't see what they've got."

"Would they—" Wim began, but Branch was nowhere near ready to be interrupted.

"Whole place is built of cypress," he said. "Inside and out. Cypress! Never seen a lick of paint. I figure it's been there eighty, maybe ninety years."

I recall how once my daddy, a mild and kindly man who hardly ever refused me, would not take me over to see some newborn blue-tick puppies his foreman's dog had one spring. I pestered and teased about them puppies for days, eight of them. I was near crazy to get over and see them before they were all sold off. But my daddy, he just wouldn't stop saying no.

Finally, one day, I went all to pieces over it, crying and carrying on. I was five, I think, or thereabouts, and *No* not a word I was much used to hearing.

So my daddy set me down and explained things. It's a rule of life, he said, that a body should never go looking at newborn pups unless they're prepared to bring one home. We already had a dog, Willard, who ate more like a horse than like the pointer he was supposed to be. We couldn't afford another such mouth around our table, Daddy said.

It's a lesson I wished I'd remembered before I told Branch and Wim—who just had to drive right over and have a look at that net house—all right, I might as well ride along.

—∞—

Sometimes now he sleeps with his eyes open.

The bed, a matched pair of golden oak nightstands on either side of it, takes up the whole far end of the room. There are windows all around, and now, while we wait for the spring trees to fill out, we can still get a glimpse of the river. The dogwoods will bloom any day now, then the azaleas, gaudy and overdressed. But Wim seems like he'd rather keep studying those rafters, straight and strong, old and reliable as Moses.

They could hold everything up for another hundred years. Is that what Wim is thinking?

Or maybe he is just asleep and his dreams no longer got much use for his eyes.

—~—

I go along for one harmless Saturday afternoon ride, and three days later I got me an old net house squatting in my yard. It sat askew and a little apart from my house's back wall. Made me feel like I all of a sudden didn't know where I was.

A week after that, a foundation was laid, and soon the two buildings were joined up by a passageway with three glass bubbles on the roof that invited sunshine, moonlight, and the stars to drop in through the ceiling.

The "layout," as Wim called it, was all his devising, glass bubbles included (only they weren't, I guess, really glass but something less breakable). I didn't say I thought Wim's vision cockeyed. But I can admit now that I did and I was wrong. Wim had a gift for looking at what wasn't there yet and really seeing it. Which maybe explains what brought him first to my sister, now to me.

The day we drove over to see the net house, Branch measured it. Then he came back and measured my house. They were uncanny alike, he crowed, snaking his tape measure through the air like a bullwhip. Just a matter of a few feet different, except the net house was taller.

"That's good," Wim said. "You don't want too much symmetry."

The logical thing, I figured, would be to line them up close together.

Or maybe T shape, Branch said, short end to long?

Wim said we were both way off track. He grabbed up a pad of paper and sketched it out for us to see the way he saw it.

I don't think Branch could grasp it. I know I couldn't myself. But of the three of us, Wim seemed the one who sheerly *cared* the most. So we didn't argue with him much.

The only thing Branch got high-handed about was that the passageway needed to be wider. "You'll want it airy," he said to Wim. Branch told me later that he meant to make sure there'd be room to turn a wheelchair. After that, I got into the argument too. "Two against one," I told Wim. "Besides, whose house is this?"

The day the connecting passageway was done, I climbed up into a live oak that stands on a slope a ways off from the house. The shape, sort of like a Z, came out just the way Wim sketched it. From up there I could see he was right. Lining the two little houses up straight would only have called your attention to how they differed. There's a peculiar kind of balance that comes from giving differences their due.

From up there in the branches, this house where I live with Wim looks comfortable with its gaps and slopes and bends. It even looks kind of artistic.

But the most important thing, of course, is how it appears down here on the ground, where I mostly am. From here it just looks natural and right, two old buildings that always been together, like an old married couple who needn't fuss about keeping in step after walking side by side for so long.

—~—

From the day I give in to that innocent ride to Currituck Sound, I was thrown to the mercies of het-up boys filling my ears with rash promises. First it was just the pair of them. A few more days went by, and I had me a whole houseful.

"Leandra, this needn't disrupt your work in the least," Wim said.

"Ought to have the whole shebang wrapped up by Christmas Eve," Branch told me.

"You'll have lights by the end of the week," the electrician promised. "Just show me now, ma'am, where'd you want them outlets?"

"New lease on life's what these thermal-pane windows gon' give you," Harley Moyock vowed the day Wim and Branch dragged me over to the C.C. Lumber and Building Supply. "And fully warrantied."

Well, we had our Christmas Eve supper on a slab of plywood with a tarp over it and half the windows boarded up. But the mess was getting straightened out by New Year's. It all seems like years ago anyhow.

—ɷ—

"Leandra?"

Wim calls out once or twice most nights from sleep. It's the pain makes him restless, I know. But he doesn't say another word. Only my name.

I never know if I should wake him. I want to tell him I am here, to make rash promises: *I will always be here . . . right here, Wim.*

But if he stays asleep, maybe the pain will seem only a part of what he dreams.

What does he see now, Wim who has always been able to see what is not yet there? I know, though he does not say so, some nights he is afraid. The darkness around our bed crowds with pictures, and I do not have it in me to imagine their colors and shapes.

"Tell me," I say. But he never will.

I'll inch slowly toward him, my arms reaching across the mattress that seems too ample by half, a grievous distance to travel. And every second is a weight.

When I pull Wim against me, his skin is icy and his bones push sharp through it and into me.

Lying in the dark, I try to picture what I am holding. He feels like one of those old wooden dolls with tongue-and-groove joints, wooden pegs to keep his knees and hips in place. His fingers are brittle. His skin is grainy.

I have always been good at finding things. I am learning to picture what is not there.

I cannot warm him. It is that, more than anything, makes me afraid.

—ɷ—

Looking back, I got a suspicion it was pushing against the house pulled Wim, for a time, back from death. Looking back now on the rush we were in is near enough to make me cry. Why couldn't the Lord, who seems to specialize in stumbling blocks and obstacles, have sent down a lightning bolt or some such to slow us down, foul us up?

A nor'easter would not have been uncommon that time of year, one vicious gale to lift and scatter the lumber till nothing but splinters was left to work with . . . sheets of plywood and windows flying through the air like playing cards . . . a good hard freeze to bust the pipes.

A building boom might have scooped up all those local boys Branch called his pickup crew, might have kept them backed up with work straight through summer's end.

I summon a picture of that huge flatbed truck dragging the net house over here snagged on a curve in the road, plumb stuck and cutting off traffic for days and days . . .

Or licks of fire consuming all that succulent cypress wood, the rafters red-hot fingers raking a cold night sky.

The windows might have been just a fraction off.

The folks from Richmond could have changed their minds or plans or dreams.

What was our hurry?

Why couldn't something have put a lag in our plans?

"We got no time to lose," I heard Branch say, grumbling to young Burley Morton, who should have been wrestling out rotten sills instead of lurking back of the shed, his hands cupped around his second Camel in twenty minutes.

Branch got all flustered when he saw I heard him: *no time to lose*. Truth told, I felt sorry for the boy, getting called on the carpet that way. But only Branch and me knew what we were about, the hard truth behind his words.

"Right as rain," I told him as the Morton boy hustled back to work with his crowbar. "No time to spare at all."

After it was over, though, when the house was all done and the shed emptied of all but what needed to be kept stored . . .

When the weeklong storm did come as it would and we had light and the windows held fast as ticks on a hound's neck . . .

When those wild boys' rash promises were all made good by

the start of the first gridded page of the new Tiny's Garage and Body Shop calendar, I began to get inklings how all that flurry and dispatch had worked against us. By then it was far too late, of course, to slow down anything.

—∞—

Though the house was supposedly mine, it was clear from the start that the work belonged to the men. And they were right possessive about it. One day I was feeling like the prize in a poorly game of tug-o-war between them, next I know I'm on the sidelines, all but forgotten. I can't rightly say I didn't mind. But mostly I was just amazed at the different creatures Branch and Wim turned into the moment they got to working together.

Responsibility seemed to divide down the middle like a head of hair with a natural part: Wim drew up the plans and Branch toted up the costs. Wim was in charge of ordering supplies, Branch rounded up the crew. The part I least expected, though, was seeing the two of them, Branch and Wim, jump in day after day to work alongside the rest of them boys. You'd have thought Branch didn't have no business to run, no family to see to. You might even have believed Wim knew his way around the inside of a toolbox.

And within two, three days, seemed like they'd got themselves a regular fan club going.

"The man has a gifted pair of hands," Wim told me.

"Never saw a fella with a keener eye," Branch said. "He'll just look at a space, then cut him a piece of board. Blessed thing fits so nice, you'd think it melted in there."

I'd come back in from the shed around eleven, maybe half past, to warm myself up and lay out some things for lunch. Branch would be up on some ladder, waving around a nail gun like there was no more harm in it than in an ice cream cone.

And Wim might be down on his knees, halfway across the room, doing something completely different—sanding a section of floor or mitering the corners of baseboards—both of them intent on the job at hand, not saying a word. There could be six other workmen around, power saws whining, hammers pounding, rotten boards being ripped out with the sound of breaking bones.

Still, in all that racket and muddle, it would somehow seem like they were talking to one another, Branch and Wim. I swear, they never stopped talking. Left me feeling right lonely sometimes, how I couldn't hear a word they said.

The first week or so it scared me, Wim working like a demon, hardly ever stopping to rest or even eat. He promised me there was no harm in it, and knowing the nature of his sickness, of course, it made sense what he was saying. He'd told me right from the start, making a poor joke of it as he would: "The bad news is there's nothing I can do to stop it. The good news is there's not much I can do to make it worse."

Branch worried some too, I could see. But the two of us could have built a wall of our worries and Wim would only have climbed right over it.

I fretted back there in the shed, sorting through baskets of scraps that always seemed to fall just short of what I needed.

"I'm keeping an eye on him," Branch said.

New color seemed to come into Wim's face. At night he slept like a baby, and he gave off a wonderful heat. Sometimes disease leaves just as mysterious as the way it can come. Isn't that right?

At seven or so, when Branch's boys started pulling their pickups into the yard, Wim would walk me back to the shed. "Now you just go on about your business," he'd say. "Forget we're even here." Then he'd look around the yard, and if nobody was watching he'd kiss me. His work clothes smelled of sawdust, and so did his hair. I'd have to fight my own hands to keep from holding on to him. But I could go back up to the house a few hours later, Wim mightn't even notice I was there.

Joy—I saw this written somewhere one time, maybe on a T-shirt or the bumper of a car—is what happens to you when you're not paying attention.

I should have *minded* those days more.

I might have listened harder and learned a few words, at least, from the silent language of two men working together to make something meant to last.

I would have slowed things down, might even have resorted to treachery, if I'd been paying more attention. Like a witch in some old fairy tale, I might have undone their day's work each night while they slept.

Once the work was done, once Wim had made his provisions for me, it was like he lost his advantage. I don't mean he's given up. And Lord knows I never will. The house was maybe a manufactured need. But I see now how the providing, it was something that stood between Wim and dying.

Now there's only him and me and the frail comforts of spring: hard rains that can't penetrate the roof, windows that open easily to softer air.

And the effortful work of keen and constant attention.

We still make love.

You might not think, to look at him, that Wim would yet have the strength for such. The blood. Or even the need.

All my life, beginning at the Vessel of Holiness Baptist Church when I was just a child, I have heard talk of "the power of love." I got the idea it was something God started but folks soon got the hang of.

When my daddy died, crushed out on that highway so far from home, Mama told me and Pammy he'd always be with us, because the power of his love would last through the end of the world and all time to come.

The power of the Lord's love can move mountains, Reverend Gaskins was always saying.

I wondered back then why a God who moved mountains like there was nothing to it couldn't manage to shove a pile of boulders off my daddy's crushed skull and shattered backbone.

I'm surely not surprised anymore at what the Lord can't do—

or just plain won't. When Wim and Pammy's baby was born like he was and died like he did, I reckon I learned not to expect so almighty much from God.

But now I am wondering how this "power of love" got to be a cliché in the first place. Hardly because it grabs any dead-sure truth by the horns.

Love is no earthly power anyhow. It's more like a surrender to a body's pure helplessness. Love is giving up any least little power you ever once had.

It's apt to be at dawn these days, our loving. Sometimes before I am quite full awake. But how could he know, me sleeping now with my eyes open too? I will feel Wim's hands begin to move up the length and rise and fall of me. And when he raises up to take what is his and to give what's left of him, it is always, each time, a miracle.

His eyes are blind. His mouth is parched and ravenous. My name flickers in his breath like a candle flame.

Sometimes I hold him too tight to me and feel my thighs cling together, stubborn and desperate. I want to tell him: *No. No, Wim.* Because my body bears its sad convictions, and one of them is that Wim can no longer spare those few drops of him that would find their way into me.

Keep everything, I want to tell him. *For yourself.*

But my body's convictions are no match, of course, for his will.

Each such loving makes me cry, for I know every time I am finding something I will never find again.

Dawn comes earlier. The sunrise tends to be garish here—vulgar, Mama would have said—and quick. The new windows almost make too much of it, the light like overripe peaches in a crystal bowl.

So little is left of him now. But we still make love. It's like something the light causes.

Every time is the last.

Each breath and thrust is a miracle of helplessness.

I speak out of turn to my coldhearted bully of a God:
"Don't go thinking You can take credit for this," I tell Him.
A time is coming when I won't even know you, Leandra.
But I will know you, I said.

—∾—

You can buy gesso at any art supply store. I know Mrs. Duncan would be pleased to send me some when I need it. But gesso don't keep well. I like mixing up my own little batches—white glue and whiting, powdered zinc and plaster of paris. The smell somehow calls to mind a doctor's office, a place you might hope not to visit but once you do, the very air has a clean and practical smell that promises you'll be patched up, taken care of.

The old doll has a cardboard body. She is dressed in a faded sailor suit and is double-jointed, a little contortionist. The orangey freckles on her nose look cancerous, and a deep gash slashes her dimpled knee.

"You look like you carried on something fierce in your day," I tell her. "Sorry, ain't you now, you didn't take better care of yourself?"

I paint the wound first with watered glue, blow it dry with the hand-held hair dryer I found at a garage sale for fifty cents. Just had a loose wire that Branch fixed for me.

After the priming, you start layering the gesso on. Hardly a thing to it, except you got to make sure each coat's full dry before you add another, which can try the patience some. You're supposed to work with a good soft brush, keep the strokes all going in the same direction, which I mostly do. But as with a lot of these delicate jobs, when you get to the last part the fingers are apt to work best. Ain't an instrument or tool made, I don't care how expensive, can match the touch of the human hand. You wind up having to sand off your fingerprints, of course. But you'll leave them behind anyhow, underneath. Your mark will always hide there.

Last night at midnight April began, with a lash of rain, a howl of wind, and a sky fractured by cracks of lightning. This afternoon ain't a cloud to be seen, though, and the air is soft and blue as the flared edge of a morning glory.

Wim slept past sunrise today, almost to light, and his eyes were closed, the lids, too, blue, and flimsy as shadows. And because he did not touch me at dawn, nor try, did not squander himself on me, my eyes don't have that gritty feel stays with you all day when you cried first thing, and my skin feels alive and hungry and hopeful, like the last time is somewhere ahead.

It is a good day, then, a thing grown rarer with time. Wim even went off by himself in the car—to the hardware, he said, though for what he didn't tell me.

I am sitting by the table, my bedraggled little sailor girl laid across my knees while I wait for another coat of gesso to dry. It's going good. There's not a hint of dampness in the air this afternoon. I study the little face, kind of bratty but pitiful, and try to guess what her name might be. Something fresh and flirty, I think. Like Judy or Trixie or Nance.

And I don't even hear Branch until he's right there in the doorway, coughing softly so as not to startle me, which of course he does.

"April Fool's," I say, grabbing for Trixie when my knees jump.

"Didn't mean to creep up on you," Branch says, but his eyes are sneaky anyway, ducking into corners, trying to see over my shoulder.

"You on the lam from somebody?" I ask him.

Branch's smile falls flat on his face. "Willy's not home?"

"Drove off near an hour ago. Discussin' nuts and bolts and such with Lyle Kinney down to the hardware. Don't guess he'll be gone too long."

Branch is studying my face like I'm talking nonsense. "You think we might talk a minute?" he says.

"I see no reason why not." I pull the second chair out from the table. "You want some tea?"

"Not a thing," Branch says. Then he glances back as if he can see out to the road, which he can't.

The lightness goes out of me. I set Trixie on the felt-covered slab of foam lying on the table, to recuperate. "Branch, what is it?" I say.

He pulls the chair out further and sits down next to me. "I need to mess in your business," he says.

"You got permission for that a long time ago," I remind him.

Branch nods but then can't seem to speak.

"Best plunge right on in," I say.

"Willy's not doing so good," Branch says.

"Well, under the circumstances I'd say you can't rightly expect him to." I sound a good bit more snappish than I intend.

Branch lowers his head. But when he looks up again, his eyes are feisty.

"You know he is dying," I say.

"I do," Branch says. "But what's got me worried is, do you?"

"Every waking second," I tell him. "And also in my dreams."

My eyes have started stinging. I look away.

Branch reaches for my hand. "But are you facing it?" he says.

"Don't see that I have much choice."

"Some things got to change here, Leandra."

"You want me to start breaking in black dresses?" I try to make it sound like a joke, but the pure bitterness in my voice comes as a shock. It was my sister's voice just come out of my mouth, and I wonder did it sound to Branch like a stranger was hiding somewhere in this room ain't got a hiding place in it.

I turn and look at him with helpless eyes. "What is it you think I am doing wrong?"

He sighs, then squeezes my hand harder. "I wish we could start this over," he says. "You think I come barging in here to give you a piece of my mind?"

I smile a little. "Reckon not."

Branch takes a deep breath. "Leandra, you know there's times Willy can't see?"

Well, I do know it, of course I do. But not with the mind I use to get me, and Wim, from one day into the next.

When I don't answer him, Branch leans forward and takes hold of my shoulders. "You figure he ought to be wandering around alone in town? You think a man suffers fits of blindness should drive an automobile?"

I start crying without a sound. Branch gets up from his chair and pulls my head against his hip.

"You want me to talk to him?" he asks.

"Wim would hate that."

"I'm his friend."

"He'd hate it anyway."

"All right." Branch is stroking my hair. "But what about you, Lannie?"

"I'm doing fine."

"Not entirely," Branch says. "Not by my lights. And things going to get worse."

"You think you need to tell me that?"

"Ssh," Branch says.

I cry a little longer, and then I've had enough.

"Today's the best day we had in a good while," I say, straightening up.

"And here I had to come spoiling it."

I look up. Branch is smiling sadly.

"You got a right." I pick up a square of flannel from the table and wipe my eyes with it. One corner is stiff with dried gesso, and it scratches my cheek. "It just makes me mad, is all."

Branch takes the cloth from me, swipes at some streak or speck near my eyebrow, then sets it down. "Fair enough," he says.

"Fair's just what it ain't," I tell him.

"I know." He sits down again. "What I need to ask you, Leandra, is where's the doctor in all this? You know you could have a visiting nurse to help out? You think you are *qualified* to take care of him with all that's coming?"

Branch stares at me steady-eyed, like he knows I mean to slap him and he means to take it.

"I know I'm not," I say.

"There's things he could be taking," Branch says. "For the pain."

"He don't want that either. Wim wants no part of any of that."

"Only maybe he's not the best one to decide, Leandra."

I shake my head.

"Do you even sleep anymore?" Branch asks. "Who is going to look after you?"

I hear a car heading toward us up the road. Wim coming back already, I think, safe and sound. But the car keeps going past the house, whoever it is speeding.

"Always reckoned *you* would," I say.

"I plan to," Branch tells me. "Only you best not expect me to keep from butting in."

I smile. "We ever have a fight that you recall?"

"Never." Branch gets up and moves to the doorway, stands looking out to the road. "I'd known how to fight you," he says softly, "we might be married now and all this wouldn't—"

"Ssh," I say. "Hush. Wouldn't neither of us wish for that."

"No," Branch says. But he doesn't sound certain.

When Wim comes home, Branch is gone. I mean to tell him—tell Wim everything. But one look at his eyes and I see the good day is over.

Just inside the door, he sinks down on the corner of the mourners' bench. The old wood creaks, and Wim winces.

I hold myself back from running to him. "I was preparing to round up a posse." I cross the room in small slow steps.

Wim smiles at me, but he can't see me. "Is it getting dark?" I whisper.

"Come closer," Wim says.

I kneel next to the bench, take the small brown bag he seems to have forgotten he's clutching—thumbtacks, cup hooks, a pack of hundred-watt lightbulbs.

I set the bag on the floor. Then I rest my head in Wim's lap.

"You'll tell me, won't you?" I say. "When it starts to get dark?"

Wim's fingers are moving lightly over my face, smoothing, leaving prints that will never be seen.

"Let's not have any more trick questions," he says.

A time is coming when I won't even know . . .

But I will know you. I will know . . .

vi

"I read much of the night, and go south in the winter."

LEANDRA CAN TELL ME, on any given day, precisely how long I have been with her here.

"One hundred and forty-seven days," she'll say. Or:

"Next month, on the second Thursday at nine in the evening, will come half a year."

I'll counterfeit amazement, even disbelief. "As long as that?" I'll say. "Can it be?"

In truth, however, my own computations are even more refined. I can transpose the sum of this sojourn into hours. It suits me to inflate the figures thus, for this brief allotment of time is the fraction of my life that amounts to something. I am come, here with Leandra, into my own.

Given days.

—ɯ—

Each early-April morning emerges like an infant from the womb: warm and moist, breathless and faintly blue. I want to reach out and slap the day into existence.

I cannot always tell if the milky haze that blurs the treeline, erases the hill, derives from the atmosphere or from my own failing sight. I shall, should I live long enough, be fully blind. The tumor, placed as it is, would be bound to press on the optic nerve, Dr. Kaplan said. It has nowhere else to go.

But the eclipse has been considerate, allowing me to take my time in making its acquaintance. Our first encounters, naturally, terrified me. The darkness was unimaginable—nothing like night in a closed room, but a limitless vacancy within, the void no longer held at arm's length. The sound of one's own breaths can be deafening.

Still, it lasted only moments. And even now, though the sightlessness descends on me more and more frequently, it makes its succinct point, then retreats, with a kind of innate courtesy.

For several months I exerted myself in the rather futile cause of concealing this affliction from Leandra. I would angle my face away from her, pretend to be lost in thought. Sometimes when she would speak to me I would not reply, miming deep abstraction. For there was something oddly dreadful to me about the sound of my own voice issuing from that absolute darkness.

But I have given up that charade. Leandra knows each inch of ground I forfeit. And like the blindness itself, she shows a delicate bent. She does not mention my lapses but simply places herself within my reach when sight fails. She outwaits the darkness with me.

For all the years we were apart (those, too, subject to my finical calculus, years multiplied into empty seconds), I was never able to compose a reliable picture of Leandra. It was not that I failed to remember her face—hardly. But when I tried to assemble her features in my mind's eye, to hold them there, they would perpetually shift, change shape. And, like trick photography, the process would harden her tender mouth into petulance, narrow her eyes with blame. Often the face left to me would be Pamela's.

I fear the darkness that lowers over me now. It is capable of cruel tricks. But now that my sight is truly failing, I can see Leandra perfectly, every line of her face like something etched by laser upon the blackness. Her body contours the once endless space through which I am, slowly, plummeting.

—∞—

"Wim?" she whispers. "You awake?"

The morning emerges, an apparition with Leandra at its center, shimmering.

She stands before the window and the air is gold, breathing, safely delivered.

"Hello," I say. Foolish, yes. A lost and besotted old man. But I do know what I am saying. *Hello.* I want never to stop coming upon, colliding with, her miraculous existence.

"How do?" she'll say. Or: "Pleased." Which is exactly what she says this morning.

And so she is: *pleased.* I can see it in her eyes, in the unrucked skin around her mouth and across her forehead. She is holding out a chipped white crockery mug, and when she leans over the bed the scent of her slept-in flesh touches my face.

"Coffee?" I say.

"You shouldn't be drinking coffee."

I grimace. "I know. What is it?"

"Coffee." And she smiles, pleased. Yes, thoroughly.

"But where is yours?"

"I'll get it in a minute." She sets the mug on the night table. "Scootch up." She bends over me again, and the oversized undershirt she is wearing, mine, slips forward, her small breasts shown entire by the stretched ribbing at the shirt's V-neck. When she plumps the pillows up behind me, my hands reach out with blind intent and I feel her nipples harden under the soft white cotton.

Leandra does not pull back, but her face is suddenly masked in sorrow. My hands drop away. She straightens up, then hands me the coffee.

"Love?" I say.

She shakes her head.

"What is it?" I say. "Just tell me."

Leandra stares into my eyes for a moment. Then slowly, as if she is bruised, she sits down on the edge of the bed.

"Sometimes I am just too sad," she says.

The obvious reply—*I know*—would be facile. My own sorrow is all I really know. Hers I can only begin to imagine.

"Go get your coffee," I tell her. "Just sit here with me a minute, all right?"

Leandra is gazing out the window. The sun, half risen above the hill, is a flat platinum disk. Her eyes look arid and bleached. Sometimes she, too, goes blind. I must not mention it.

When Leandra turns from the window, her face is composed. She stands, the muscles in her slender legs tensing, braced as if on the deck of a boat in rough seas. When she raises the white shirt and pulls it over her head, her body comes to light. Unfamiliar. Harder and leaner than the body that, an hour ago, dovetailed with mine in sleep.

"Leandra, there's no need—"

"There is." She takes my coffee cup from me, sets it aside, turns back the covers.

Her eyes are too slow to close. For a moment I glimpse myself in them—brittle, emaciated, weak.

"Oh, Wim." Leandra's voice is my own, the voice of the limitless dark. "Just look at you." Her fingers trace the ridges of bone that delineate me.

"Don't," I whisper. "Leandra . . ." Cowled clavicle, hipbones the ridge of a shallow bowl, bars of bone that cage my vital organs: what I amount to. *Don't.*

"I need to not mind being so sad," Leandra whispers. Then she is in the bed, an anguish of twisted limbs to bind me like roots, her hair flowering over my face.

"How else," she asks me, "am I going to learn?"

—ww—

Mine was not, when we buried my infant son, a conventional grief. There was something almost furtive in it, as if the evidence of some harrowing crime were being disposed of. I wonder now if there may not have been more than a little relief mixed in with my sorrow.

When I went in to see him, during those few hours that constituted my son's lifetime, his deformity was concealed from me under white flannel. I imagined the cloth to be an unbearable weight upon a heart that could not have been much larger than a thimble. I asked that he be uncovered.

"I should be able to look at him," I said. "As he is."

Dr. Hathaway made it her business to dissuade me. When that didn't work, she forbade it.

"There are things no one should have to see," she said, this flinty old woman who so rarely flinched from anything.

"He is my son," I said.

A moment passed before she nodded, a reluctant concession.

"There is almost never an instance where there is nothing I can do." She took hold of my arm then, her fingers scoring muscle, striking bone. "This is what I can do."

"You don't have the right," I told her.

"No, I just have the power." She was pulling me from the incubator, from my dying child. "The authority," she amended.

She sensed, I think, that I was ready to lash out at her.

"It is my prerogative"—she smiled sadly—"my *privilege,* to keep you from looking upon what you well might never for the rest of your life stop seeing." Her voice was scarcely audible above the hum of vital machinery.

Resistance left me suddenly, as if something had ruptured and hemorrhaged. Drained, I followed Dr. Hathaway from the Neonatal ICU. Outside, in the corridor, my back against a transparent shatterproof panel that separated me from my child, I first, as a man, wept.

When I finally lifted my head, the doctor was gone. Leandra was coming toward me, her footsteps steady and soundless as she moved down the long antiseptic hall.

A Grieg melody filled the windowless consultation room with elegiac implications. Kaplan, white-coated, entered the room briskly, walked to the console, and turned the radio down. He studied me with dispassionate eyes. "You're not looking too bad," he said.

"Thank you." I smiled. "You're not, either."

"Irony agrees with you," he said. "How are the headaches?"

"About the same."

He nodded, settled in behind his desk, and picked up a prescription pad. "I'm going to give you something for the pain. It should help for a while. You'll let me know when you need something stronger?"

He held out the prescription. I hesitated before taking it. "What?" he said.

"You still haven't told me how long I've got."

The soft music soared, hovering for an instant above melancholy.

"Six months? A year?" Kaplan lifted his well-tended hands in a pantomime of futility. "I'd simply be guessing. What good would it do?"

"It might help me decide what . . . portion of my time I'm willing to spend in a stupor."

"These will just make you a little drowsy," he said.

"Great," I said. "But later—"

"Later the pain will start calling the shots, Mr. Cantwell."

"The hell it will," I said.

The doctor looked up, startled.

"My Hemingway impression," I told him. "It probably still needs some work."

Kaplan pressed his thin lips into a thrifty smile. "I've seen worse."

"I've gone a few rounds with pain," I said. "I didn't do badly."

The doctor studied me for another moment. "In your case," he said, "I just might put my money on the full year."

It made me feel good, deciding not to cower. It might even, I thought, turn out to be what I had instead of God. Pretty, as Jake Barnes so quotably said, to think so.

That Hemingway was a cynical bastard.

—ꟽ—

I'd forgotten how small she was.

Pamela had complained bitterly, throughout the pregnancy, about her size. It was heavy labor to breathe, she said, carrying that unaccustomed weight. She developed a whole vocabulary of exaggeration to describe herself: colossal, stupendous, gargantuan. If I made light of her verbal extravagance, she turned her semantic arsenal on me: beast, wretch, bully. If I offered sympathy, she locked herself in the bathroom in a storm of tears.

It was her rage, though, not the pregnancy, that made my wife a giant. Dr. Hathaway had in fact expressed dismay at how little weight Pamela actually gained. Her face was full of hollows, her arms and legs sapling thin. The mound of belly that eventually grew out in front of her seemed to have little to do with the delicate body that carried it.

The delivery had been by cesarean section. Once again Pamela's blood pressure had plunged and she'd been slow to emerge from anesthesia. She was far from robust, Dr. Hathaway said. It would be best to keep her in the hospital for a while, where she could be watched.

From the moment she was delivered of our child, Pamela looked unimaginably small to me. Her face, taut and peaked against the pillows of her hospital bed, seemed not much bigger than a fist.

When once, in sorrow and longing, I reached for her, she felt panicky and insubstantial as a bird fighting my hands. Apart from her fury, there seemed nothing to grab hold of. I wondered if fury so consuming could even leave room in her for grief.

Still, it was the grief I tried to reach out to. "We have to help each other through this, Pamela," I said.

I was alone with her in a small private room with walls the shade of winter pallor. The drawn blinds were spattered with silver-blue reflections from the soundless television.

Our child had expired perhaps twenty minutes earlier. Pamela had never seen him.

"Would you like me to tell Mrs. Cantwell?" Dr. Hathaway had grown formal in the face of death.

"I'll tell her," I had said.

"I could go with you if—"

"No," I said. "Thank you."

Then I'd asked the doctor to tell Leandra, who was waiting down the hall.

Pamela was staring at the tin-colored screen, where a shining automobile was blithely scaling an impossible precipice.

"Pamela," I said, "did you hear me?"

Her midnight eyes glanced briefly off mine.

I turned off the television. "Neither of us can get through this all alone," I said.

"I thought we already did," said Pamela.

It was then I tried to touch her.

The distress was all in her body, frenzy in her flailing hands. Her face was as blank and dim as the television screen.

In shock, perhaps . . . she would need time . . . the doctor didn't have to talk me through this.

I pulled a chair up close beside the bed and just sat there for a while, staying with her. There was something almost peaceful about the respite, my own sorrow allowed to flow freely below the surface for a time.

Eventually Pamela went to sleep. She looked so small in that bed.

I waited until I could be sure her sleep was sound. There was no need to rush. Leandra would stay, I knew, no matter how long it might take me to get back to her.

—~—

I have been given a sentence:

I have ——— to live.

Guesswork is required to fill in the blank. My existence is become a questionable proposition.

Still, the particulars have no bearing on this central fact: the subject of the sentence, completed or not, remains the same:

I.

"There will come a time," Dr. Kaplan says, "when you'll no longer be aware of your identity."

I nod, a reasonable man—my identity still in evidence.

"You must not regard it as a defeat, Mr. Cantwell, if the pain—"

"Defeats me?"

"We need to be realistic," Kaplan says. "That's all."

> *These fragments I have shored against my ruins . . .*
> *Datta. Dayadhvam. Damyata.*
> *Shantih   shantih   shantih*

—~—

"I need to go out this afternoon," Leandra tells me. "Will you be all right for a while?"

I am swiping egg yolk from a speckled blue plate with a triangle of soft toast. Some days I am tempted to believe not a thing in the world is wrong with me. Before I even got up this morning I sensed that my legs intended to hold me, my eyes could be counted on. I am full of appetite. Even my headache seems benign—a simple custom to be observed, no more than that.

But the idea, so sudden and unexpected, of Leandra's absence touches the back of my neck and the pit of my belly with cold.

"Where are you off to?" I do not sound as casual as I'd hoped.

"Just a few errands." Her eyes are oddly fickle, flirting with the breakfast things, the spring-green window, the mild disorder on the shelves. "Branch would carry me, he said."

"I might ride along," I say.

Leandra says nothing.

"Unless I'm not welcome?"

"A good bit of traipsing around," Leandra murmurs. "Not very interesting, I'm afraid."

I nod. "Not the usual itinerary of gourmet restaurants, world-class museums, pagan festivals?"

Leandra smiles, yet her eyes evade me.

I despise the man who presses her, as if he is unknown to me. "Give," I say. "Leandra?"

"There's something we want to get you," she says at last.

"Ah, a surprise."

She gets up from the table and goes to the sink, her back to me there. "You might say."

The set of her shoulders, her nervous hands in a choke hold on the spatula, afflict me with remorse.

I move in close behind her, rest my rough chin on her smooth hair. "Don't let me cow you," I tell her. "I'm harmless."

After a moment Leandra drops the spatula into a dishpan of soapy water. Steam rises. She turns around and tucks her face into my shoulder. "I'll be back before you know it," she says.

"Let's not get carried away."

When I lift her face between my hands, she closes her eyes.

"Harmless?" she whispers. "Am I supposed to let you get away with that?"

—~—

She is back before I know it. Afternoon, as often happens, has not been as kindly as morning. The pills I now take, sparingly, for pain will not permit me to stay awake. The sleep they induce is deep and dreamless, a little rehearsal for death. Waking is a desperately arduous act.

When I open my eyes, the first thing I see is a blue-and-silver shadow in the corner of the room. I stare at it, patient, until its parts coalesce. Light refracts off the silver spokes, making the wheels appear to spin.

Leandra is cooking. An unsavory odor of singed bird flesh, the sound of hot spitting oil, terrorize my senses, and I want to cry out, *No,* as if I have finally found my way into a nightmare.

Weakly I defeat the bed's hold and falter toward the bathroom. The vomiting is violent and drives me to my knees. "All right." Leandra's hands grip my shoulders. "It's all right, Wim."

Then at last it is over and she is washing my face with a cool wet cloth. I try to struggle to my feet, but she presses me down. *Take your time.*

I barely have the strength to speak. "Your idea?" My throat burns. My tongue is thick and foul.

Leandra's fingers dig into the base of my neck. "Mine," she whispers. "Yes, mine."

"And Branch?"

"Ssh. Here." She grasps me below the arms and helps me to sit on the edge of the tub. "I asked him to help me," she says.

I nod. "Obliging."

"It was my idea," Leandra says. "I want to have it here for you when . . . in case you need it, Wim."

"And if I don't?"

Leandra crouches in front of me, her eyes leveling with mine. "It isn't bought, just rented." She keeps hold of my shoulders. *For dear life,* I think. If she let me go, I'd surely fall . . . my fall the proof she is waiting for, she and Branch. For one terrible instant I hate her.

I lose my balance, reach out with both hands, and cling to her warm bare arms.

"You're wasting your money."

"*Your* money." Her eyes are wet, but she won't stop smiling. "Turns out you don't need it, well, then we'll have something to laugh at," she says. "You see anything wrong with that?"

"I hate the fucking thing," I whisper.

Leandra tightens her grip on me. "Already got some use, then, ain't it?"

—∾—

By the time Pamela came home from the hospital, I knew she was lost to me. Time might pass and grief might ease and rage abate, but that would make no difference.

She hated me.

She would never let me go.

I had failed to protect my wife from what would destroy her. It wasn't as if I hadn't been warned. I suspected the future I faced was precisely the one I deserved.

By the time my wife returned home, of course, I'd been forced to confront the fact that I loved her sister.

That Leandra may have loved me as well, that was mere suspicion—my greatest dread and keenest longing, most wayward of my hopes.

I would hear her pacing in her room late at night, the wall between us thin and essential as membrane.

I never slept.

In the morning, while it was still dark and cold, I would hear her in the kitchen, punching down dough, beating eggs, tearing away the skins of tangerines and grapefruits.

When the smells of yeast and citrus and coffee wafted under my door, I would finally close my eyes and, for a few moments, rest.

It seemed to me that she never stopped cooking, though the two of us, together, barely ate enough to . . .

"Keep a bird alive." Leandra would say, smiling. "You got to keep your strength up."

"And you," I'd say. "What about you?"

"Me? Strong as an ox . . . eat like a horse . . . right as rain—you name it."

She taunted and teased me with her homely speech, her shop-worn expressions, knowing I was no match for them—knowing, I think, that in this way she could nearly always make me smile.

It was, otherwise, difficult to talk. And if we did not talk, it grew difficult to ignore how little we ate.

My throat was always blocked with something. I could not distinguish between anguish and yearning.

"You are what you eat," Leandra would tell me.

I am next to nothing, I thought.

But I was lying to myself, of course. Even as I grew insubstantial with grief, there was desire to give me heft, to delineate me.

What I amounted to was all hunger.

Across the table, morning after morning, night after night, Leandra watched me with famished eyes.

But how could I be certain what she wanted? She might simply have harbored the belief that I had explanations to offer . . . or hope . . . some comfort of a brotherly kind.

The night I came awake at Pamela's piano, stabbing that single raw note through the dark, everything changed, of course. Leandra and I barely touched, just leaned against one another for a few moments in the chill. But it might as well have been a violent act of possession that slammed us together. The thin and vital tissue that had separated us was irreparably torn.

Violation, penetration . . . my vocabulary for those few moments may seem overblown, but it is accurate. *Transgression.* And the altered nature of our relation was not mitigated by our refusals to acknowledge it. We struggled through meals in difficult silence or awkward conversation. Leandra continued to pace at night. The wall between us still, ostensibly, stood. It had been breached nonetheless, and we both knew it.

I suppose that one small infraction might have been erased eventually, had our conduct otherwise remained blameless. For Pamela was soon again in the house and demanding our full attention. Her silent refusal to thrive seemed only to thicken the air of complicity.

Leandra cooked more than ever. She did so much cleaning that Josie complained she could hardly find a thing to occupy her and even, for a time, left us. But my sister-in-law had found an unsuspected soft spot in Josie Andrade's severe Yankee heart. Soon Josie was back, her spare alto conversation harmonizing in the kitchen with Leandra's lighter, more supple tones. I could hardly understand a word they were saying, yet the pitch of grief, the vibrato of sympathetic affection, carried to me, and I knew a pained and sudden envy for the fluid tongues women seem born with.

Pamela, however, remained cloistered in silence.

I returned to teaching.

Summer began, sluggishly, to bestir itself.

There were a large lawn, a few small flowerbeds to tend. I took down the storm windows, put up the screens.

We might, had Pamela remained quiet, have found our status quo: a conventionally miserable unconventional little family. Still life: childless couple with maiden sister-in-law, posed frozen in a doorway festooned with black crepe.

Following her discharge from the hospital, Pamela had kept to her bed for several weeks, stringently fasting and breaking her vow of silence only to make known her most vital and immediate needs—water, say, or an extra blanket. And of course, *Just leave me alone.*

There was no earthly reason now for her not to get up, Dr. Hathaway told me.

She simply didn't care to, Pamela indicated, when pressed.

The doctor—an obstetrician, after all—could no longer offer house calls. The last time she came, she slipped me a scrap of paper with the names of three psychiatrists on it. Two of the three were women. All of them were "highly competent," Dr. Hathaway said.

"A shrink?" Pamela was hardly inclined to be open-minded on the subject.

"It's only natural you'd be depressed, Pamela."

"I am not depressed," she said.

I kept the scrap of paper in my wallet, behind my organ donor card, on the off chance I might decide to see one of the psychiatrists myself.

Soon Leandra delicately broached the subject of returning to North Carolina. "Pammy Jo don't need me."

"You don't know that, Leandra."

"She told me so herself—not a thing for me to do here anymore, she said." Her face was tranquil, but her eyes made no bones about hurt and shame.

"Leandra," I said gently, "look at her. Do you really think your sister is any judge of what she may need right now?"

She glanced away. "I wish she would cry," she whispered. "Pammy needs—"

"Yes, she does," I said. "And what about me, Leandra? Do you suppose I could manage this"—my gaze wandered around the spotless kitchen—"alone?"

"Might be without me here the two of you'd be talking."

"Do you honestly think so?"

Leandra sighed.

"Please," I said. "I can't let you—"

"But what if it's me causing the trouble?" She looked down at her hands.

"You know better, Leandra."

She raised a wan face. "I'm not sure I do," she said.

"Pamela shouldn't be alone," I said.

"She has you." Leandra closed her eyes for a moment. "Which is how I know she'll be all right."

"Leandra . . ." Something started to come unraveled inside me, to shred. "Leandra, look at me," I said softly. "Do I appear to possess the strength and comfort your sister needs?"

She took a step toward me, stretched out one hand as if to touch my arm, then pulled back, her face slanted away.

"What Pammy needs and what she thinks she needs don't quite match up sometimes," she said.

"What your sister needs and what I've got to offer don't often tally, either." My voice, bitter and bridled, might have been my father's. "Leandra," I whispered, "*I* need you."

Her face hid nothing of what the admission inflicted upon her. Perhaps my own concealed even less.

"Do you hear me?" I said. "Please."

Finally, Leandra nodded. "But I got no business here," she said in a low voice. "We both need to remember that."

Before I could answer, Leandra slipped into the hallway. I heard the door to her room, ten paces away, click closed behind her in the dark.

—⁓—

In mid-June Pamela began to get up for an hour or two each day and play the piano. She could not, given her long estrangement from the instrument, have done much of anything that would strike me as more startling or eccentric.

After years of lessons we could not afford, long days of practice that often reduced her to tears of rage and frustration, Pamela had seemed to develop a violent enmity toward the fine (albeit used) instrument it had taken us four years to pay for. The last months she'd played, Pamela had appeared to be attempting to beat the old Steinway into submission rather than to produce anything like music. Chopin was banished, Mozart and Bach were exiled. She took up Tchaikovsky and Rachmaninoff, grandiose repertory that lent itself, in amateur hands, to all manner of excess. Pamela stomped on the pedals with her whole weight, levitating from the slightly wobbly bench, and left a few of the ivories chipped.

Now, however, the tantrums of high feeling appeared to be over. Tragedy and romance had lost their place of honor in Pamela's repertoire. Chopin returned, and with him Scriabin, Debussy. Liszt . . . but only the more studious and exacting études. She applied herself with particular devotion to a concerto that sounded as if Shostakovich had composed it with Stalin pacing a tight perimeter around him. Pamela played its constrained passages slowly, repetitiously, as if fulfilling a tedious obligation. The music laid a thin veneer of composure over the shattered house.

—∞—

Such a brittle and transparent coating was bound, of course, to crack under pressure.

One sun-splashed Sunday in late June, I'd just finished cutting the grass and was out in the garage, cleaning and oiling the blades of the lawn mower before putting it away, when I heard screams, the sound of breaking glass.

I ran in the back door and through the kitchen. The shrieks and shattering seemed to be coming from the living room. A voice that didn't sound quite human seemed unable to stop screaming.

My wife, wrapped in a dark-violet caftan, was standing on the piano bench. Her face was livid and contorted, her hair a wild disorder covering her eyes and sticking to her wet lips.

Accompanied by long arpeggios of wordless fury, Pamela was reaching into the high shelves of the nearby étagère, plucking out the pieces of handblown glass we'd collected, hurling them, one by one, across the room. At her sister.

Leandra, her face as white as the woolen carpeting, the linen slipcovers, stood frozen on a widening glacier of shattered glass. Her head was bowed. Her hands, hanging at her sides, made no attempt to protect her from the hard bright bubbles flying toward her head. Blood trickled from a small gash on her left cheek. Her eyes were closed.

A large pear-shaped vase, swirled with color like ribbon candy, sailed above Leandra's head and exploded against the wall, showering us all with brilliant splinters.

Pamela went on screaming, as if still frantic to get our attention.

An iridescent glass apple, rose gold, burst in her hands. Blood bloomed on her palms, blossomed from the tips of her fingers. One small red petal dropped to the floor.

"Get out," I whispered. "Leandra, just go."

Leandra did not move. She did not open her eyes.

My wife's screams, her blood, meant nothing to me.

I grabbed hold of Leandra's shoulders and pushed her ahead of me from the room, through the house, out the back door.

The car stood in the driveway, the keys in it. I'd planned to wash it when I'd finished with the grass. Without thinking what I was doing, I put Leandra in the car and drove off. I believed I could still hear my wife's screams when we were miles away.

Beside me, Leandra sat rigid. The cut on her face was superficial, a trickle of blood already drying on her cheek like a long, dark, jagged scar.

I kept to back roads, making mindless, arbitrary turns now and then. I had no idea where I might be going, but I have the impression, now, that I may have been making wider and wider circles around the house, moving away from Pamela slowly, obliquely, perhaps concealing my intentions from myself.

We drove for at least twenty minutes, I think, before I said a word.

"Are you all right?"

Leandra, her eyes still closed, nodded.

"What happened? Can you tell me?"

She said nothing.

"All right," I said. "Never mind."

She began, quietly, to cry.

I started to turn down the road to the covered bridge, then realized a beautiful Sunday in early summer would likely be drawing a crowd. I sped through the intersection and kept going until I reached a nearly concealed dirt road that cut off to the east.

The lovely old farm stretched along the backside of the town reservoir, fifty acres or more of what must once have been grazing land, now overgrown. Crumbling stone walls gridded the woods. The farmhouse had been perfectly preserved for three centuries. The property was posted, but the couple who owned it never left Manhattan, I knew, until just before the Fourth of July.

I drove down past the house across the bumpy pasturage and nosed into an alcove of pines near the water.

Leandra had stopped crying. Her eyes were still closed.

"Can you tell me now?" I said.

She shook her head.

I got out of the car and went around to open the passenger door. When Leandra didn't move, I reached inside the car, took her hand, and guided her out. She put up no resistance. I kept hold of her hand as we walked to the reservoir's edge.

I found a small swell of earth that was not too damp. I sat Leandra on a large rock there.

"Wait here. Leandra, will you wait for me?"

For the first time she seemed to see me then. She was trembling. She wrapped her arms around herself.

"Just for a minute," I said. "All right?"

"Yes." Her voice was no more than a whisper.

I came back with an old plaid car blanket, which I spread on the ground, and a gray hooded sweatshirt. I wrapped the sweatshirt around Leandra's shoulders. Then I sat down on the blanket.

"It's warmer over here," I said, "in the sun."

She sat down on the ground beside me, her back half turned. A chicken hawk arced through the sky, then made a sudden straight drop behind the treeline like a stunt pilot going into a stall. The dark water glittered.

"She was playing," Leandra said softly. "But only scales. I thought it was all right."

I waited.

"I should know not to talk when she's playing," Leandra said.

My knees were drawn up in front of me. I leaned forward, resting my head on them.

"Always been afraid of her," Leandra whispered. "You know it?"

"Yes," I said. "So have I."

I didn't realize I was crying until I felt Leandra's hands on my shoulders.

I wept for what seemed a long time, making no sound, but my body racked by some force that left me, at last, exhausted.

Then I was still, except for the shivering. The sun was lukewarm. It was never really summer there until mid-July.

"How'd you come to find this place?" Leandra said.

"Pamela found it. A long time ago."

"Pammy Jo always could do that," she said. "Find beautiful secret places. When I found one myself, always somebody'd got there before me, seemed like."

She paused and I heard, far distant, the percussion of a woodpecker's industry echoing over the water.

Leandra laughed softly. "Used to sneak around after her," she said, "see where-all she'd go. Pammy'd mostly get tired of a place soon enough. Then I could have it for my own."

I felt the sweatshirt, warmed by her body or the sun, laid across my back.

I raised my head. Leandra wound the sleeves around my shoulders, dried my face with one cuff.

I gazed out over the reservoir. The water, the blackish blue of my wife's eyes, looked freezing.

"Some of them places so lovely," Leandra said, "it's a wonder she could bear to give them up."

I looked at her then. Her gray eyes, lightened by sunlight, slightly swollen with crying, were guileless. She was hardly more than a child.

I reached into my trouser pocket for a handkerchief, wet one corner with my tongue. Then, my eyes intent on her, I began trying to wipe the blood from Leandra's cheek.

She flinched, pushed my hand away.

"Does it hurt?" I said.

"It hurts when you look at me," she said.

"I won't look, then," I said. "I swear."

I tried to turn my eyes away. Leandra tried too. It was more than we could manage.

I dropped the handkerchief on the ground, saw the wind take it. I cupped the back of her head in both hands, her straight fine hair woven through my fingers. My mouth moved over her face, and the taste of salt coated my lips, then my tongue.

Leandra's hands pressed against my chest, as if to push me from her. Then her fingers were clutching my shirt, pulling me close. "No, Wim," she said. "No." And: "I am so truly sorry."

It was she, I think, who unbuttoned her blouse, I who lowered the straps of the soft cotton camisole underneath. But perhaps not.

I tore at my shirt. I wanted, at first, just a single moment to feel her skin against my skin. No more than a moment's warmth. And my mouth . . .

But it was not enough, of course. That could hardly have been enough.

—~—

The day's light had all but died by the time we returned. We did not speak, or touch, in the car.

I pulled in close to the back door. No lights were on inside. Leandra moved quietly ahead of me through the shadows of the kitchen. At the end of the hallway she ducked into the guest room, glancing back at me once, her eyes filled with shame.

I tried, pointlessly, to reassure her with a smile.

The door clicked shut.

In the living room, shards of glass glowed pink and orange across the white carpet, absorbing the light of the setting sun. The keyboard was covered, the bench overturned below it. A milk-glass vase lay on its side on top of the piano, in a pool of water and scattered jonquils with broken stems.

It was Leandra, finally, who found her. Pamela lay on the bathroom floor beside a bathtub brimming with scarlet water. Two flat black razor blades, slightly rusted, were on the edge of the tub. She had evidently held her wrists in the water until she lost consciousness. There was only a little blood around her on the floor.

Leandra called the police. I could not leave the bathroom until they arrived. *Come away,* Leandra said. *Come away now, Wim. Close the door, sit down somewhere.* But staying there, with my wife, seemed the one decency I might still observe.

The coroner was a tired-looking man in rumpled golf clothes that seemed, under the circumstances, unnaturally bright. He interviewed me first, then Leandra, in the kitchen. His questions were mercifully blunt and brief. When I told him about the recent birth and death of our infant son, he nodded smartly, perhaps relieved to have found a neat explanation for a potentially messy situation. Statistics on postpartum depression were included in his condolences.

I did not contradict him, or make any claims for my own culpability.

"Extremes of despair," the coroner said. "You'd be amazed, Mr. Cantwell, how many women, even women who deliver healthy babies, can just . . . and even those right there in the same house don't always . . ."

All that screaming. But it wasn't quite true, I suddenly realized, that not a single word was intelligible to me. . . .

Don't think you can go now, Wim. No, Wim. Please. Don't think you can just walk away and leave me here.

Pamela appeared to have been dead for at least an hour, the coroner said.

I'd have sworn I didn't, at the time, hear a word I could have made sense of.

My sin the sin of betrayal—or simply that most standard of sins, pride. Whatever possessed me to believe my stunted, measly love could penetrate to the core of her need, could adequately clothe such naked need?

And was it merely that she craved someone to vouch for—not nakedness, nor the beauty that concealed the need, but simply for the need itself, unadorned?

Is somebody there, Wim? Can anybody see?

—ʌʌ—

There is only the slightest scar, a tiny pale star just below Leandra's left cheekbone. A person would have to know it was there in order to spot it, I think. That one cross-stitch of skin stays white when the rest of her face, exposed to the sun, turns golden.

Pamela died with a long red slash low on her belly, only beginning to heal. Though I knew it could not be so, I imagined her blood flowing from that wound rather than her wrists . . . a bloodbath, and I its sole witness.

Leandra chose the dress her sister was to be buried in, a simple raw silk sheath the shade of terra-cotta. Pamela had worn the dress just once—a faculty dinner at my school. It looked nothing like her, in fact. Being my wife was a part that, on occasion, she dressed for.

The suit Leandra wore to the funeral, another of Pamela's wifely disguises, was black linen, a poor fit on Leandra, though I'd have said, insisted, the sisters were just the same size.

Pamela had scarcely been outdoors in months. Her hair, untouched by the sun, had darkened. The fire had gone out of it. Though one good summer might have brought it back.

In the mornings, when Leandra intends to work, she draws her hair back and confines it in an elastic band. The faint silver strands at her temples show only then. They never fail to startle me. She is—what? Thirty-one? Pamela was thirty-one when she died. Leandra's birthday is in August. Pamela's was in March. Leandra is already the older, but too young, by far, for graying hair.

Leandra wore white when we buried my child—a shirtwaist dress as plain as a nurse's uniform, a cheap pair of white patent-leather shoes.

Pamela dressed mostly in rich vivid colors—aubergine and garnet, celadon and teal. She had a gift for choosing what suited her, for altering what did not.

Leandra's clothes are faded to the hues of shadow, lavenders and grays and dusty blues, prints that have lost their definition.

We rarely speak of her sister now.

But we continue to listen, as if we might yet attend to her every word.

—⁂—

When we returned to the house after the funeral, Leandra's bags, already packed, were standing by the door. Her plane would leave from Hartford at five o'clock. Driving into Boston would have been impossible at that hour.

"You cannot go." I'd said it several times.

"I cannot stay." Leandra had corrected me gently.

"Yes," I said. "I know."

I went outside to check the oil in the car. It would be a long trip.

When I returned to the house, Leandra was in the kitchen, making sandwiches. Neither of us had eaten for several days. She had changed into a gray skirt, a white blouse, faded blue tennis shoes.

I set an oblong jeweler's box, black velvet, on the counter beside a loaf of bread.

Leandra looked at it, not me, with heartsick eyes. Her face had taken on the pure opacity of a moonstone. "What's this?"

"Something I want you to have."

She shook her head, picked up a knife, pared the red wax from a wedge of Gouda cheese.

"Please," I said.

"No." Pale-gold slices dropped onto the bleached butcher block.

I picked up the black box, pulled back the springed lid. The antique wristwatch inside was rose gold. The Roman numerals on its pearly face were small and hard to read.

"I got it for Pamela," I said. "You should have it."

"I never wear a watch." Leandra's hands were trembling. I took the knife and set it down. "I don't want anything," she said.

"Just take it away, then, please."

She looked up at me finally. I hated myself for the helplessness

I saw on her face. I grabbed her wrist and clasped the watch around it. "I don't care what you do with it," I said.

After a moment Leandra nodded. She did not look at me again.

When Leandra had gone, I found Pamela's black linen suit hanging in the closet, slightly set apart from the rest of the vibrant clothes, like a stern teacher overseeing a roomful of unruly pupils. I leaned into the closet, bringing my face close to the jacket's dark lapel. It seemed to me that I could smell Pamela's perfume, Leandra's hair . . . a fanciful notion, surely.

I did not go home that night, after seeing Leandra to her plane. I stayed in a motel in Windsor Locks, as if remaining near the airport kept Leandra in reach. In the room above mine, someone was pacing, and the television stayed on all night.

—≈—

The modest trickle of blood on her thigh had stunned me. I might have wiped it away, but by then my bloodied handkerchief had been taken by the wind. Years afterward, I continued to dream that she occupied a hidden room in my house, Leandra and a child whose cries were muffled by a door I could not locate. Reared in darkness, my son . . .

There was hardly any blood on the floor.

Too many years by too little light . . . it takes a toll on the vision.

Leandra's face was half healed already by the time she left.

I cannot stay.

I know.

And then, before you know it, the damage is done.

All night someone pacing up there. Dim blue light.

Don't think you can just walk away and leave me here.

Now, in memory, I carry a picture of my wife that is both indelible and vague. I tend to remember Pamela more as someone I once saw than someone I knew.

Vivid.

Unforgettable.
Obscure.

—∞—

"Wim?"

Leandra is beside me in the dark. I cannot see her. We are not touching. This bed is too big to suit me, she says sometimes.

I can see nothing. I feel her there. I can barely remember, thankfully, the time when she was not.

. . . memories draped by the beneficent spider...

Dying makes one's history something of an abstraction, it seems.

"I'm here," I tell her. "Right here, love."

"We probably ought to talk about a few things," she says.

I cannot.

Yes . . . I know.

My blind fingers grope along the edge of her pillow, find her face, search for the small white star. But it refuses to be found.

Her arms slip around me, drawing me close. When she whispers, her breath is warm against my neck.

"You think He blames us?" she asks. "When it was Him set the trap in the first place?"

I need not, after these months with her, ask who she means. "Was that what it was, a trap?"

"Probably ain't the most respectful way of putting it." She laughs softly. "Reckon the Lord's well used to my loose tongue by now."

"He hears you—you truly believe that?"

"I count on it. Don't you?"

I shake my head, stirring up the pain. For a moment the blackness goes red and loud. "I honestly don't know, Leandra."

"Isn't it maybe about time to start asking around?" she whispers.

Even now, in the North's dead of winter, we have nights mild enough to sleep with a window raised. The birds, flapping and parrying in the stripped mulberry out back, sound clandestine.

"I've never stopped asking, Leandra."

"Asking yourself. But that's not the same."

"Is the light coming up?"

"Not for a good while yet."

"I simply couldn't love her enough, Leandra. I never even came close."

She touches my face. "Couldn't nobody do that," she says. "Not for what she needed."

"That doesn't excuse me."

"No." Her hand slips from my cheek. I grope and find it, a thin-skinned knot of knuckle bone I cannot untangle. "Nor me," she says. "I'm not sure it's excusing we need anyhow. Maybe only forgiving."

I smile. "Where your God comes in, no doubt."

"You know anybody else is up to the job?"

You come to mind, I want to tell her. But Leandra would never stand for that. "I don't see a surplus of candidates," I admit.

Leandra's laugh warms the air between us. It is the warming perhaps that prompts my small concession:

"Do you ever think maybe it's work we're just not cut out for?" I ask her. "It could be forgiveness is a talent—a skill only a deity could master. Like only an angel can dance on the head of a pin."

"That's where faith took you?" Leandra sighs. "What in the world am I going to do with you?"

I start to reply, then think better of it. After a few minutes I feel her body easing back into mine, her fingers loosening. I picture her hand opening like a rose, blooming scarlet between my chalky palms.

It is an act of faith, even in darkness, to close my eyes. When they open again, I believe there will be light, another whole day's worth, and my eyes to see me through most of it.

In time my every breath matches itself to one of Leandra's, rising slow and falling deep. I am asleep when her voice calls me back:

"How much farther you think you can go without God, Wim?"

"I'm in the dark," I remind her.

"Ssh," Leandra says.

"How would I begin to look, a blind man in the dark?"

"No need." Leandra lays her palm across my forehead, and the pain boiling beneath my skull drops to a simmer. "It's only a matter of letting Him find you," she says.

—~—

Grief, it seems, is indivisible. I have always been grateful for that. I would not have cared to see a strict accounting, a balance sheet of what my losses came to, how they broke down. Nor would an itemization of my deficits have been edifying.

I have loved only two women, cared considerably for a third. For none of them have I shown much profit, I'm afraid.

When I told Clio I was leaving, she replied, not unkindly, that I had never really been there, after all.

It was a claim I chose not to dispute.

"Your sister-in-law?" she said. "The girl down near Charleston somewhere?"

I nodded, mute. No more sense in quibbling over the fine points of geography.

"I knew it had to be someone." Clio sounded oddly satisfied: an annoying loose end lopped and tied.

"The house is in your name," I said. "As you know. The rest—"

"I don't need a thing," Clio said. "You must be aware of that?"

I looked at her, my wife of six years. Clio has grown, with age, sturdier, more handsome. She has broad cheekbones, deep-set eyes, a face that, at fifty, is curiously unlined. She is the only woman I have ever seen shown to true advantage by a mannish haircut. She possesses a perfectly formed skull. Her body is long and generous, her lovemaking straightforward and athletic. Clio's sheer self-possession has provided a kind of protection to me.

"I'm surprised," she said, surprising me. "You've never seemed the type."

"The type?" I assumed she was referring to Leandra's youth. I was disinclined to defend myself.

"You never *go* anywhere," Clio said. "However have you managed an affair?"

I was unaccountably shocked.

"You've kept her stashed around here somewhere? I suppose I might have paid more attention."

"I have not been unfaithful, Clio."

"No?" She smiled.

"I haven't seen Leandra in ten years. We don't even speak on the phone."

"Love letters seem so . . . passé," she said. "Even for you, darling."

I shook my head. "You don't understand."

"I don't," she admitted. "That hardly matters now, does it?"

We were sitting in the den, what had originally been the guest room. Clio was not keen on overnight company. She'd had a small fireplace added when she revised the room. We sat on either side of the fire, one of the season's first, in matching wing chairs with crewel-embroidered slipcovers—a couple posed by an unimaginative photographer to suggest domestic harmony.

Clio leaned forward, wiped a speck of dust from the cherry butler's table between us. She picked up a cut-glass ashtray, then set it down again. Neither of us had ever smoked.

"You're not making this up, are you?" she said. "This business about dying?"

I smiled at her, full of sudden fondness. "A splendid notion. But no, I'm afraid not."

She studied me for a moment. If there was not quite sorrow in her eyes, there were certainly sympathy, authentic regret.

"If you haven't seen her in ten years," she said, "how can you be sure she'll . . . ?"

"Have me?" I rested my elbows on my knees. "I can't," I said.

Clio stared at me for another minute but clearly found no reassurance there. Her gaze drifted past me, to the bookshelves. "Don Quixote," she said softly. "Is that it?"

I shrugged. "Perhaps."

"Poor Dulcinea," she said. Then, as if regretting the implied bitterness, Clio reached across the table and touched my knee.

"I don't even know what to wish for you," she said. "If you find what you want, that will only make dying sadder." Her fingers pressed into tendon. Muscle jumped in my thigh. "Won't it?" Clio asked softly.

I looked into the fire. "I don't know," I said.

A backdraft from the chimney tossed a little puff of ash against the brass fire screen.

"I didn't exactly plan this," I said.

"No," said Clio. "One wouldn't."

Her hand slipped from my leg as she stood up. Her back to me, she leaned over the fire, the heels of her strong hands pressed to the mantel's edge.

"I'm sorry," I said.

Clio shook her head. When she turned around, her face was neutral, slightly flushed.

"You could always come back," she said. "Assuming old Rosinante is good for a round trip."

—∞—

"You watch me like a hawk."

Leandra is thin and wan and electric with energy. The less I keep awake, the more she keeps working. Were I not here across from her at the table, keeping an eye on her, she would eat not at all.

I myself eat less and less, am able to keep down little of what I get down. Perhaps every third day now I am too weak to get out of bed until at least late afternoon. Soon, I know, it will come down to one day out of two, then . . .

"I watch you," I prompt her, "like . . . ?"

"An eagle?"

"Try lynx," I suggest.

"Never saw one." She takes a deep breath. "You been minding me like a Baptist preacher in a beer hall," she says.

"Colorful." I nod. "Really quite nice. But at odds with our meaning here. I want you to indulge, not abstain."

Leandra pauses, thinking. "You start minding your own p's and q's," she says, "reckon we wouldn't have to go through all this, would we?"

"Ah, but what would we talk about then?"

"I'm waiting for you to tell me," Leandra says.

I raise the dented lid to a tarnished pot. The cabbage, cooked white, is studded with bits of brick-red side meat. Fighting down nausea, I spoon some onto her plate. "Try this. It's tasty."

"How would *you* know?" Leandra says.

"I know what I know." I smile.

"You are wasting away, Wim."

My smile turns unforgivably jaunty. "That gives you no license to do the same."

"Would that be so bad?" Suddenly Leandra's eyes are wet. "*Would* it?"

"I don't want to hear that." My voice is low and furious.

Leandra bows her head. "I know." Then she looks up. "Starting to seem like half a world stands between us, Wim. How am I supposed to get across it?"

"Leandra, I don't—"

"I keep looking for a way between what you don't want to hear and what I got to say. Looks to be a mighty narrow path."

"I'm sorry."

"Reckon I know you don't intend it. What I don't know is how to keep on my feet and keep hold of you at the same time."

"You shouldn't have to keep hold of me."

"You expect I'm apt to let go a second sooner than I got to?"

On the stove the teakettle begins to whistle, then, unattended, to scream. I get up unsteadily, remove the kettle from the burner, turn off the flame. When I return to the table, Leandra has pushed her nearly full plate aside. A tiny porcelain hand with only two fingers lies palm-up beside her crumpled napkin.

"Feels like I'm losing you before I need to." Leandra's eyes are dry now, but her voice is thick with tears.

I sit down, scuffle my chair closer to hers. "I might be all right at the dying," I tell her. "I really might. It's doing it in front of you that seems to be my downfall."

She stares into my eyes. "You think it'd come easier with somebody else?"

"Maybe without anybody, or just . . ."

"Among strangers?"

"Disinterested parties." I try to smile.

She waves a hand, as if swatting my words from the air.

"I'm not sure I can stay here, Leandra."

"You made a promise."

"And in good faith." I nod. "But keeping it proves . . ."

"Hard?" Leandra picks up the doll's hand and studies it. "Hard don't give you the right to go back on your word. Hard don't cancel a thing."

"No," I say. "But you could."

She stares at the fractured hand for another moment, then slips it into the pocket of her overalls.

"Not in a million years," she says.

—~—

It astonishes and amuses me now to remember how virulently I hated him.

The day I first met Branch Goodlin, I succumbed to a bout of frantic jealousy—a dying man of fifty-four hilariously miscast in the role of a sullen sixteen-year-old, all rage and hormones and inadequacy.

I found his handsomeness insipid, his good health rude; I mistook his frankness for stupidity. Branch had been here before me and would be here long after. I wanted to soil and bully and make a fool of him, to beat him to a bloody pulp.

He wanted, Branch says, to do the same to me. We don't discuss why. We don't need to.

When we worked together, rebuilding these rooms, making them sound for Leandra, we might have been brothers, Branch and I. Now he watches my decline with helpless heartsick eyes, treating me with a son's deference. Branch Goodlin, my junior by a generation, is the closest thing to a friend that I have ever had.

It is Branch who is there, not Leandra, the first two times I fall. For which I would pour wine to the gods, were either—wine or gods—palatable to me now.

On the first occasion, it seemed to both of us mere civility to act as if the fall meant nothing. I was not hurt. An inconvenient rag rug was a more convenient explanation than a spell of dizziness, a sudden loss of strength. Branch is a sizable man, perhaps six foot one, a hundred and eighty-five pounds. I was nearly the same heft until a few months ago. Branch picked me up and set me on my feet without the slightest show of exertion.

"You all right?" he said.

I nodded.

"Women set out them little rugs like booby traps," Branch said. "Rather you'd break your neck than track in dirt."

We didn't look at each other.

"So you think property values haven't hit their peak yet?" I said.

Branch didn't blink. "Looks to me," he said, "like we might be in for another good year or two."

By the time Leandra came back from the shed, her arms filled with packing cartons and bubble wrap, Branch and I were hunched over the table, studying a surveyor's map.

Leandra's smile was indulgent. "You boys planning a trip?"

"Looking for buried treasure," I said.

"Buried, my foot," said Branch. "We are sitting pretty. This here pile of gold's right out in plain sight."

—~—

The second fall, this afternoon, was a little harder to gloss over. The right side of my body, from hip to knee, is bruised to the palette of a cyclone sky. It is only a matter of time, I suppose, until

Leandra spots the evidence. A blood rose is budding above my left eye, concealed by the slant of a painter's cap.

Leandra had not, so far as I knew, planned on going out. We'd had a good morning, making jam of the two pails of blackberries she picked yesterday. But the day was hot, the toast and broth I had for lunch did not agree with me. I was back in bed not long after noon, lulled by Dr. Kaplan's little capsules.

When I awoke the house seemed cooler. It must have been four or so. I opened my eyes to a milky light dappled with blind spots. I assumed the shadow in the bedside chair was Leandra, naturally.

"Nice life you got here, bud." Branch's voice sounded hollow. "Ain't had me a real nap since Carol Jean signed me up for matrimony."

I smiled. "Fortunate you found a wife who offsets your natural indolence."

"Can't hardly sit down for a minute." Branch's face was coming into focus. "Give me the heebie-jeebies with them lists she's always makin'." His grin was as counterfeit as his grousing.

"So you skulk over here to laze around," I said. "Nice arrangement."

"Long as I can get away with it."

"Good God, is that a necktie you're wearing?"

"Rotary," Branch said. "The best I can say is they gave us bread pudding for dessert. I suspicion there mighta been a bourbon bottle drug through the sauce."

"You country folk do know how to cut loose," I said.

"Yeah boy. And you shoulda heard the speaker—fella sellin' some new line of dog food down to the Feed and Grain. Showed slides and all." The grin was authentic now. "Regular barn burner," Branch said.

"Sorry I missed it," I said. "Where's Leandra?"

"Carol Jean carried her off somewhere. I wouldn't want to guess."

"Errands?"

"Whatever-all they mean by that." He nodded. "Do her some good, anyhow, to get out awhile."

I didn't say anything.

Branch stopped smiling, "Leandra's all right, Willy. How about you?"

"Not bad," I said.

"You hurting?"

I shrugged. "Had enough rest?" I asked him. "It's time I got up."

"Good," Branch said. "Maybe give me a chance to grab the bed before the girls get back."

Laughing, I sat up and lowered my feet cautiously to the floor.

"Give you a hand?"

"No, thanks."

As I tried to stand, the whole lower half of my body seemed to go numb. Branch wasn't quite quick enough to catch me. I collapsed, striking my head on the corner of the night table as I went down.

"Aw, damn." Branch sounded terrified. "Damn it all to hell, Willy."

"I'm all right," I said.

"Your head's cut up. Don't know as we ought to move you."

"I'll move myself," I said. "Just give me your hand."

"You sure?"

When I looked up, I couldn't see him. I smiled. "You're enjoying this, aren't you?" I said. "Me on the floor at your feet."

"You are a contumacious old coot, you know it?"

Branch grasped me under the arms and pulled me up, then lowered me to the edge of the bed.

I sat still for a minute, getting my bearings. The darkness was thick and smelled of decay. Branch kept hold of my shoulders. I felt a trickle of blood trailing past my left ear.

"I'm all right," I said again.

"Damn, I hate this." Branch let go of one shoulder. I could sense his bulk, looming over me. "How many?" he said.

"What?"

"How many fingers am I holding up?"

"Don't tell me," I said. "Marcus Welby, M.D., right?"

"Can't see one blessed thing," Branch whispered, "can you?"

"I can get along without the sight of your pushy beak for a minute or two," I said.

"Cut it out, Willy."

"It comes and goes, Branch. You know that."

He was quiet for a moment. Both of us were breathing hard, our breaths overlapping.

"I got the idea it comes a good bit more than it goes these days, don't it?" His big rough hand clamped around the back of my neck. Then I felt him blotting the cut on my head with tissue.

"Damn," I said. "I hate this too."

"Leandra know?"

"Some," I said. "It's pretty obvious."

"You reckon they could do something about it?" Branch said. "In a hospital, I mean?"

"No."

He sighed. Then his hands slipped from me and I felt him moving away.

The darkness was easing to a mottled appaloosa light. I imagined myself galloping through a landscape riddled with shadowy obstacles, dangers passing in a blur.

I heard Branch's footsteps coming toward me again, accompanied by another sound, faint and unfamiliar, a glide with a little squeak in it.

Then it stopped. "Can you see me?"

"Yes," I said.

And I nearly could. His white shirt was like a sun dog in a frigid sky, his tie a dark slash bisecting his chest. He stood near me, but so far above, leaning down over a boxy blue-and-silver cloud.

I reached out and touched the padded arm of the wheelchair.

"Get in," Branch said.

"Absolutely not."

"Trial run," he said. "That's all."

"Son," I said, "you are getting way ahead of yourself."

"I don't think so," he said. "Come on."

"You wouldn't be in such a rush if it were your ass about to be deposited in that insult of a conveyance," I told him.

I could see his face now, enough to see him flinch. I pressed my advantage. "Would you?"

His eyes, perhaps because they could see more clearly than mine, backed down first.

"Bully boy," he said.

"I'll let you know when I'm ready to be an invalid."

"Right. And in the meanwhile you got a runty little ninety-eight-pound woman with a half-broke heart to pick you up? Sweetheart of a deal," Branch said.

I closed my eyes.

"Get in," he said.

"I'm not ready."

"I know." He set the brake on the wheelchair, put down the footrest. Then, with no trouble at all, Branch Goodlin pulled me up from the bed, turned me around, and forced me down into the soft sling of seat.

"Fuck this," I said. "Fuck it."

The long passageway into the other room quivered with light. I imagined Branch's strong blunt hands fast on the rubber grips.

"Release the brake," he said. "On your right. That's it."

At my back, Branch leaned down and kissed the crown of my head, exactly on the spot where I have always known my hair would first go thin, just as my father's did. It has, insofar as I can tell, yet to happen.

We lurched forward, bumped the doorframe.

"Hang on, boy," Branch said. "Now you are really going to go places."

—∞—

"On the Fourth they'll have fireworks," Leandra says. "Out along the highway, where the old fairgrounds used to be. You never seen anything like it."

I see them already, scribbles of light, pink and green and mandarin trajectories plummeting, dying out before they hit the ground.

"Oh, Wim, you got to see!"

Gold and silver spider mums bursting into bloom against the blackness, sharp petals of light endlessly falling.

—∞—

Wrenched rhyme—the device of treating groups of words as if each were a single word:

Frail unset moon,
Pale sunset soon.

Give it here.
Live it dear.

Et cetera.

Rhyme, I saw, could not be wrenched from a prosaic soul.

Or perhaps it could, but rhyme was simply not sufficient.

Never enough.

For years it was the light by which I lived, poetry. I would die without it, I thought, a somewhat puerile conjecture that now, in the end, will hold true: *I shall die without it.* The heat and the light and the life of me, my failing at it the best of me, and finally the death, the end of me: *without it.* For I found it a pushy and discommoding thing, poetry, with which to share a life. The true poet's vocation leaves room for little else. Was it room I could not spare . . . or simply fear that, in the end, the room might prove empty?

The two rooms I now occupy with Leandra are open to the sky, receptive to all whimsy of light and weather. . . .

Shall I depart by corridors of light? They say we do. . . .

They say we are hurled headlong into such brilliance as the living would deem unbearable. . . .

They say those we embraced in life stand bathed in radiance as they receive us . . . and those we betrayed, or merely failed, no matter how spectacularly, are found folded within wings of longanimity, and the very firmament reeks of pardon. . . .

Isn't that what they say?

—∞—

Leandra sits now at a distance from where I lie, as if fearful of pilfering the air that keeps me alive. I still have moments of perfect clarity. She is wreathed in shadows, attired, festooned in shade.

A squat lamp with a punched tin shade draws a spotty scrim of light between us.

Her small white hands lie palm-up on her knees, slightly bowled, as if just by waiting she might catch something of which she might make use.

Now Leandra no longer works as she keeps vigil over me. Like a postulant in some arcane religious order, she has renounced industry—vanity, perhaps?—as she awaits the coming of grace. She does not sew. Neither does she weep.

"Oh, stop it," I say. "For God's sake."

"What, love?" She bows over me. Her hands cannot help themselves. She bastes the hem of the bedsheet to my chin with invisible stitches. "What is it, Wim?"

"Dreaming," the he I am become mutters. He is irritable, terse. "Don't mind me."

A needle of pain stabs somewhere deep in my skull. The pain has no point, no edges. I can no longer determine where the pain ends and I begin. But no—isn't it the other way around?

"Where is it?" Leandra whispers.

That's for me to know and you to— "Hah," I say.

"Just tell me *where*. Wim?"

"Haystack," he mutters. That ought to keep her busy for a while.

I think that under the covers I have an erection. I'm sure I do. I've had it for days, for weeks. Leandra would surely see, if only she did not insist on keeping me covered with so many blankets. Muffling my passion. Perhaps she is afraid. Maybe she looks at me when I am asleep, pulls back the sheet and shudders and adds another blanket. Keeping my need under wraps, weighting it down. My chest and groin are slick with sweat. I reek. My blood is boiling.

"Your mouth," the old man says. "Try that." Then he giggles, old fool. He is addled and mean. He is filthy.

Leandra, my pilgrim soul, devout, bends lower, nearly prostrating herself over this altar where so swiftly I become relic.

But he is no believer in sacrifice, this profane old man. One bony hand devils out from under the blankets and makes a grab for her breast.

Leandra pulls back, too quick for him. He has frightened her. For shame. He appalls her. He laughs.

Her hands enshroud me again, sweet flesh and supple tendon firmly winding rotting linen, binding finger bones turned to powder.

"No."

"Hush," Leandra says.

I close my eyes. The old man's ugly smile masks the remains of my face.

"You are doing this on purpose." The stern sister's face looms over me. "Aren't you?"

Such purity. "Your mouth," I say. "Just look how hard—" I try to throw off the blankets but cannot lift them, cannot find . . .

"You get yourself straight back here right now," Leandra says. "I mean it, Wim."

Raising holy hell.

(Come in under the shadow of this red rock),
And I will show you something different from either
Your shadow at morning striding behind you

Or your shadow at evening rising to meet you;
I will show you fear in a handful of dust.

Sometimes now in the night Leandra reaches out for me. I know she is asleep. She has the smallest hands. The soft pouch of my flesh does not begin to fill them. Her art does not suffice here, does not even serve. Spare parts . . . perhaps what her curved hands have been awaiting, there, just outside the dim pellicular light.

The white sea widening on a farther shore the bird the beating bird and I the drowned Phoenician Sailor . . .

(Those pearls that were his eyes. Look!)

—~—

The baby may have been, I see now, more real to his aunt than to his parents: not a territorial dispute, a nightmare, or a dream, but simply a child. She had unabashed designs on his love. She wore her mourning for her nephew, my son, in her eyes. Her eyes grew dark as widow's weeds.

Her mouth collapsed around her grief for her sister—my wife. Her lips rarefied, lost color. A full confession, indelible, could be read upon her face.

Jets keened in the air above us as she moved away from me. We must not see each other again, she said. I watched her pass through a detecting device, a blank and empty doorway without defining walls or messages. There was a shriek. Leandra recoiled. A wide-hipped woman in a strict blue uniform halted her, summoned her back. She was, for a moment, detained there, within my sight.

A reprieve, I thought. I started toward her.

Without looking back in my direction, Leandra removed her wristwatch and dropped it into a red plastic bowl. A nosegay of keys, fished from a pocket, was confiscated like contraband.

A second security guard stood at the other side of the vacant portal. Noisy static came from a black plastic box clipped to his belt.

Leandra passed in perfect silence through the gate. Passed with flying colors. Her belongings were returned to her. She walked to a nearby trash barrel and dropped watch and keys inside.

The present falls away, the present falls away . . .

The male guard kept his eyes on me. To look away, I thought, would constitute an admission.

By the time I had passed scrutiny, Leandra was far down the polished corridor. I could not, had she turned around, have seen her mouth or eyes.

She passed, unscathed, through long knives of white light. The floor looked treacherous and slick. I lost all perspective. Leandra grew larger as she moved away.

The guard was eyeing me again. I nodded. We were not quite on speaking terms. He crossed his arms on his chest and glanced elsewhere.

The passageway was not endless, after all. Leandra vanished through a door. Her body was a grief, indivisible. The door was a black chasm.

Into the eternal darkness, into fire and into ice . . .

"Hey."

He must have circled, come up from behind. The squawk box, still now, was in his hand.

"Man, are you waiting for someone?" he said.

—w—

The last time I saw my father, he told me I was not likely to amount to much.

"Folks spend half their lives saying things they don't half mean," Leandra says.

We are listening to the news. Or, rather, she is. I am listening to her listen. I cannot see her. I hear the growing stillness in her, her poise against the pull of all that would do harm in the world. My death, already, has changed her.

A conservative gubernatorial candidate is elucidating his stance on capital punishment. *I'd be pleased to flip the switch myself,* he says.

Leandra turns down the radio.

"You believe in purgatory?" she says.

Trick question. I believe in Dante, I want to tell her. "Purgatory." I smile. Leandra well knows I've been unable to summon up a single conviction about an afterlife, even now that the matter has taken on a certain immediacy.

"I figure there's got to be one," she says. "A place we can stop to eat our words before we go barging into heaven."

These people need to see, the politician says sotto voce, *that we mean bidness.*

"And hell?" I say. "That's reserved for those with an eternity of words to eat, I suppose?"

"You don't go to hell for *saying* things." I watch her come into focus. "You got to do some serious evil to get yourself there." How easily she smiles. "You got to mean *bidness,* if it's hell you're after."

I sigh.

Her smile wavers and fades. "What I'm saying is, you got to *intend* the harm."

I close my eyes. "Most of the harm we do—we *cause*—is inflicted without an inkling of our own intentions. We just don't think—"

"Wait." Leandra is pressing down on my chest with both hands. "I am not finished, Wim."

Her hands are forcing air from my lungs. My chest feels hollow, and the air is scarlet water.

"You got to intend the harm first. Then you got to spit in the Lord's eye when He offers you forgiveness."

I open my eyes, finding myself suddenly defenseless against her deep gray gaze. Her image quivers and drifts, submarine, inundated. I try to speak her name and cannot.

Gradually, her hands let up on my chest, and I start breathing again.

"He got forgiveness to spare, Wim, you hear me?" Her mouth close to my ear. "He mostly don't take no for an answer if He can help it."

"I hope you're right," I say.

Leandra eases down beside me on the bed. I lie on my side, facing her, my knees half bent. I imagine I look like a man who jumped from a tenth-story window and died before hitting the ground.

Leandra, her back to me now, inches over, fitting her body to the angles of mine. I am become all angles. Her head is tucked under the sharp point of my chin.

"I know what you're doing here, Wim," she says softly. "Even if you don't."

My smile is wrenching. I don't know why I put my face through it when she's not even watching. "I'm not doing much," I say.

"Don't make light of me."

"Yes." My face eases back into the shape of woe. "All right."

"You think it's me needs to forgive you, or can," she says. "It's not."

"Did you ever stop to count your losses, Leandra? Figure out who to charge them to?"

"It don't figure out that way."

What we got here is a gov'mint's been spending money like a drunken sailor on shore leave, the candidate says.

"What you got to do, Wim, is forgive yourself . . . for what couldn't be helped."

I remember the cool blue absolution of Dr. Hathaway's eyes. "That is not up to me," I say. I am not up to that.

"Maybe not." Leandra shifts closer, her backside pressing into my groin. "But we, all of us, got to take care of a good many things that ain't exactly up to us."

I say it's them *ought to pay, not us.* The radio crackles.

We appreciate your candor, sir. The woman newscaster sounds slightly stunned. *Thank you for talking with us.*

No problem, the candidate says.

"Leandra?"

"I'm here." She fills my arms, defines my body.

"Did Pamela *have* to die, do you think? I mean, if we . . ."

"She chose."

"But if . . ."

"No," Leandra says. "I know what you mean to be asking, just don't know the answer. I only know we sinned against her—we did—and then spent the rest of our lives being sorry."

"The rest of *my* life anyway."

Leandra rolls away, comes to rest facing me from a distance. I think that if I could only see her face I would know something I need to know. But what?

"You think I'm going to stop being sorry," Leandra whispers, "with you gone?"

"I didn't mean . . ."

She touches my cheek. "I know that."

"I haven't been as sorry as I should be, Leandra, these last months."

"Nor I. The Lord understands that too, I reckon."

"He gives us a lot of leeway, this God of yours."

I can hear her smile. "Ain't that just what I been trying to tell you?" she says.

Serenade—a love lyric, similar to *aubade* but set at, or addressed to, evening.

"You need to get some sleep, Lannie."

"No, not now."

Their voices are so close that I imagine them beside me in the bed. Imagine how Branch's hands first soothe, then arouse her. The skin between his knuckles with a fine gold down, but darker, coarser where the known quantity of his brother body, still young and no stranger . . .

"I don't know what to do that can give you—"

"Just what you're doing, Branch. I—"

"You've got to let me—" How his hands possess her.

And her body's unfurling like a fiddlehead in earliest spring, all tenderness, and Branch's boy's hands' gentle straining toward the roots of . . .

An insidious tenderness.

There in the bed, right beside me.

Hands that can do anything.

"Willy?"

"Ssh," Leandra says.

"Is he . . . ?"

"He dreams," she says.

"Leandra, couldn't I just—"

"Maybe later, all right?"

Their voices move away from me at the approximate speed of light.

Light is something I remember. There beside me in the bed. Buried deep. Remember perfectly.

There.

Light.

In her.

I dream.

His heart outside his body, as if it could not wait to give itself away . . .

I would, in Leandra's heaven, meet him at last, my son, no helpless infant now but an angel, full-blown and potent. Introductions performed by a benign and paternal God, who would then with divine tact stand back to see how, on our own, we hit it off, to hear my boy's offer to show me the ropes of eternity. And my own exhausted anecdotes of a world gone sour . . . but no, I too would be an angel, not some tedious old man full of grievances and aches, were only Leandra's vision of Kingdom Come . . .

I know what you think, Wim. The fortune-teller's distant smile reaching the Sweet Hereafter. *I know what I know.*

I can, to a point, almost envision it, eternal bliss rendered domestic, one great family reunion where sins are checked like coats in the vestibule, peccadilloes as easily lost and forgotten as umbrellas. But such fancies shun one indispensable baffle, of course: Pamela. How should I, even with angelic countenance, once more come face-to-face with my bride, she slaughtered, I maimed? No vision of heaven has the largesse to contain such mercy as we, each for the other, should need. It is here, then, that agnosticism serves and faith fails. . . .

What it is, Leandra whispers, *is pride, Wim, pure pride in you insisting on no greater forgiveness than such as you can find in yourself. Don't you know the Lord laughs at our puniness just like we got to laugh at how a baby's first step lands him on his rump? You got any idea how we tickle Him, Wim?*

A smile spreads slow and showy as dawn over my face.

"You're awake," Leandra says. "High time. And just what have you got to be smiling about, you don't mind my asking?"

"You admit that He laughs at us, then?"

"Laughs?" Her voice is cautious. "Who laughs, love?"

"Your magnanimous God, creating us for His laughingstock. I suspected as much."

"Dreams, darlin'." Leandra folds her hands, my face like a prayer between them. "Right glad if the Lord was in them, though."

"Ridicule," I mutter, hoping to rile her.

"Cool?" she says. "Let's get you another blanket."

"Wait," I insist, but my angel has flown.

Leandra gone . . . but not Pamela. Nor God.

"Forgive me," I whisper.

If anyone hears, it is only Leandra, who has returned to blanket a cold drift of white wool across my sunken belly and chest.

My arms buried, I sink into stillness. A hard freeze edges up my neck and touches my chin. My lips benumb, and crystals glassify the corners of my eyes.

There will be no more tears. The voice is my father's, the laugh it ushers in Pamela's. My mother, as always, remains mute.

Up in Massachusetts, the ground that nourishes my son's stunted bones, that holds them precious, will soon thaw. May some headstrong unruly flower decorate the soil I can no longer tend. I myself plan to go up in smoke. Indeed, I insist on it. Have I made that wish clear?

"Leandra?"

"Ssh," she says.

"The goddamn earth won't—" But the will the words make hash of lapses, and I am left in a shiver.

"Hush." The warmthless blanket weights my shoulders. "There. Is that better?"

A maceration of syllables, all notional sense cowering in the darkest corners of . . .

"Love?" Leandra says.

Love.

"Is there anything you need?"

Love:Need::Conundrum:Oxymoron.

"I don't know," I confess.

Then I am amazed once more to find myself unheard by a creature so adept at listening.

. . . I could not
Speak, and my eyes failed, I was neither
Living nor dead, and I knew nothing,
Looking into the heart of light, the silence.

It is shamefully easy, now, to feign sleep. And what could it cost me, her belief that I still find rest these nights?

Gladly do I eat crow, imploring her God to make of my breathing a sweet ballad, something concocted of air and what is left of me and His mercy, made of next to nothing and sung to her alone.

Its refrain must be repeated and repeated. Repeated again, then: "Are you asleep?"

Finally, assured that I will not wake, Leandra switches on the lamp. "Wim?"

She listens for another moment. Then, at last persuaded by my impersonation of slumber, my high priestess performs her nightly ritual:

Reaching down into me, Leandra lifts out my soul and holds it up to the light.

vii

THOSE EYES, maybe they don't see much anymore, but they are brimming over with something. Not tears, I mean. Nothing that easy. Nor love, though there is surely, always, that.

No, Wim's eye is on something now, he is *keeping* his eye on it, like one of those contests youngsters get into, where if you blink or look away first you lose.

Wim's got his eye on something, and now I'm the one, seems like, don't see. I stare into his eyes like any minute now I will glimpse what it is goes on in his mind. I don't blink or look away. I know it's something there.

—∾—

I try not to put much stock in "deserving." It's a notion don't wear so well running up against life. Wim no more deserves to die than I deserve to lose him. But my sister's death looked to me, back then, like something I deserved. For I was still that much of a child, and prey to childish notions.

God ain't about to kill off one person just to punish another. I see that now, of course. Even plain human love mostly ain't apt to be that petty. And wouldn't love, boundless love, be pretty much what God comes down to?

Truth be told, I doubt punishment is ever the Lord's main concern. Straightening us out, more likely. As to Final Judgment, I know what the Bible says. Bible's like an old person: plenty of wisdom in there, but mixed up with a lot of muddled overwrought things got to be taken with a grain of salt. All creation come from the mind of God. I know that part is right. What don't make a lick of sense is the idea of eternal damnation dreamed up by a mind that's pure mercy.

I've told all this to Wim. I can't seem to stop trying to steer his gaze toward heaven, where he ought to be looking now, instead of back at a past can't be changed. I don't expect it's heaven Wim doubts anyhow, just his own welcome there. I figure I must be here to change his mind.

"Ain't the Almighty always been more a doer than a talker?" I asked him a few weeks back. "Still, there's a few things He's told about Himself in no uncertain terms. 'I am a merciful God'—you remember that?"

"I also seem to recall what comes along with it." Wim gave me a tease of a smile. " 'I am a *just* God.' Your leaving that part out was an oversight, I imagine?"

"Justice?" I sniffed. "Reckon that was something the Lord come up with early on, a little experiment," I told him. "Nothing to do but toss it out, once it was tested for a while."

"You are an apostate," Wim said. "A heretic."

Not knowing what he meant, I didn't pay much mind. Not then. "Sticks and stones," I said.

Wim grinned like a bandit.

"Stack up justice alongside human nature," I told him, "it don't take God to see you got an idea ain't going to work. Pure justice got to run things, be sorry little call for heaven."

He laughed outright then. He would. "I didn't realize you took such a dim view of humanity."

"Dim's not what I'd call it," I said. "It just seems plain that getting things wrong and taking them hard is how most of us learn what we need to. If telling us was all it took, the Lord wouldn't had to lift a finger since He handed Moses the Ten Commandments."

"So sin and folly are like remedial classes—God just covers the tuition?"

"Any idea about God can be made to sound foolish, Wim. Our minds are bound to fall short of Him. Not to mention our words."

Wim reached for my hand. "I was joking," he said.

"Reckon I know that," I told him. "But I am not."

He was sitting on the mourners' bench, just stopping there to rest on his way to the bedroom after sitting outdoors awhile. He'd come in flushed with the mild winter sun. His lips looked bleached now and his eyes showed pain's dull blind shine.

"Here I gone and got us stuck up past our knees in muddy talk," I said, "when you ought to be lying down."

Wim tightened his grip on my hand. "What were you trying to tell me?"

Never mind, it can wait, would have been a lie, of course. But I knew he wasn't ready to believe me. My talk of God still mystifies him same as his big words always done to me. I try to believe there's time yet and that maybe, like me, Wim remembers things later, leaves allowance for second thoughts.

Sometimes I'll look up Wim's words in the old Webster's I still have from when I was in school. *Apostate* means renegade. *Heretic*'s somebody holds beliefs opposite what's taught in church. I reckon Wim wasn't far wrong then in his name calling—even if it was a case of the pot calling the kettle black.

My sister dying for *my* sins? Pammy did no such thing. Not for Wim's sins, either, though we did surely lapse into sin, a helpless human fall. We wronged my sister, no two ways about it. Wronged her and ourselves and each other, and all in the pained sight of God.

But it wasn't our wrongs or weakness Pammy Jo died of. Fact is, my sister died by her own hand and we can't know why, not exactly or fully, not ever. Which is all by itself, the not knowing, terrible punishment.

When the Lord calls us in to talk over our lives, each one separately, without each other to lean on and hide behind, all three of us got some betrayal to answer for, some weakness to own up to.

And some love to excuse us.

That's what I think. And what I want Wim to know.

"Tell me, Leandra." Wim's eyes were clear. The pain was, for the moment, lending him back to me.

I sat down beside him on the mourners' bench. "It's me, not God, can't tolerate your doubting Him," I said quietly. "Reckon you know that."

Wim thought for a moment, then nodded. "What I don't understand is why."

"You being afraid," I said. "It's the least thing I can abide."

"Don't you suppose everyone's afraid of dying, Leandra?"

"Only the ones don't know what to expect."

Wim tried to quash a smile, but wasn't quite able.

"You think I don't know what you're going to say?" I tried to smile too. "Nobody leaving this world knows what to expect, right?"

"And I know what you're going to say—that you do." Wim didn't try to hide his smile now, nor how sad it was. "Given another year or two, we'd be reading each other's minds so well we might forget how to talk," he said.

Another year or two . . . given . . . The extravagance of the notion knocked me, for a second, dizzy.

"Leandra?" My eyes were closed. "I'm listening," Wim said. He sounded so far away. "Don't think I've stopped listening."

"How on earth am I supposed to let you go, knowing you're afraid?" I whispered.

I could feel him waiting beside me on the bench, trembling.

"And what is pure mercy, anyhow, to be afraid of ?" I said.

—w—

It was one of my childish notions that when my sister came home from the hospital, bereft of her baby, love would heal her . . . would lift her right up off the bed.

Wim's grief was too great to bear. Pammy was bound to see that, I thought, and would in her own grief be drawn back to her husband. I pictured a rent in the dark curtain my sister lay behind. I saw how the threads of her love and sorrow would cross with the threads of Wim's, like weaving.

The tearing had been dreadful. The mending was apt to be hard. But with it my sister would want me beside her. Surely Pammy would start to see me, I thought, would beckon me near her again.

But when my sister came home from the hospital she seemed not to see me at all. When I spoke to her she barely answered. I may as well have been calling out, reaching from the moon.

Wim it was who needed me. That much was clear. Except I reckon I must have needed him too, which made a little more complicated what can never be excused.

I will try not to make excuses when the Lord calls me to account. And if I am honest I will have to tell Him how even now I got more than a little gratitude mixed in with my shame. For in some way I think that sin saved us, Wim and me, kept our hearts whole in our bodies, kept us alive. I am a heretic, I guess.

Now Wim is dying. He didn't choose to. So I reckon it must be the Lord's will. It would be easy to see the pain, the widening sweep of Wim's suffering and losses, as his punishment. And mine. But like I said, I just can't believe the Almighty's mind works that way.

Wim don't believe, he says, in salvation. How could he, when he thinks the end of this life is the end of everything?

Sometimes Wim is, like Pammy used to say, too smart for his own good. Don't want to be hoodwinked, taken in. Even by heaven.

Now, though, his words are deserting him like rats jumping off a sinking ship. His ideas are crumbling to dust.

These nights, as I keep vigil over Wim's slow, hard leave-taking,

I do not sit here alone. The mourners' bench is crowded, mine just another puny body squeezed in amongst the sick and the sorry, the quick and the dead, all of us waiting for nothing less than the pure mercy that's been promised us and that we can count on even if our faith is no match for our stubborn and addled hope.

It's that the Lord looks at finally, I reckon. Our hope.

The one human thing that's as boundless as His love. It's been there inside us all along—our salvation.

There is, Wim says, no such thing as salvation. But tell me: what else did he come here hoping to find? How otherwise does he summon the strength, still, so little left to him, to reach out with his soul and his body to mine?

I know what he's seeking, what those eyes keep watching for.

It's love Wim recollects as he loses track of everything else, the salvation in it.

—w—

I sit beside the open windows now and talk a blue streak. Here's summer halfway out the door, and I'm trying to hold off its leaving. You wouldn't walk away, would you, while somebody was in the midst of talking to you?

It isn't really summer I can't stop talking to, of course.

I can tell when Wim is listening to me. The corners of his mouth go soft. His head, without leaving the pillow, strains up just a bit, a fledgling with appetite.

He mostly won't answer me now. Can't, I reckon. I don't know whether it's pain holding his tongue, or fear, or how he's losing words about as fast as he might have learned them. He must have been a mighty quick child. Sometimes when I ask even simple things now I get no answer. Makes me lonesome some. I know he listens, though.

I'll lean down over the bed to try and get his goat.

"Scarce as hen's teeth," I'll whisper to him. "Comfortable as an old shoe." And: "Older than white thread."

I bandy about all that is sacred and clamorous—pennies saved and stitches in time and carts and horses and beggars and wishes. "If wishes were horses, wishes could fart," I heard Branch's daddy say one time. His laugh was like a foghorn. Then Branch's mama got all put out with him for talking uncouth in front of a young lady, which was me, so I had to quit smiling quick.

Wim's face got a mind of its own now. I can tell he is smiling by these little tucks dug in around his mouth.

" 'Honey, I am older than white thread,' my granddaddy used to say. I was always askin' how old he was, and that is what he'd tell me."

The smile gets waylaid somewhere beyond me. "You're listening, aren't you?" I say.

Wim's eyes go cloud-wrapped, and I catch a chill.

"You know, don't you," I whisper, "that you are a right beautiful old man?"

He resembles my granddaddy now a bit, does Wim. White whiskers on his chin and that faraway look. His bones so tight against the skin it's a wonder they don't poke through. I feel him bleed in the center of me.

Sometimes I forget he can't see me. I stare into his eyes like you do when you're asking a body something important and you don't intend to let them put you off, want them to feel it weighing on them before they answer.

"Wim," I ask him, "will it be soon?"

The corners of his mouth tuck in. His face tilts up, hungry.

"I want you to tell me," I say. "You hear? Don't think you can just go wandering off whenever you please."

You know how the light from a lighthouse looks when you are a good distance from it? The light in Wim's eyes is like that, white and sharp and stubborn and blind, piercing through—outshining—everything. So bright that, even across all that way, it makes you want to close your eyes.

It's almost like that light is talking to you, calling out. Go on about your business, it says. Make tracks if you care to. I'll still be shining here. Whenever you look back, it's me you'll see shining.

Branch stops by every morning now, on his way to work. He cannot stay, he says, just wants to know how Wim passed the night. And me—do I need anything?

"Peaceful." I'll tell him. "Quiet." And: "Not a thing, thank you kindly." Not always, strictly speaking, true.

I'll offer him coffee.

"No time," Branch says.

I'll give it to him anyhow, heavy with sugar and cream. On the better mornings Branch will drink his coffee by the side of Wim's bed, our bed, in a frame of sunshine. I'll keep to the other room then, busying myself with some little chore. I like the sound of their voices, Branch's mouth going a mile a minute like he thinks he can talk death out of something . . . the halting murmur Wim makes now and then, picking through what words he's got left to find one or two he can make do with.

The headaches are worst in the morning, apt to ease as the day wears on. Some mornings Wim got nothing at all to say for himself, poor Branch left to do all the talking on his own.

"Got to get a move on," Branch will say. "Shove off, hit the road, make hay while the sun shines. The early bird . . ."

I picture the crimps around Wim's mouth. He would laugh if he could, I just know it. He'll let Branch get away with anything.

"I'll be around." Branch backs out of the room. "You keep on being a trouper, Willy."

When he comes out into the front room, Branch's face looks starchy. He tries to smile at me, for me, tries so hard, not really getting anywhere. He winds up shaking his head.

Then he yanks his shoulders into line. "Color's better this morning," he'll say to me. Or: "He was looking right at me, I swear."

"You think so?"

"I'm sure of it."

Branch comes up close. He smells like a husband in the morning, all aftershave and soap and coffee. Sometimes I think how he could be, have been, my husband—not wishing for it, just wondering what it might be like. I really can't picture any such thing.

When Branch and me was seventeen, just getting ready to graduate high school, his daddy died. Mr. Dexter Goodlin was a big stalwart man with yellow hair and round pink cheeks that shimmied. He recollected every joke he ever heard and had an uncommon relish for trucks and children. His yard was always full of them.

After our own daddy died, Mr. Dexter tried to pull me and Pammy into every family gathering and outing and shenanigan went on over there in that big slouch-roofed white house. Pammy Jo didn't go around much, but me, I couldn't keep away. Reckon I always could conceive of myself better as sister to Branch than wife.

When Branch's daddy took sick, I kept to their place as much as I could, looking after the younger children, cooking or ironing, just trying to help out. The Goodlin family lost their noisiness, seemed like overnight. Mr. Dexter turned color, his skin gone near as yellowish as his hair used to be, and all his hair fell out.

It was something in his liver, Branch's mama told me. Last time I got to go in and see him before he passed on, Mr. Dexter told me a joke about a coon hound could read. I can't recall how it went, only how it tickled him to tell it and how hard it made him cough when he got to laughing, how loud that coughing sounded in a house gone suddenly mum.

When he was laid out at Twadell's funeral home, Mr. Dexter looked like a small clay figure in a suit and necktie. A poorly doll. Branch cried once during the calling hours. I walked him out quick to the parking lot. His crying came hard, like the sound of grinding metal.

He's taking Wim hard, Branch is. Sometimes when he comes out of the bedroom it hurts me to look at his face. He knows what's going to happen, but he can't accept it, he wants to fight. Only he don't know who to hit or pick an argument with.

And also Branch worries for me, I know. He won't say it, of

course, but I reckon he sees death as a kind of profanity, something a woman ought to be sheltered from. He's maybe forgot those last months I had care of my own mama, what-all needed doing for her—diapers and such as that. "Lannie, why don't you let me . . . ?" Branch don't know what to do. He wants to spare me. I tell him, *Just what you're doing, being here.* I play Wim's radio all day long. Won't stand for this house going mute like Goodlins' did that year. If I can't stop another thing, I can at least put my foot down on such silence.

"We're in for some weather," Branch tells me. "You scoot on down to Miz Fulcher's place and call me if you need anything. Got a phone in the van now too."

I smile. "Takes more than a bit of weather to rattle me, Branch."

His chin, shaved smooth as a skipping stone, juts out a bit. "How long I been telling you you need to get yourself a telephone?"

"Since 1979 at least." The smile is starting to make my face ache. I let it go. "Phone's not apt anyhow to do us the smallest good."

Branch shies, shakes his head. "You plan on getting more mulish when you're an old lady?"

"Wouldn't surprise me one bit."

"I may not be up to it," he says.

"We'll cross that bridge when we come to it."

For a second I forget who I'm talking to. I wait for the words to get pounced on. But Branch don't do that, of course. Don't even laugh, just ducks his head a little.

"Go on about your business," I tell him. I picture a strong beam of white light guiding me through the day. "Me and Wim will be fine."

Branch starts for the door, shoulders a slump in his bright-blue blazer. Then he traces back and gives me a little peck on the forehead.

I hold on to his lapels for just a minute, breathing in that husbandly smell. A perfume of hot iron and starch rises from his white shirt.

Then I let him go, give him a little push toward the door. Can't hardly afford, right now, to try to hold on to anything for long. I don't want to forget how to stand on my own two feet.

Branch backs slow out the driveway. Two soft toots of the horn are muffled by a rising wind as he swivels out onto the road. The northeasterly sky looks tea-stained. I turn from the window before his van disappears around a bend. Before the sound of his engine has died, I've turned up the radio.

As a youngster I used to imagine my memory was a huge white screen like in a movie theater. I'd need only choose a part of my life to relive and there it would be, playing out before my eyes, giving back everything I might have lost or missed or plain misunderstood.

Or maybe not cherished enough. Failed to hold precious in the present it belonged to. I had, as a girl, whole days with my daddy I could return to, live inside, behaving beautifully, when need was severe.

Now, though, memory seems more like a thick dark curtain. Lord knows what-all's behind it, and for every moment you'd rejoice to retrieve, there are a dozen you'd as soon leave lost or hid in the dusty dark. You can't always pick the things that are readiest to come back to you, is the tricky part of remembering.

In the years since Pammy died, memory's been only too willing to yield the stranger my sister somehow became. When I turn round quick, her face is behind me. Bitter and blameful, her voice wakes me up in the night.

When a glimpse of the girl was what I'd plead for, though, memory turned mean, tight-fisted. I could think about Pammy Jo, even talk to her like I always did. But I couldn't *see her* anymore. For years my real sister stayed back in the dark somewhere, caught behind that curtain, and nothing I could do would coax her out into the light.

Seems like Wim brought Pammy Jo with him, though, when he

came. That very first night I got at long last back the sister I been pining for since she got on a bus in Norfolk and I stayed behind for Mama and third grade.

The Pammy I can again recollect these days seems no kin to the one came later. Where did that woman come from? I wonder. If I watched the screen long enough, pushed back behind the curtain and brazened through the dark, might I find the connection, trace a route through the thin air my true sister, beautiful and brave, vanished into?

Everything she said and did, everything Pammy Jo *was,* seemed like a promise. Folks needed only look at her to start counting on things they hadn't put stock in for years. Like a princess in a fairy tale she was, and not just me and Mama saw it. The school superintendent, Mr. Larry Fordyce, who taught in Currituck County for forty-odd years, declared it was a teacher's plumb luck to run into such gifts in a youngster . . . maybe every other lifetime, was what he said. The Women's Club give Pammy every scholarship it had. The man come down from Virginia Beach to take the senior portraits placed in my sister's hand a business card with raised gold letters: *Ever you get the hankering to try modeling, honey* . . .

Well, when I try to tell it, sounds like I just fell off the turnip truck, I expect. A stranger with a camera, some printed cards, and maybe not the best intentions . . . a tired-out teacher and a flock of well-meant ladies looking to do some local good . . . ain't as if the world my sister set on fire was a big one or irksome to light. Still, a body seeing Pammy then—not just her beauty, but the spark in her, the way she went about things—would surely know what I mean. She had only to take a step toward you to make you feel picked out, raised up, rewarded. If she'd said she intended to drape the moon in crepe paper, nobody who heard her'd think twice before asking did the ladder need steadying from down below.

Only now that I myself have some acquaintance with love can I begin to imagine how it might have felt for a man to find her heart set on him. It must, for Wim, have been a fearsome thing, a kind of enchantment thrown over his life like a net, strands of beauty and wonder and sorrow all knotted together. . . . He is yet trying to sort them out and free himself.

Wim told me one time, not so long ago, that Pammy made him "miserable with love," words so at odds with themselves that I was tickled into a smile. But then I noticed Wim's face, the misery still plain on it after twenty years.

"I'm sorry," I said.

Wim smiled sadly. "I'm absurd," he said. "I know it."

"I wasn't—"

"I know."

"Except if it brought mostly misery, maybe what it was wasn't love exactly."

"Maybe not." Wim looked away.

I circled behind his chair, leaned down to lay my cheek against his back. "You loved her," I said. "We both know that."

"I loved what I thought she was," he whispered. "That's not the same thing."

"And she loved what she wanted you to be."

He didn't answer.

"It wasn't you made Pammy do what she done." My hands stayed clamped on his shoulders. "You ought to've known it way before this."

"I do," Wim said. "I always have."

"Then how did your shoulders come to be so stooped with blame?"

"Had I been capable of the kind of love she . . ." His voice dropped. "If I only could have loved her the way I love you."

I took hold of his face then and turned it toward me. "An old man and a young man ain't got the same heart," I said. "It's a different love's going to come from a man nearing death than one's just started his life. You loved her with what was in you then."

"I wasn't a child."

"No. But she was."

"Pamela was—"

"I was *there,* Wim. You think I didn't see what become of my sister?"

A sudden spate of rain I never saw coming scattershot the windows. Wim's knuckles paled as his fingers gripped the arms of his chair.

"I doubt you know how close I came to hating her," I said.

Seemed like we both stopped breathing. I thought in the terrible stillness how during hurricanes you're supposed to crack a window or two lest a sudden change in pressure cause the house to explode. Slowly I took in a scant breath of air, let it out slowly, then took in another.

"Hating her for refusing me the smallest chance to love her," I said. "For using death to maim the both of us, the way she—"

"You were only a girl," Wim said. "You could hardly—"

"That's right," I said. "Exactly. But we're all getting lost all the time in our lives, don't you think? And having to find our way back mostly on our own? Sometimes I wonder can we help one another at all."

"We're supposed to try," Wim said.

"Indeed we are," I said. "Only I expect the trying's more to get our own bearings than to straighten out anybody else."

The rain was falling harder, coming straight down. Wim's head was bowed. I turned and looked out the window, where the bald spots in the yard were turning into pools like pewter plates.

Wim whispered something.

"What?" I leaned toward him.

"You think I am going to see her, don't you?"

"I know you are," I said.

"How can you be so certain of something so . . . ?"

"Flimsy?" I smiled. "It's us are flimsy, Wim, not heaven."

"And you honestly can't see what a dubious prospect your heaven is?"

"I can't," I said. "And I'm grateful if it is that I can't."

He stared at me for a moment, then shook his head.

"I know you'll get to see Pammy because the Lord give us every chance to undo our wrongs. I'll be seeing her myself one day."

"I'm afraid your universe has more of sense and kindness to it than your God's does."

"Hush," I said.

"You're worried He might hear me?"

"He'll know you mean no harm."

Wim smiled.

"If I had the least doubt about heaven," I whispered, "you think I'd stand for you dying?"

"You believe you could stop it?"

Outside, the rain was hastening dusk. I reached down and grasped Wim's hands, pulling him to his feet. Unsteady, he leaned against me.

"God or no God," I said.

—∾—

I do not doubt Wim loved my sister, nor wonder that his love lost its direction. I fear to ask, even of myself, how then he could love me. Did he hunger for simplicity? Is that what I've had that he yearned to possess? Perhaps it has been as simple as that.

And what of me? Might loving Wim have been no more than a way to stay close to a sister who shoved me away? Branch has suggested as much. But that goes back to when Wim just got here, before Branch got to love him too and so had room in his heart for cool dark inklings.

Whatever is inside us, I reckon love makes a jumble of it all. And maybe we should be thankful—never yet saw a life run on pure good sense that had much of joy in it. Might be, anyhow, that love, like hurricanes, is just one of the Lord's reminders that it's still Him running things. It's bound, no matter what, to bring a shambles wherever it makes landfall. And if there's a lull in the middle, if a feeling of stillness and even peace should come, anybody heedful would have more than a hunch they were caught in the most dangerous part.

I wonder did Wim and my sister—sometime before I got there, before the storm of sorrow the baby brought upon them—did Wim and Pammy live for a time in the eye of love? I want it to be so, and so that is how I, who was not even there as a thought, will remember it, even if Wim does not.

And maybe right now, this last bit of time with him, is the eye of my own particular storm, a caught breath, a lull before the worst of it. What afterwards, I can't help wondering, is liable to be left of me? Reckon that is one of Wim's rhetorical questions, because this love is set loose now and can't be called back or staved off. No, I am all awash in it, no flood I can imagine cresting, no squall I'd hope to belay.

I set the basin of water on a three-legged stool beside the bed. This milking stool used to be in my granddaddy's barn, older than white thread and kept long past the year when the cows were sold off for cash money at tax time. The pasturage around here ain't good for much, truth be told. Worn out or maybe never good for much in the first place. The soil is sandy, the waters bitter. Store-bought milk just wasn't the same, my mama always used to say, her voice a grieving.

One springtime a few years back, I got to feeling ambitious and figured to strip the milking stool, refinish it. I am fond of its sturdy no-nonsense shape. How you couldn't tip it if you tried.

The stool was oak underneath, like I suspected. But the rusty red paint on it was about the stubbornest thing I ever run into. There was maybe milk in it, a recipe for paint used in olden times, and it holds on forever. Wouldn't nothing get that blood color to come up out of the grain.

I soaked and sanded till my hands got so rough I hardly had call for sandpaper. Use you a cherry stain, Mr. Purdy over to the hardware said. Them red streaks will blend right in. But I didn't care for the notion of oak trying to pass for cherry—no better than the paint, to my mind, a false note.

I sanded some more, then let the poor thing be. Red lines trace through the wood like a biology book picture of a body showing where the veins are . . . color shady and false and obstinate as memories twisting through your days, a complicated tangle you wouldn't exist without.

"You awake, darlin'?"

Wim smiles at me. I think he can see, a little bit.

"Leandra," he says. "What are you up to?" It is midafternoon. His voice is breezy and clear as a bell.

"Thought you could stand a bath, is all."

He makes a sour face, too big and silly, like that Uncle Miltie on TV used to tickle Mama so.

"Got the water nice and warm here."

His bony fingers dig into the border of the blanket. "Water is never warm," he says.

"You expect me to take that for scientific fact?"

Wim shivers and squinches up his face.

"Mr. Wizard," I say. Me and Mama used to watch all that old silliness from back before I was born, after Branch's uncle Rudy got the cable TV franchise for this part of the county and Branch talked him into hooking us up for free. Right miffed, Branch was, when I told him I'd got rid of the TV after Mama was gone. I give it to that old folks' home out the Bright's Grove Road. Been a lot less fuss there since, I'm told, now the ladies can watch their soap operas and Oprahs without depriving the menfolk of their ball games and such.

"Mr. Wizard?" Wim says. "When did you say you were born?"

"None of your beeswax. I'm plenty old enough to look upon a man's nakedness, is all you need to know."

Wim sighs. He loves his baths, I know that. It's me looking at him now that discomfits him. Less my seeing what is there than marking what is gone. He looks like I reckon you'd expect: a body pared to the bone, skin so thin any but the lightest touch could split him open, make him bleed. To shave him now is a fearful thing. I'll dawdle around it for days, stalling for time and steadiness of hand till Wim gets to looking mossy and worn as an old grave marker.

"You just lay back and let me have my way with you, you hear?"

He smiles a baby's shaky shapeless smile. His cheeks and chin are smooth. Branch did what I never thought to ask and run the razor over them yesterday while I slipped out to the store. Branch got him the trustiest pair of hands a body could hope for.

"Cold," Wim says.

"Warm," I say, prying his fingers from the blanket. I believe it's slipped his mind he's holding on. *What makes thunder and lightning, where rainbows get their colors from, storms brewed off the coast of Africa* . . . I pull back the covers, strip off his damp pajamas. *The human body is seventy-four percent water, Mr. Wizard said.* Wim closes his eyes.

Is it water he is losing, only that? The skin so lax and roomy around his bones now that I can feature my own bones slipping in to rest beside what is left, to warm . . . *My God, you are a beautiful old man.*

For a moment I forget the cooling water, the green washcloth, the blue sponge, the floating bar of yellow soap worn to the shape of my palm. My fingers delve into the twin hollows between neck and collarbone, rest there for a measure of his pulse's music, then two.

"I'm not about to let you catch cold," I whisper close to his ear. His eyes keep closed. "Won't abide no chill anywhere near you." My palms smooth down the length of his long ruined body. His skin is the shade of light-brown sugar, soft as old kidskin. I rub cream on it every day. My hands have never been so soft.

Wim don't have much hair on him . . . less now, but never much. I remember a man used to work with my daddy on the road crew. In spring the men'd take off their shirts and never put them on again until maybe November sometime. This one man, name of Jarvis Grandy—his boy Anthony was in my grade in school—he had hair all over his body, ran right down his back like a bear's, and you could hardly see his skin.

But Wim, he just has these two little patches, shaped like wedges of pie and nearly matching. One is on his chest, the other down below his belly. The hair is fine and dark and silvered, too soft for something so wiry, not like any animal I can think of.

The water must be cooling fast. I've near forgot why it's there. My hands wash over Wim's body, stroking lighter where the hair is, as if the gentlest touch might wear it clean away.

Wim's breathing slows, evens out. When I think he is asleep, I catch the soap like a slippery fish, squeeze out the sponge.

Tepid water seeps across his skin, washing away the tracks left by my hands. But I know my touch is still there, deep, so deep, in the grain.

—

A voice sends dreams packing . . . and I would, with my wits about me, offer thanks. For I'll have no truck with such dreams as choose me to visit these nights.

I have fallen asleep beside him, the lamp and radio left on. A sharp-edged disk of too-bright light slices a half circle into the mattress. The music Wim might finally hear God in brings discord to the room.

But it wasn't the music nor the light snapped me awake. It was Wim, his voice like wires vibrating in a high wind.

"Pamela?"

He is not accountable, of course. Cannot be blamed. This is God's doing. *Pamela.* But my own fault. You got to be careful what you tell, even when you pray. I should never have told Him the one thing I could not bear.

There, says the Lord. *You see? You can. Bear anything.*

"Pamela." Wim's hands beat away the blankets. He is naked underneath. Not decent. Ribs like rungs on a ladder.

"Yes, love." My first lie to him? All I have to give . . . don't let him, Lord, *not now* . . . don't let him see my empty hands.

His grasp, freed of the covers' confinement, is ferocious.

I pull away, sit up in bed, undo the mother-of-pearl buttons at the front of my nightgown. The buttons are so tiny I'll be able to use them on a doll's dress one day. I will go on making things. I will have to.

I pull the nightgown up over my head. So much, already, between us, and the warmth draining out of him so fast . . . the cloth, another barrier, is not to be tolerated.

"Pamela?" He frets.

I wrap myself around him like a blanket. "I'm here," I say.

She is here.

I close my eyes and see a sky the shade of a golden-eyed cat's stubborn stare. A gust of wind pelts the windows with grit.

Wim tries to ask me something, ask me *for* something, but the words are blown to debris.

"Yes," I whisper. "Yes, love."

It is a promise I'm making him, a promise good for anything. May he be allowed to keep it with him when he goes, I think to ask the Lord, maybe striking a bargain. But it is hard just now, I admit, to conceive of Him as somebody I'd care to do much business with. Each day I ask for just one thing: just one more day; no miracles, no special treatment.

"Cold," Wim murmurs in a near-drowned voice.

"I know," I whisper. "I know."

Must be sheer force of habit takes over then, because before I know what it is I'm doing, I find myself back on sociable terms with God.

You just go ahead and take him, then, I say. *Whenever You are ready. Reckon we both know You got to, soon. Why drag things out when it's bound to hurt him? Don't got to be God to see when a body's had enough.*

Then, just when I'm feeling right sheepish for giving the Lord a piece of this mind He Himself made and so knows inside out . . .

right that second's when the power shuts off. Just like that, the glare and the music gone.

Then out of the darkness and out of the blue I hear, clear as a bell, my name. *Leandra.* Wim's voice sounds young and sturdy and dead certain.

"Leandra."

"Yes," I say. "I'm here."

Thank the Lord, like they say, *for small favors.*

I do, in passing.

Then I wedge my body under Wim's, keeping him afloat. The water is already rising.